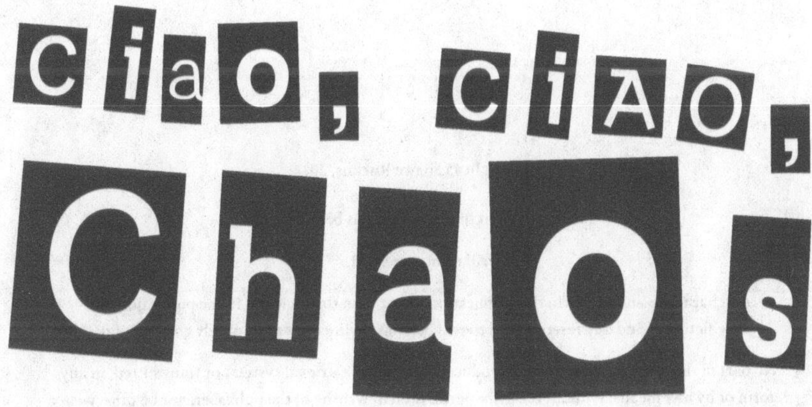

Ciao, Ciao, Chaos

SHAWE RUCKUS

UK Book Publishing.com

Editing, design, typesetting and publishing by UK Book Publishing

www.ukbookpublishing.com

ISBN: 978-1-916572-90-4

MERCENARIES IN SUITS

Begin the *Mercenaries in Suits* series with Book 1, *A Chinese Remedy*, and join Chance in a world of mystery and mayhem in this 2023 Readers' Favorite Book Award Urban Fiction finalist.

Part-time fixer Chance Yang is often reluctantly drawn into a mystery. And, as the globetrotter finds, the deeper he delves into these cases, the harder it becomes to uncover the truth.

When the sister of an Asian tycoon is found dead, can an unlikely consultant from China discover whether she committed suicide or was murdered? Chance's life is upended as he is drawn from Tokyo to London, where he finds himself falling for a woman he's been hired to protect.

Soon, Chance finds that the cases that he's been enlisted to investigate are never as straightforward as they might seem. Especially when his boss, Felipe Kazama, always seems to know more than he's letting on...

In Book 2, *The Learning Curve of Pain*, Chance is caught between his personal feelings and the demands of his job, as his investigations lead him from the sunny shores of Spain to the posh boroughs of London.

As life leads Chance back to London, he encounters Detective Nigel Weatherby of the Metropolitan Police. Referred by his flamboyant former boss, Felipe Kazama, the Detective is searching for answers into what should be an open-and shut-case of murder.

Chance must go undercover to infiltrate the lives of a wealthy and powerful family as he searches for answers that may be best left buried. Undeterred by the death threats he receives, can Chance live with the price that must be paid to see justice served?

In Book 3, *All Body Bags and No Knickers*, even a family holiday offers no escape from murder when Chance journeys with his new wife Catherine from London to northern coastal China.

On the annual Ghost Night, when spirits wander, the couple never imagined death would stalk their idyllic honeymoon destination. When three naked bodies are discovered in a nearby seaside ruin, was it murder, an act of revenge, or an affair gone wrong?

The answer to these questions may hit closer to home than Catherine could ever expect or than Chance is willing to admit. As the couple chases clues, the bride realises that her new husband may have terrible secrets to hide...

What readers say about *A Chinese Remedy*:

"Chance and Felipe make an engaging duo that readers will surely welcome in sequels." – **Kirkus Reviews**

"Ruckus creates the illusion that we are part of the case and we are figuring it out along with the characters." – **Readers' Favorite**

"A thoroughly entertaining yarn packed with intrigue and a slightly off-kilter narrative style that adds an element of dream logic to an otherwise recognizably contemporary London landscape." – **IndieReader**

"Easy to read as you have your coffee or tea, maybe before bed and just forget that time is passing at all." – **Amazon**

"Fast paced and fun. It reminded me of a Quentin Tarantino movie." – **Amazon**

What readers say about *The Learning Curve of Pain*:

"The final act provides a shocking character turn and a memorable denouement." – **Kirkus Reviews**

"A pretty interesting, classic set-up that holds promise for an intriguing yarn and some deft detective work." – **IndieReader**

"Will the secrets remain hidden? By all means possible, the truth is what stands out the most. In the leafy London borough, the search for answers is only one step toward uncovering the mystery, though let it not deceive you." – **Readers' Favorite**

"A mystery within a mystery." – **Amazon**

"I do recommend this book to those who love a good slow-burning mystery." – **Amazon**

What readers say about *All Body Bags and No Knickers*:

"With memorable characters, immersive descriptions, and astonishingly clever sleights of hand, All Body Bags and No Knickers is a literary mystery, a travel guide, and a delicious thriller standing on each other's shoulders in a trench coat." – **IndieReader**

"An entertaining mystery with a paranormal twist." – **Independent Librarian, Edelweiss**

"The book's ability to transition between sorrowful and humorous moments provides readers with an emotional rollercoaster, adding depth and unpredictability to the plot. This is, without a doubt, an enticing page-turner that keeps readers hooked from beginning to end." – **OnlineBookClub**

"Buckle your seatbelt for this mystery because it will keep you guessing all the way. Mystery fans everywhere will want to add this book at the top of their reading list." – **ReaderViews**

"It helped me unwind and simultaneously piqued my interest with the details of past events that the novel revealed progressively. My initial feelings of calm and mild curiosity were quickly replaced by excitement as several hints began to divulge what had transpired in the past and the identity of the true suspect." – **Readers' Favorite**

"The couple's travels in China are filled with sights, sounds, smells, food, and fun. The author's descriptions of their different activities and excursions were better than a travelogue and will tempt readers to make their own travel plans." – **Reedsy Discovery**

Ciao, Ciao, Chaos

CHAPTER 1

OCTOBER 2016.

LONDON, COVENT GARDEN.

SLINGSBY PLACE.

Part-time florist Catherine Roxborough was afflicted.

She had married Inner Mongolian-born Chinese M&A consultant, Changxi Yang (known as Chance Yang to an inner circle of friends), a scant three months ago.

Having received an invitation from Chance's aunt, the couple had embarked on a trip to northern coastal China during the summer. Everything had been lovely on their honeymoon, and they had visited a vibrant seaside city in Shandong Province, reconnecting with Chance's long-lost family and making many more new friends.

Everything had been lovely, that is, until the fateful Ghost Night, when three of Catherine's new acquaintances were discovered dead in a seaside ruin. Everything had changed when Catherine learnt about the possible involvement of her husband's cousin in those awful deaths.

Now back in London and returning to the familiar minutiae of her life, Catherine found it easier not to think about the horrible incident. Even her colleague Orla's helpless laughter and wittering had proved to be comforting.

"We went to Brittany. Bejesus, I didn't even know abalones have teeth!" After sharing her mother-in-law's tips on how to make perfect, crunchy toast points, Orla squeaked, "Cat, how was your honeymoon?"

"Oh." She pulled herself out of her reverie. "It was...alright," she said. "We had this dessert in Hangzhou where they made fresh lotus seeds profiterole-style."

"Was it crunchy?"

"Very much so," Catherine mused. "We also had sorbets made from loquat and waxberry."

"Yet you look done in," her colleague observed astutely. "Did anything go wrong?"

"No, no." She put down her floral scissors. "It's just jetlag and..."

Not everyone abets perjury when they go on holiday. Perhaps more than perjury...

But heck, she didn't reckon justice the same way her godfather, barrister Cecil Stone, did.

"I should get going," Catherine said, a bit lamely. "See you in the morning."

"Alright. Call me if you need someone to talk to."

"Of course."

Catherine returned to their locker room, put on her tweed jacket and a trilby, and headed to Catherine Street, where Chance and his friend Dominic Turner had set up a jazz bar. For the last time that summer, they would gather in that howff and have a meet-up on the rooftop before the ember months set in.

When Catherine arrived, she saw Patricia Bennett, her godfather's partner, and Sophie Stone, her godfather's daughter, were already there, with Sophie's young son Brendon reading an illustrated guide on chirping insects. The mother and child had recently moved back to London for Sophie to take up a research position at the nearby King's College London.

The young researcher smiled apologetically to her. "Cathy, I'm sorry for all the trouble I've caused you two."

Before returning to England, the couple had learnt that Sophie had hoped to move into Chance's rented flat on Kean Street as the new academic year began. Chance pulled some strings at NP Properties, so Sophie and Brendon had settled in before he had had the opportunity to clear out his belongings.

"No problem at all," Chance said as he appeared. "I've already moved most of my things to Catherine's place anyway."

"I'm afraid we used your utensils to make tortellini."

"Keep them if you want."

Brendon said, "We put all your goods and chattels in a box; you can pick it up anytime, Uncle Yang."

"Right. I will sign and date the deed of surrender David prepared and return my keys and key cards promptly. How are you finding the place?"

"All Sir Garnet. It's lovely, quiet, close to work and everything on top of the low peppercorn rent," Sophie said. "Mrs Robinson has been kind enough to invite us to supper. Sarnai also minds Brendon from time to time when he explores the open-air atrium."

"But I don't like Mrs Suntook." The boy closed his book and pouted. "She told me off for bringing my Twiggy to the atrium. She keeps nagging that the apartments should be 'pet-free', but my ghost insect is for scientific observations!"

Catherine remembered Mrs Merete Suntook, an elegant lady who frequented their flower shop and who always wore satin gloves. "Does she live there on her own?"

"Yup." Sophie took a sip of her cocktail and added, "I think she mentioned that she and her husband keep their flat as a pied-à-terre. Now, she's gone back to Melbourne to sort out some family matters." Sophie sighed. "Sometimes I feel sorry for her. Mrs Suntook seems a very lonely lady."

Patsy puckered up but said nothing.

"I feel really sorry for Mrs Robinson as well," Sophie said. "Perhaps misery does love company."

They all knew of Hannah Robinson's sad story.

She had moved to London from the States with her husband Eddy, who was once a foundling but later became a legal counsel for a fintech. Half a year ago, Eddy had suffered a stroke in a hotel lobby in a red-light district in Brussels. It was also the day of the Brussels Bombings – he later died because the ambulance couldn't make it when surrounded by so many casualties.

Eddy's death baffled Hannah because he had lied to her and nearly everyone about his whereabouts. She was thus determined to find out why he had ended up in a wrong location at a wrong time, so she had asked Chance for his help in tracking Eddy's digital trail.

The search led them to obscene online videos featuring Eddy, so they concluded he was a Lothario. Yet, when Chance contacted the uploader of the videos, he turned out to be Eddy's long-lost twin brother, Liam Killingback, with whom he had been meeting in secret. And now, Hannah Robinson was embittered with herself once again for not having trusted her late husband.

"And just to think…" Sophie relived that dreadful day. She herself had been injured slightly during the Brussels Bombings while attending a conference at a local university.

They fell silent for a while before Patsy asked, "Had you already met the…actor then?"

"Yes, I had. He seems a nice fellow." Sophie admitted, "I know Father is not very keen on the idea."

"You can move back anytime you wish," Patsy offered. "We will be more than glad to have you."

"That's very kind of you, but you deserve some space to yourselves–"

"Soz, people, for cutting it so fine!" Felipe's voice preceded his arrival. "I was at the Swingers–"

"Dang it, Felipe!" Patsy put down her teacup with a clack. "We've got sensitive ears here!"

"Patsy! Just where do all your prurient interests come from?" Felipe took off his natty leather jacket and plonked himself down on a chair. "The Swingers is a newly opened indoor golf venue in Shoreditch. Look it up if you don't believe me." He then said, "Why are you nitpicking today, Patsy? Didn't you get your Monday morning moan? I've heard that the English moan about their work every Monday."

To the general population, Felipe Kazama was a half Nikkei Peruvian investment banker with a flamboyant dress code, a galling mouth, and a Harvard Business School MBA degree.

To Chance, Felipe Kazama was a dangerous man. You never knew when he was lying, when he was joking, or when he was telling the truth. Or how terrifying the truth might be.

Roddy, the bartender, appeared. "What else can I get you, Nurse Bennett? Another bumbo, maybe?"

"I'd like a diet coke, if that's okay."

"On its way."

"Patsy, diet coke has no soul."

"Stop saying these beastly things!"

"One Vimto for me, Roddy, and one for yourself as well." Felipe threw Patsy a wink. "Don't you find me a handsome beast, Patsy? Aren't you gonna tell me that the Kingdom has missed me and my swag sorely? And did you enjoy grinding my gears every day?"

"Gah!" She threw him his car key. "Why didn't you bring your girlfriend and *finally* introduce her to our clique?"

Felipe looked at her as he swirled his Aston Martin key ring. "So you two can play Aunt Sally with my name taped on the dummy?"

"I've never–"

"Now, no need to deny it." He crossed his legs. "We separated due to irreconcilable differences, natch."

"Ha!" she barked. "With such brisk mood as yours, no wonder you are getting high-toned and hectoring us with your foul humour. I wouldn't be surprised if she *chucked* you for a true gentleman."

Once again, the rest watched back and forth as the two parried.

"Well, Patsy," Felipe considered, "you are not entirely wrong in calling me a 'nutter' or a 'ratbag'. It takes a lot to satisfy me. As they say, not everyone can pull off a long-distance relationship."

She huffed indignantly. "I shouldn't wonder that you were always short with her."

He gave her a crafty grin. "And with just which eye did you see that I was short?"

She nearly threw down her napkin. "What is the *matter* with you–"

"One diet coke for the lady." Roddy returned. "Anyone want to try some homemade passion fruit jelly?"

"Oo! I want some!" Brendon exclaimed.

The bartender offered the trifle pots around, and Patsy snatched the last two. "*Oopsy*, Felipe, surely you have no objection if I keep one for Cecil? He has such a sweet tooth."

"Go and snaffle it for your oldie goodie then."

As the others tasted the sweet, Felipe said quietly, " I remember an urban legend about a serial kidnapper who targeted young girls and cut off their hair as a souvenir. He'd make jelly using the gelatin from their hair. So, *enjoy*."

"Bally botheration!" Patsy threw down her spoon and pushed the pot away disapprovingly. "Didn't your mother teach you appropriate table talk?"

"Didn't yours teach you the beauty of thrift?" He took up the pot and her spoon. "It seems that I could only proffer myself for this *extremely* challenging endeavour."

"Huh! With such brusque table manners, no wonder I saw someone tailing your Aston," she said spitefully. "Most probably your *deeply **vexed** ex*."

This caught his interest. "Oh yeah? When did this happen?"

She rolled her eyes. "This summer bank holiday. We were nose to tail on the way back from Leavesden, and this Mondeo followed us all the way to Kensington."

Felipe sent Chance a look as the latter tucked this information away. Could it be that inexcusably rude bloke again?

"We have had many kerfuffles, Patsy, but this time you might be correct. Most likely a fling who regrets letting me go." Felipe thought. "October in London is a great season to be in love. Do you have any colleagues I can wolf whistle at in full cry?"

"Never!" She rolled her eyes. "The girls in my ward are all going steady."

"Sisters before misters? Don't jump to conclusions so quickly. Who said owt about Janes only?"

"You better not make a game of these things!"

"Woah! That's one way to kill a mood. What makes you think that I'm joking, goody-goody Patsy? It seems that I'm not living in your heart of gold at all." Felipe chuntered loudly as he furiously squished his jelly. "Anyways, I'm tired of your chop logic." He stood up and gathered his jacket. "I guess I'll try to pull a pretty bird at the nearest Scottish Widows branch. See you later."

Felipe left, and Sophie explained to Patsy on the side, "The first time we met him in Phuket, he was with his partner. A personable crooner, if I remember correctly."

"I'll check on him." Catherine went out and saw Felipe smoking by his car.

"Are you alright?" she asked.

"Call no sandboy happy." He puffed. "It's you that I'm concerned about. Cathy, you have worry written all over your lovely visage."

She made up a ready excuse. "Well, I'm only nettled because my fanfic got flamed the other day, so I've decided to make them available on request only."

"You know what to do for the best," Felipe said, "but if you need a father confessor to confide in, you know where to find one."

He watched as Catherine nodded slowly and went back in without another word. Then he clipped his cigarette butt and sat in his sports car. The seat was unadjusted. Inside the cupholder rested his two carved walnuts where he had left them two months ago. He looked around. There was half a bag of Murray Mints in the map pocket; he took a sweet and imagined a few things.

***

Later.
Their gathering ended, and the couple drove back to their snuggery in Holland Park.

Catherine unlocked the door, and Mr Darcy was waiting quietly by the umbrella stand with his furry tail curled back. She bent down and picked up her large ginger cat. "Who's the cutest in the world?"

For some unknown reason, the cat's front paws were slightly wet.

Chance followed her as he put his car key in a salver. "Do you feel peckish? Should we cook something now?"

"I can wait." She let her cat go. "Let's finish unpacking first."

They busied themselves with small tasks, and Catherine brought out two boxes of pastries with sweet rose petal fillings and two jars of lotus root powder. "Remind me to take these to the Academy tomorrow for Melody and Orla."

"Of course." He put away their laundry. "What should we have for dinner?"

"Maybe some garlic chicken? I can toss a salad," Catherine suggested. "I don't know why, but yesterday's rib stew didn't taste as good as the basted ones we had in Yantai."

"Boar taint is to blame." Chance washed his hands and put the kettle on. "I'll make sure to give the meat a good soak and simmer beforehand next time."

Catherine opened the fridge. "How's it going?" A small penguin-shaped electronic device they brought back from China greeted her inside.

Mr Darcy jumped onto the counter and pricked up his ears.

"Things are okay." Catherine took out a salad bag and some endives from the crisper in her fridge and set to her task. Then she murmured both to herself and to him, "It was nice seeing everyone again."

Her husband concurred.

She glanced at the cat calendar she had pinned on her fridge door, thinking how, four years ago, a girl dying on her hospital bed had scribbled on a few calendar slips, hoping to get her last messages across.

They worked silently for a while as Catherine washed and juiced two lemons. She said, "Mr Darcy's paws were a bit wet just now when I held him. Do you think he might have taken a too keen attitude to the new bidet in our washroom?"

He smiled. "I hope not."

She smiled back thinly. "I know it might not be the most romantic birthday gift, but it is convenient and highly practical."

"I agree. And just to be safe, I'll wipe his paws."

Her salad was ready, and then she recalled, "Do you think Coach Sidney would tail Felipe's car out of spite?"

Chance frowned and sighed. "I don't think so. To be honest, I'm not sure if they were ever dating." He swallowed a thought. "And it's still too early to name the culprit. It could be that rude bloke who threw up on my car."

They ate, showered, watched an episode of *Keeping Up Appearances*, and Chance called Yining, a friend's daughter spending an exchange term in a school in Somerset. Nothing was awry at the girl's end, except complaints about the frequent fry-ups offered at her school's canteen and the rainy weather. She also shared with him accounts of the scenery she had seen and some local folklore she had heard on a recent outing to the Brecon Beacons National Park.

Then the couple retired for the night. Chance felt the tingling sensation of an incipient migraine, but soon nodded off.

Sometime later – he didn't know precisely when – his sleep was disturbed by agitated urging. **"Darling, wake up!"**

Catherine shook him awake. He struggled with opening his bleary eyes in the dim, roseate light.

"Y...yes?"

She whispered; her breathing rushed. "I heard *someone* **speaking** downstairs!"

He was now wide awake. "Sssh..."

They pricked their ears and could hear occasional mumblings from downstairs.

"Blast!" he cursed softly, his mind working on the possible identity of their intruder(s). Then he put on a bathrobe and told Catherine, "Stay here and call the police."

"Wait!" She stopped him, rifled in her bedside drawers, and pressed a taser into his hands.

He tightened his bathrobe sash, tucked the taser in, and stealthily moved out of their bedroom.

They had not talked much about the repercussions of their Holmesian truth-finding in China. *Could it be...?*

Chance descended the stairs one at a time, making sure his bare feet made no noise on the polished parquet floor. Now he could hear the maunderings better: they sounded like a man giving instructions. Faint lights came from their kitchen, disappeared, then came on again.

He put his hand on the taser and recalled how dextrously Felipe had used the device. Now he regretted not having practised with it.

*"**Do not move!**"* He dashed into the kitchen, and the sight in front of him nearly knocked him for six.

***

Mr Darcy was sat in front of their fridge, his paws swinging the door open and closed as the small penguin device inside responded to the motion.

"How's it going?"

"What's for dinner?"

"Close the door, please."

"Don't eat too much after nine."

Chance didn't know whether to smile or swear at this stunner. He released his bated breath, tucked his taser back in, and hefted the cat up resignedly. "Well. Now we know the culprit..."

Catherine was right, he thought, in calling her furball the cutest mischief maker. The cat's paws were wet once again. He looked around and found several imprints by the lower compartment inside the fridge, where a sheen of water droplets had gathered.

"Close the door, please," the small penguin-shaped device repeated.

He shut the door as the ginger creature nuzzled closer to him like a clingy sloth. "I suppose we haven't properly introduced you two. Was that why?"

Mr Darcy meowed as if assenting.

"It's a birthday gift from my sister so I don't feel too lonely. You and I are both creatures of habit. Did you feel lonely when we were away?" He carried the cat and returned to their bedroom, almost bumping into Catherine halfway. She wielded a cricket bat and was still on her call. He explained what had happened, and they then apologised profusely to the operator.

They double checked that all the doors were locked, and all the windows were latched securely, bringing the cat along. Then they went out to the garden. Nothing was out of place under the light-polluted night sky.

Later, they returned to their bedroom and Catherine said, "Mr Darcy, you gave us *such* a ***fright***."

She smoothed her cat's whiskers as Chance dabbed his paws with a tissue.

Catherine smiled poignantly. "Poor thing, were you curious about all the new gadgets? Tomorrow we shall make some proper introductions."

They settled back, and she mused, "Let's not travel for a while."

He flicked off their bedside lamp. "Of course."

A moment later, she murmured, "I can't sleep."

He felt the cat kneading softly in between them. "Me neither."

"I'm worried."

"Me too." He hesitated. "Although you said what happened changed nothing between us, it still has changed us, and in a big way."

He heard a pensive sigh, then Catherine said, "There's something I haven't told you." She turned to face him. "I've missed my period."

"Oh, Catherine–"

"I'm not pregnant," she said. "At first I thought it was only late, but it didn't come. I think I know why. It happened after my parents passed away as well. I was distraught and sorry for myself for a long time."

He waited.

"Now I'm worried whenever I think about what happened and what might happen."

"What worries you more? The righteousness of his revenge, or whether he would succeed or not?"

She sighed again. "I suppose the latter. You know, I don't reckon justice the way my uncle or Cecil does."

He offered honestly, "I worry about the consequences."

"The consequences?"

"Very few people know what happened," Chance said. "The last thing I want is to put anyone in danger."

The next day, Catherine sought Felipe out after lunch, and they met near a toffee stall in Southbank.

The weather was set fair, and as Felipe removed his sunglasses he said, "Cathy, you and my buddy are hiding something serious from me and from everybody else."

"Everything's alright."

"Now you are leading me on," Felipe said. "Just like how once you shied away from admitting that you wanted to visit La Specola."

She turned to watch the river; the rushing water seemed soothing. Catherine had never understood why cornball films liked to feature a scene by the Thames, but at that moment she knew.

Finally, she said, "Something happened during our honeymoon."

"Let me guess." Felipe played with his cigarette case. "You saw an alien?"

"No." She laughed weakly. "I'd rather we had, though."

"Then what happened?"

"If I tell you–" she made up her mind "–I must have your complete confidence."

"When did I ever fail you in that regard?"

So, Catherine told him about the three awful deaths at that seaside ruin, the distraught young man who had fled to South Korea, the avenging husband and father who was after him, and the tragic twists and turns weaving through the years.

She finished her story with lots of 'maybes', and Felipe considered and said, "Don't worry, Cathy. If someone so loves to represent God, then God must grant his every wish. It's time for the vultures to gather."

CHAPTER 2

That noon, Chance went to his former flat on Kean Street in Covent Garden to collect his personal belongings.

Sophie and Brendon were out on a school visit, but she had no objections to Chance using his old keys, so he parked his car near Aram, a modern furniture store, and got out.

He arrived at a glass door beside a red brick wall daubed with graffiti of half a clown's face, found his key card, swiped open the glass gate, and took the lift.

"Ninth floor," the usual synthesised sound announced as he stepped out.

The small, open-air atrium was quiet. He went into his old flat. The curtains inside were open, and he could see the BT Tower afar amidst rents in the scudding clouds.

The corrugated box where Brendon had collected Chance's bits and bobs stood by a pier glass. He smiled inwardly as he remembered how the boy had referred to them as 'goods and chattels': a legal term he had learnt from his grandfather, for sure.

Chance went through his things quickly: an odd sock here and there, a set of entangled earphones, some bath bombs, and finally, a large frame of mezzotint artwork featuring circles and squares – a housewarming gift from Felipe.

He heaved the box up, took a final look at the panoramic view of Covent Garden, and left.

"Good to see you." As he locked the door, Sarnai Ganbold, Hannah Robinson's cleaner, came out of the refuse storage. "I hope you had a nice time in China?"

"More or less, thank you." He looked around. "Is Mrs Robinson in?"

"She's at the gym," Sarnai said. "She has moved on just as you have moved out. A Mongolian saying says that the pastures stay the same, but herds come and go."

"We have a similar saying in China." He heaved the box further up; the mezzotint was heavier than he thought. "How was your summer?"

"It was nice, but summer here is so short." She shrugged. "But it's British summer, what can we expect? At least I'm good with the cleaning robot now. It saves a lot of my time." Sarnai tilted her head and added somewhat unwillingly, "and recently..."

"Yes?" he prompted after a few seconds.

"Recently, I feel like I'm being watched..." Sarnai confessed ominously.

"Being watched?"

"And being followed..." Then she said briskly, "The other day, when I picked up my daughter from school, she said someone had tried to pass himself off as her father's friend, and he told her to come with him. But my girl was sharp enough to see through his lies. You see, her father doesn't have any white friends."

Chance chewed over her account. "If there's anything I can help with, let me know."

"It's not like I'm rich or anything, so I don't know who would…" Sarnai said a little lamely. "Anyway, I better go. Mrs Robinson's sister and niece are visiting soon, and I must prepare their room. At the moment, it's a cleaner's nightmare."

Chance took the lift downstairs and saw a slovenly-looking plumber waiting behind the double glass door with a foldable ladder on his shoulder and a tool bag in his hand. The man gestured to Chance, signalling if he could open the door for him from the inside. Chance moved through the lobby and pressed the green 'Exit' button on the marble wall.

"Cheers, mate." The glass door opened as the man entered.

Chance gave a slight nod in acknowledgement and, in the same instant, felt the bottom of his box giving away.

"No!"

The man quickly caught his mezzotint as a confused Chance chased after his bath bombs, now rolling all over the lobby floor.

"Sorry about that." A moment later, he returned.

"Always tape them boxes underneath, and they stay sturdy," the plumber told him.

"Will do next time." Chance thanked him again and lugged his belongings out.

He secured the mezzotint with the back seatbelts, put the rest into the trunk, and removed a large buff envelope from his glove compartment where he had gathered the keys and key cards to be returned.

Then he went to the apartments' main reception on Kingsway and delivered the envelope.

"Thank you, Mr Yang." A staff member from NP Properties confirmed the items. "David will be in touch if anything is amiss, and for now—" she typed and clicked something on her desktop— "I have removed you from our mailing list. I wish you a good day."

"Thank you."

He got back to his car and sat in the driver's seat. Something kept niggling at the back of his mind.

His phone buzzed; it was an automated email from NP Properties thanking him for staying with them and telling him not to hesitate to reach out if he had any questions.

The mailing list...

Something sparked in his head, and Chance remembered that the front reception had always sent out emails to the tenants regarding upcoming maintenance schedules. They even did so that time when the RSPB came to collect the nun pigeon that took refuge on Hannah Robinson's balcony and that one time when roadworks were being carried out on Drury Lane in late August when he was away.

Why hadn't he received any communications about plumbing work this time?

***

Chance looked through his inbox; there were no maintenance-related notices for that week.

"Recently...I feel like being watched..."

An uncanny feeling crept over him. He remembered what Sarnai had said and sprang from his seat.

He ran up to the glass door, forgetting that he had already returned his key card, then dashed to the main reception again. "Sorry, I've forgotten my doormat. Can I quickly borrow the lift card again?" He made a mealy-mouthed excuse, and the receptionist agreed unwillingly. "Please return it before lunch hour ends."

"Will do!" He hared off for a few quick steps then returned. "Hmm... do you know if there is any maintenance happening in the apartments?"

"Not to my knowledge," the lady shrugged. "Although occasionally there might be some minor work and small upkeeping."

"Thanks!"

He went through the less-used entrance inside the office building that led directly to the apartment lobby.

"Someone had tried to pass as her father's friend..."

He pressed the 'down' button several times, but the lift seemed stuck on the ninth floor. Chance tried not to recall what had happened when that lift stuck in March as he sprinted up the emergency stairs. He got to the ninth floor and saw a ladder placed between the lift doors, preventing them from closing.

Clack!

He heard something breaking as he entered the atrium. The door to the Robinsons' was shut. He walked up to the wooden door and checked the refuse storage with his peripheral vision. There were no temporary notices posted there.

He readied himself and knocked hard on the wood. "Sarnai? Are you in?"

The door opened a slit, and the plumber poked his head out. "What do you want?"

"I need to speak with Sarnai."

"Who's Sarnai?"

"The cleaner who works here."

"Eesh," the man said, "she's gone. Got some better-paid hourly this afternoon."

"The lift was on this floor when I came up, with a ladder *stuck* in between its doors."

"Must 'ave taken the stairs." He joked, "Ladies like to exercise their buttocks. As for that ladder, I'll get it shortly."

"I came up the staircase and didn't see her." Chance heard some small noises, one tiny click, another, and it stopped. One click, another, and it stopped again.

"You must have missed her," the plumber concluded as he raised his volume. "Now, matey. I've got no time for small talk. Still got work to do." He tried to close the door, but Chance quickly intervened.

"Why are you here, anyway?"

"To replace a hose connector. The current one is up the spout." He furrowed his eyebrow. "The last bloke bodged the job, so they sent me. Now, are we done?"

Chance heard the small noises again. "Let me in."

The man clenched his jaw. "What if I say *no*?"

"Then you will bear the consequences."

***

Tasing a man down was a lot easier than he had thought, Chance reflected as the man stumbled and fell in front of him.

He kicked away the spanner the imposter had hidden behind his back, found a spool of sturdy waterproof tape in the man's toolkit, and tied him up. Then he strode into the living room. Sarnai had her hands and feet bound and her mouth taped. A broken carafe lay beside her feet.

"Oh!" Chance rushed towards her and cut her loose with a pair of kitchen scissors. "Are you alright?"

"Thank every blue sky that you understood!" She sniffled. "999 is too long...then I remembered you call 110 for police in China..."

He quickly assisted her up. "Are you hurt?"

"My neck hurts, but nothing serious." She glanced towards the door. "What happened?"

"I have him under control. Do you know him?"

"No." She shook her head vigorously.

"Let's find out who he is."

Later.

He vaguely dreamt of eating spaghetti, only the sauce was too salty, and the noodles overcooked. Then, as he was brought back to consciousness a degree at a time, he realised that a wet mop was prodding his face.

He coughed and stirred. "What the–"

Someone brought down the mop again, and he choked his words back.

"Who sent you?" The Asian man squatted beside him.

"No one." He gauged his appearance; he didn't remember seeing him when he tailed her.

"Did you follow my friend from Leavesden to Chelsea?"

"*What?! NO!*" he cried out. "I don't even know you!"

The woman demanded, "Did you follow my daughter after school?"

"Well..." He lost momentum.

The Asian man frisked him. "Who sent you?"

"Look, this has nuthin' to do with–"

The mop again: "Were you the one following me?"

"I did–"

"Who sent you?"

"No one–"

The mop again. "*Who* sent you?"

"I said no one! For God's sake! Can't you put away this *bloody* mop?!" The veins on his grubby face were protruding. "This has nothing to do with you. This is between her and me!"

"What do you mean?" The woman froze. "I don't know you."

"I know who *you* are and what you've done!"

"Let's call the police," the Asian man suggested calmly. "They have far more experience handling stalkers than us."

"Yeah, go and call the police so we can unveil this *killer*! This *vile* woman!"

He saw the pair looking at each other quizzically.

"Do you think he's certifiable?" the woman asked. "I saw yesterday on the news that someone had escaped from a hospital."

"I'm not mad!" he scoffed. "You must be! Have you forgotten what you've done so quickly?"

The woman tilted her head. "What did I do?"

His patience was wearing thin. "You don't *remember* what *happened* on the morning of the 19th of September?"

"The 19th? Last month?" the woman recalled, and her expression grew tense. She found her jacket, took out her smart phone, and showed him a photo. "Is this Nokia your phone?"

***

"That's reet," the man coughed.

"Do you know him?" Chance asked her.

She responded gingerly, "I've never met him. I don't understand what he has to do with me–"

"I–"

"I suggest you speak *only* when spoken to." Chance took out his taser and put it on the carpet beside him. He then asked Sarnai, "What happened on the 19th last month?"

"Oh, that day–" she hesitated as she recalled. "I came into work, and I cleaned the dust box of the cleaning robot and washed Mrs Robinson's gym clothes. Then, I went out into the atrium to brush the door mat and saw a cell phone near one of her terracotta pots."

"Yes?"

"That day, Mrs Robinson told me earlier that people were coming to fix something in the atrium, so I thought he must have left it." Sarnai continued, "There was a number scribbled on the back of his phone, so I called it. The call went through, and I asked the person on the other end if they had lost their phone, and a woman said no. Then I asked if she knew whose phone it was, and she said no again. I told her how I had found her number, and the lady said, 'I give out at least five thousand cards every year. Do you suppose I remember all the recipients?'"

Sarnai turned to Chance. "Then I needed to go to my next spot, so I left his phone at reception."

"You did nothing wrong."

"Don't listen to this *lying* hag! That's not true!" The man wriggled his hands. "You need to hear *my* side of the story!"

"Go ahead then."

"Let me up first."

Chance found a dining chair, hauled the man up, and secured his hands behind its legs.

He cleared his throat. "That day, I came here to work. The last bloke bodged, so the firm sent me instead."

Sarnai told Chance on the side, "I remember Mrs Suntook complaining about a drain leak in the atrium and how it wasn't fixed."

The man continued, "It was my first time at these apartments. I finished the job and went to the next one on my schedule in Hammersmith. I have a personal cell and another one for work, so I only realised I'd lost my personal one on the Tube, but then my company contacted me to say that someone had found it."

"No discrepancies so far," Chance said.

"What matters *most* was what happened in between." He sighed. "I have a boy with my ex, and we've grown distant after the divorce. But beginning this year, Johnny, my son, got in contact again. They moved to Dar es Salaam. He didn't have a particularly happy childhood, and he got into drugs. Sometimes he'd call for advice and... money. The number I wrote down was for a famous rehab instructor in London."

They waited for him to continue.

"On the 19th, Johnny called me in the morning, agitated. I told him I'd come and fetch him, he could get clean, and we could start again. But by the time I went to collect my phone from the reception, he was dead."

Sarnai gasped, "He *died*?!"

"He and his girlfriend were out for a drive. They crashed, and he didn't have his seatbelt on, so... The girl drove and had hers on, but she was also injured quite badly. She's pregnant, and she is still in the ICU." The man scowled at Sarnai. "So you are *responsible* for *three* lives!"

"I am very sorry to hear about your son, sir. But I do not know why you should lay this blame on me. Perhaps you don't know, but the previous tenant of flat number five died in there, and I found her body. I am a parent myself. I would never wish that kind of thing to happen to anyone's child."

"Just do it, *just* go on playing silly!" he shouted. "When I got my phone, I had a dozen missed calls, all from Johnny, but his last call went through. Someone had answered his call on my phone. Lindsay said she was distracted because Johnny had a tiff with '*me*'! She said that 'I' told Johnny to 'fuck off and die'! ***Except it couldn't be me!***"

"I didn't do it! I promise!"

He raved, "But you were the *last* person to touch my phone!"

Chance stepped in. "Could it have been someone at reception?"

"No. The call came before she handed it to them." He dipped his head. "It took me days just to figure out who that cleaner was."

Chance advised him, "You better consult the police."

"They will never take it seriously. They will only laugh in my face that another junkie is gone."

"The local police in Dar es Salaam, then?"

The man lost momentum again. "They are already on the case because Johnny and his girl were joyriding."

"Have you got any ID?"

"In my bag."

Chance searched and found a driving licence attesting that he was Ikenua Joseph from Havering. He also found a few foolscap-sized maintenance logs in his bag.

"I'll cut you loose now, but don't do anything rash." Chance released him.

"Not as long as she's still holding that mop." Ikenua Joseph stood up and exercised his swollen wrists.

"It wasn't me. Honest to Tengri!" Sarnai put away the mop and sent them an apologetic look. "I'm sorry that I didn't tell the truth earlier. That morning, I got a call from my daughter's teacher that she had a touch of fever. I had a friend who was visiting town, so in the end, she said she'd cover this spot for me. I brought her here and left–"

"Where is this friend of yours then?!"

"Please let me finish. Sometime later, I got a message from her that she had found a phone in the atrium, and she didn't know what to do with it. She doesn't speak much English, so she sent me the number on the back of your phone, and I made the call. We wanted to find the owner before giving it to reception because I could lose my job if anyone found out what I did." Sarnai thought quickly. "When did that call happen? You said someone picked up your son's last call – when did that call happen?"

"Eleven-o-three." Ikenua Joseph rummaged through his bag and took out a pile of papers. "I asked someone to help me print out my calling history. Here, this highlighted line tells the time." He showed it to them. "And whoever answered my call also deleted the very same call record on my phone."

"May I?" Chance asked as he reached for the sheets and scrutinised the pages momentarily.

Sarnai responded, "My friend didn't do it, I assure you. I was supposed to be here at eleven sharp, but we were late by about ten minutes because our bus had to take a detour. And as much as I hate to say this, we weren't the only ones here that day. We saw Mrs Suntook leaving the building when we came in. Mrs Robinson said she would go to a flotation tank session in Vauxhall that morning, so she told me to use her spare key and do my work. We arrived and saw Mrs Suntook leaving and walking down Drury Lane."

Then Sarnai remembered something. She took up her phone, made a call, and conversed in Mongolian for a few long, agitated minutes.

Later, she led them out to the common open-air atrium. "My friend found your phone here." She pointed to a corner of the gutter covered by small pebbles. "And when she found it, it was turned off."

"It was turned off when I went to collect it, but I thought its battery had drained." Ikenua Joseph stared blankly. "Where is this other woman now?"

"In Australia, I think."

He demanded more. "What else do you know about her?"

"Her name is Merete with three 'e's and her husband is the CEO of a medical group in Melbourne."

They fell silent and could see the small tip of the slowly revolving London Eye.

"I'm sorry," Joseph offered half-heartedly.

"If you still doubt what she says," Chance said, "perhaps I can get you the CCTV footage for the lift on the 19th. On one condition, of course: that you don't harm anyone."

CHAPTER 3

Sarnai let Joseph go. Chance called Felipe afterwards and told him what had happened and what he needed.

Felipe said, "I suppose I can ask Enid a favour, and if she won't oblige, then her boss, and if he won't, the boss of his bosses." He then added, "Sorry about what happened during your honeymoon. I once joked that the phrase 'all fur coats and no knickers' is not as vivid as 'all body bags and no knickers'. But perhaps, for now, it is too vivid to be any good."

"You know," Chance took a breath, "I've been thinking... I know Mercury has a branch in Seoul. Can you pull some strings and help me track him down before the irreparable happens?"

"I can try to rustle up some info, but no promises."

"Thanks."

Chance drove back to Holland Park, contemplating what had happened.

Catherine seemed to be in a better mood. She looped a song, 'Lay Your Love on Me' by Racey, in the background, as she combed Mr Darcy with a durian-shell-shaped silica cat groomer they had brought back from China.

"Earlier, when I introduced Mr Darcy to Pingu – by the way I decided to call that small penguin device in our fridge Pingu – and he said, 'don't eat too much after nine', and Mr Darcy meowed as if he'd lost all his snack privileges, and then I explained that Pingu meant overeating in the evenings, and they made up."

Chance washed his hands, made a cup of plain black tea for himself and a rose tea for her. "I haven't thanked you."

"For what?"

"For connecting the dots." He watched her sway to the rhythm as the cat purred.

"I told you, sometimes I have a feeling for things." She gathered the fallen cat hair and smoothed her cat's Henry's pockets. "And I haven't thanked you for sharing your secrets with me." She crimped the tiny fur rolls and put them on a small plate. "What would you do if you decided to keep quiet?" Catherine looked up searchingly into his eyes.

"I don't know," he said, with a certain gravity in his tone. "Maybe I would just keep quiet."

She sensed that he was at war with himself. "Then we'd miss out on the opportunity to unravel the truth."

"Well, there has never been only one version of the truth."

"That I disagree with. There will always be an unvarnished, indubitable truth. But as they say, a trouble shared is a trouble halved. How's your day been?"

"Alright."

Catherine stowed the plate away in a drawer. "I've been thinking about doing some cat hair felting later. Oh, and Sophie is planning a soirée this Friday. To celebrate her new job and everything," she said. "I bought some artichokes and, Mr Yang, we will leave you the task of making dessert tonight."

"How about baked nectarines with peanut brittle?"

"That sounds lovely."

He finished his tea, refilled their tea caddy, and gathered the ingredients. Then Catherine sneaked up on him from behind like a cat and encased his eyes. "Guess who?"

He played along and replied jauntily, "My naughty catling?"

"Busted." She hugged him and gave him a smooch on the face. "Hmm...you smell divine. Like a freshly peeled mandarin."

"I thought we were leaving dessert for later?"

She laughed and tickled him. "Cheeky tiger." Then she confessed, "I've talked with Felipe."

"So I've heard." He turned to face her.

"How?"

"I called him after..."

He didn't want to drag her into yet more trouble, but then he didn't want to keep another secret. So, he told her.

"Poor Sarnai..." She searched his face. "Are you hurt?"

"No," he said, "but we need to be careful now. Danger could be next door."

"You mean I should be concerned about the curtain-twitching Mrs Ferguson?" she joshed.

"You know what I mean."

"Yes." She mused, "I'm not afraid, and I hope that Mrs Suntook didn't do anything wrong. But after this summer, I came to realise that life is not all roses and cherries and can be more bizarre than anything in books."

"But still–"

"When my parents died in that car crash, I blamed myself for not going with them that night. Then I blamed that driver for drunk driving. One gusty night I went to his house and saw his bereaved daughter. Then I cried for a long time and left." Catherine sorted the coriander leaves that Chance planned to use as garnish and said sagely, "Felipe told me that for every hurt, there is a leaf to cure it[*] ; and for every wrong done, there is karma to correct it."

***

Three days later.

They drove to Kean Street that Friday night. The spot where Chance usually parked his car was occupied by Felipe's Aston Martin. Chance had uncanny feelings about going there as he recalled how Sarnai had once asked him:

"Do you think there is something wrong with this building? With so many deaths associated with it?"

The CCTV footage he got access to had proved Sarnai's account, and Ikenua Joseph told them to contact him as soon as Merete Suntook returned.

The couple took the lift to the ninth floor. They could hear Felipe and Patsy bickering as they stepped out.

"Patsy! There's no need to be hotter than a two-dollar pistol. As much as we are pyrophiles, let's save the sparks for later."

"You know what you are?! You are a *textbook **classical*** predator!"

"I learned at Harvard Business School that there are three types of predators: the power predator, the persuasion predator, and the opportunistic predator. Enlighten me: which category should we put Theresa May in? In the third or across the board?"

---

[*] 'For every hurt, there is a leaf to cure it'
Felipe quotes from the poem 'In Perpetual Spring' by Amy Gerstler.

Brendon sat on a bench in the open-air atrium with a popgun in his hands, and Catherine approached him. "Why are they arguing again?"

The boy offered, "Aunt Pat had a button fall off her coat, and he mentioned something about buttons, and she called him 'reebald'. Then he asked her if she had any press studs, and she flew off the handle."

"You're entirely too clever by half!" they heard Patsy shouting. "You're three kinds of fools all in one!"

"Do I sense you deflecting? Don't tell me how much you've done for your country, Patsy the Bennett. Ask what it *did* to you. You may care for the NHS. The NHS doesn't give a ***stuff*** about you. Let's not forget that Thomas Guy made his first fortune smuggling Holy Writs from Holland without imprimatur."

"You just have to make *everything* ***insufferable*** for me!"

"Patsy! Do you know who you are addressing? You are talking to a man who once dined with the man who saved Japan."

Patsy stormed out. "Tell him to pipe down and naff off!"

They went in, and Felipe took the muselet off a champagne bottle. "Ah, the love-struck birds are here, and we can let the bang-up times roll. Cathy, let them prosecco socialists enjoy their prosecco, and we can bask in our wonder water. Do you know that writing wine names in round and rugged letters will make the wine taste different?" He regarded a large photograph of the International Space Station that Sophie had put up. "And I've heard if you have a bottle of Château Pétrus languishing in your cellar, it can get a flavour boost by spending a year on the ISS."

He poured her a glass. "Come on, let's celebrate. Tonight is also my leaving do."

"Oh, are you leaving London?" Catherine placed the petite cocotte they had brought for the potluck on the countertop, along with two small jars of home-made pickled walnuts.

"Nope, though I've decided to take indefinite gardening leave. This meant I had to move out of my corporate housing. But luckily, I have a friend willing to lend me his penthouse suite next door, so I still have a place to stay."

Chance sent him a doubtful look.

"In light of *recent* events," Felipe gestured casually, "Jayden commissioned me to find out if we can see aliens from these balconies. A glass for you as well, buddy?"

"No thanks."

"Suit yourself. As they say, 'tis better to sleep with a sober cannibal than a drunk Christian."

"If you can't be good, Felipe." Patsy came back. Her nose was red, and her voice coarse. "Be *careful* then. I've heard that aliens tend to abduct unwanted ones, especially those who spout."

"Patsy, do you know the number one secret that no one wants to admit? That we are 'aliens' to other planets. By the way, do you know there is a book titled *The English: Are They Human?* Maybe you are an alien yourself without knowing. Supporting aliens is supporting diversity."

She found a tissue and blew her nose hard. "Why do you have to be so...*so* contrarian!"

"It's a sin to feel sinful, and I've decided to live for fun–"

"For Chrissake, will you *please* quieten your cleverness for once?!"

Brendon hid behind the couple, and Catherine intervened before things escalated. "Will Cecil be late?"

"He's not coming. Got a meeting with a client at Boodle's."

"Patsy, don't you find me a trouper compared with your crabby dull dog? Does he even do dad jokes?"

"You *villain*!"

"Why, pernickety Patsy, you gonna spank me and make me wear a brank?"

"Whew! Lovely seeing everyone's already here." Sophie returned from her shopping. "I'm starting my shakshuka now."

A moment later.

As Brendon helped his mother to crack the eggs, Chance recalled, "I remember a CGCU event at Imperial, where you have to build a plane from paper and sticks to carry a raw egg from the Queen's Tower to the lawn."

"Oh, yes. I did enter the Egg Race once, but we didn't manage to save the poor egg. Should have chosen more aerodynamic modules early on," Sophie said. "Cathy says she bumped into you once when she visited me on campus."

"She did, and she left quite an impression on me."

"I'm glad that I helped in matchmaking you two in a way. What did you think of the Egg Race?"

He said, "I couldn't bear to see eggs cracked for no good reason. Honestly, I consider it a waste of food."

Sophie added some sweet paprika and stirred the pot. "It's amazing seeing how quickly China's space programme has advanced, especially given how the US banned exporting relevant hardware and software for use in Chinese space missions for nearly two decades."

Felipe commented, "China will have its own space station in no time."

"Just when did *you* become an authority on space?" Patsy mocked him.

"Patsy, perhaps you don't know, but ickle ol' me holds an MSc in astrophysics with distinction." He grinned. "Everybody loves to date men who are good at physics and motion."

She rolled her eyes sharply.

"In any case, perhaps I may not be an authority on space-related discussions and discourses, but you know who else is not cut for the sinecure?" He toasted to the air: "your BBC pundits, who predict that the Isle of Man would be a likely place to put the next person on the moon, after the US, Russia, China, and India. Really, what do these BBC respondents do other than see a man about a dog? I might even buy it if they said Peru."

Patsy said flatly, "Here's something that we are proud to have in the UK and I doubt is available in Peru. Strong institutions and thriving business environments that support and embrace entrepreneurship so people like Richard Branson can develop ambitious space programmes like Virgin Galactic—"

"Virgin Galactic is basically a rocket of burning rubber – no pun intended."

Sophie laughed, "I wish I could say otherwise, but this much is true."

Felipe swirled his champagne flute expertly. "By the way, Patsy, do you know what happens if someone dies on the International Space Station? They put the body in a body bag and hang the bag out to freeze, so it becomes smithereens."

"That's it!" Patsy let rip. "I'm done speaking with you!"

"Please don't give me a rocket. Come on, and there's no joy without annoy. When you gaze at the stars, Patsy, you might not look at any celestial bodies but satellites. The art of living is to not overthink."

"How's the school searching?" Catherine emerged from the washroom and asked her friend as the latter cooked while munching on Jaffa cakes.

"I don't know if I want to send Brendon to a school. Home-schooling worked just fine," she responded. "But I did get an exciting piece of information. Kensington Wade, the first school to offer a dual English-Chinese education, will open next year. Might be something that you find useful."

They smiled in secret as they turned and watched Chance engage Brendon with questions about his ghost insect. Sophie asked, "Do you think he will be a tiger dad?"

"I think he will be a softie."

Her friend smiled. "I just remembered what Hugh MacDiarmid said about reproducing the ancient Greek temperament."

Catherine said, "You've reminded me, though. I still need to sign up for my Mandarin Beginner's course at the Modern Language Centre at King's. I promised his aunt to learn so we can converse more directly next time we meet. And I can attend the evening classes right after my afternoon shifts at the flower academy."

"Do pop into my office when you are around."

"Right, they have delicious chips and wraps at Chapters," Catherine salivated. "Now with my more flexitarian diet, I'd like to taste all the goodies that I've missed."

They heard the boy announce proudly, "Last year I wanted to become a zoologist, but now I want to become an entomologist!"

"Smashing little chap. Your Aunt Cathy might tell you that being an entomologist is not as charming a profession as a psychiatrist." Felipe sipped his champagne. "Sophie, I don't see any demerits in home-schooling, and interest is the best teacher for a third-culture kid. Not to mention that British education is bleak at the best of times. And now that we are neighbours, I can teach him to live like a boss."

"Huh!" Patsy retorted. "I wouldn't entrust any child to you within a mile."

"For your record, Patsy, I cared for, cooked, cleaned, and looked after my three *hermanas* before they came of age. I would never leave a child alone." He looked at her. "I can teach Brendon the appurtenances of the life of a consultant. Perhaps you could teach him the life of a croupier?"

"Stop your braggadocio and stop showing off your sybaritic lifestyle."

"But Patsy, life is not all chalk and smooth talk. Finance is all about looking forward, accounting is all about looking backwards, and marriage is all about looking miserable." He prompted, "Brendon, tell your Aunty Patty what we were doing this afternoon."

"First we watched *Johnny English*. Then we read a story on courtly love and King Arthur, and I drew." The boy ran to a sideboard and took out a sketching in crayons.

Felipe prompted him: "And what does the yarn teach us?"

"That decent persons don't go after their friends' wives and girlfriends," the boy announced. "And here is King Arthur, wearing his green hat."

Patsy glared daggers at Felipe. "Brendon, ducky, you must have got it wrong. King Arthur should wear a helmet or a barbute, not a green hat. He's not Robin Hood."

"He wears one because he is a cuck–"

Someone knocked, and Chance went to get the door.

"Look who's here!" Hannah Robinson was delighted to see him. "Hope you had a lovey-dovey honeymoon?"

"More or less, thank you."

"I saw the lights were on and just wanted to say hi to Brendon Boy." A lean fellow appeared behind her, and she introduced him. "This is Travis; Travis Newman, my gym instructor. The flophouse he is staying in got flooded, so I'm letting him stay the night."

"That sounds terrible!" Sophie said. "Why don't you two join us for supper?"

"Oh, please don't let me disturb your evening," Travis said timidly.

"Absolute piffle! The more, the merrier. Come on in."

They came in, and brief introductions were made.

Catherine shared with the group what had transpired between her attention-seeking furball and the penguin device in her fridge, and Brendon laughed until he had tears in his eyes. "At least my Twiggy won't do that." He then showcased his ghost insect to Travis like a prize.

Travis took out a gym circular from his messenger bag. "Brendon, would you like to learn how to fold an origami ladybird? Though I'm afraid it will not be red and black."

"Sure! There are many colourful types of ladybirds." The boy put down his net cage.

Travis passed the boy another leaflet. "Just follow my instructions then. First, we need to make a square..."

They watched as the two trialled and errored with each fold. Finally, the ladybirds were made, and Sophie used a black marker to add a few dots on the paper insects' wings.

"There are also ladybirds that don't have dots on them." The boy marvelled at his creation as he held it and ran around the room. "If only it could fly."

"'That's easy." Sophie took up a sheet of paper, folded a dart-like plane, and glued the ladybird on top. The paper plane glided smoothly and quietly.

"Ace!"

A moment later, the boy calmed down, and he asked Travis, "Do you know how to make other insects with paper?"

"Sadly, that's the only insect trick I know," Travis said. "But I do know how to fold paper cranes. Once, I folded a thousand of them for a sick friend, wishing she could recover."

"Oh, that's very sweet of you."

"I want a puppy to keep me company," Hannah Robinson reflected. "But I don't want all the responsibilities."

"Why have a dog when you already have a clean bot?" Travis took off his jacket as he observed the room.

Hannah mused, "I suppose you're right. And my sister Wren and her girl are visiting soon, so I'm looking forward to that. I haven't seen them in a coon's age!" She apologised quickly, "Oh, I shouldn't have said that; I hope no one takes offence."

"I once had a gosling as a pet," Patsy said. "It waddled and followed me everywhere and helped to remove weeds from my uncle's lawn."

"My cousin Essie received a filly every year for her birthday until she was twelve. Anything to drink?" Catherine asked their new acquaintance. She found him a gauche youngster.

"Tap water will do."

Felipe brought him a jug of mineral water as he said, "I have a friend who has a clean bot and a Labrador that was not housebroken. So, one day, he got back after work and found that his dog had pooed, and the clean bot had wiped its poo all around the house. Boy, was it a shitshow!"

Patsy pulled a face. "Can't you *stop* giving us *rank* details–"

The oven dinged, and she went indignantly to check her shepherd's pie.

***

The dishes were ready, the table was laid, and the group started their supper.

"So, which gym do you work for?" Catherine asked Travis.

"I'm not working there, strictly speaking. I'm volunteering at the gym that's near the Duke of York's Theatre."

"The one in May's Court?"

"No." Travis dabbed his mouth with a napkin. "More down the Strand. I lead a few classes on meditation, mindfulness, and nutrition. I'm a certified nutrition coach."

"I see."

"Which florist are you based in, if you don't mind me asking?"

"The one in Slingsby Place."

"Aah. The one with flowers that cost a bomb. They are certainly out of my price range."

"Well, we have them brought in via air freight daily. We also offer reasonably priced pick-and-mix gift bags. Recently, we launched a weekly bouquet subscription, which is a big saver."

Travis turned to Sophie. "What do you teach at King's, Ms?"

"I teach an introductory module on avionics and also training on COMSOL," she said, "though my main research area is in rover obstacle avoidance."

"I bet. No wonder you can fold such cool planes."

"You should see the rovers that Mum has built!"

"Well," Travis said, "I have someone in my gym class doing a course on aerospace medicine at King's. Being a flight surgeon can be stressful, requiring a high level of exactitude."

Patsy offered, "I'd say that being an A&E nurse is just as stressful, but luckily, my hospital has its own gym and pool for us to unwind and relax. Does your gym have a pool?"

Hannah explained, "They have an indoor swimming pool with underwater speakers. They also have treadmills and spin bikes that can generate electricity. The power generated is used to provide hot showers for the homeless. Seeing that tangible impact is very rewarding, to know that you are doing them the world of good."

"A free hot shower can mean a lot to people who sleep rough. My boss gained this insight when she met a specialist rough sleeping advisor at an event," Travis said.

Hannah concurred, "This scatty bag lady comes in, and I can't help asking how things are for her. Gosh, she had such a hardscrabble life. I bet some of them really want to shed their past like a snake sloughs its skin."

Travis then said, "Being a healthcare professional in the UK is tough work. A couple of months back, I was in Leicester, bunking up with some med students. They all agreed that systematic failures and shortcomings led to the tragic case of Hadiza Bawa-Garba GP and the death of her infant patient."

Patsy nodded slightly. "It was a heart-wrenching incident for all parties involved."

Travis added, "Though there was some debate over the nurse's treatment. She was removed from the register instantly, right? But when I did some ethnographical research in Blacon, I recalled another case relating to infant death resulting from embolism in a hospital in Cheshire where a nurse was moved on to clerical work."

"I'm not sure if I know about that particular case," Patsy answered. "I suppose it all boils down to the benefit of the doubt. I do hope they will have the young GP's gravamen reconsidered and her case re-examined."

Hannah said: "Travis has been quite a recourse to me these past months, teaching me to conquer my fear and overcome my worries." She remembered, "Felipe, you got your MBA from Harvard, right? Travis is your alum. He did his undergrad degree there."

"Glad to hear. Which house?"

"Currier House."

"Interesting, the one where Bill Sikes, I mean Gates, stayed."

"I hope you don't mean 'interesting' in the British way. What were your most memorable Harvard days?"

"There are many crazy alcoholic memories that I can't share with the tender ears here."

"Well." As he sat up straight, Travis said, "I got my AB in Government from Harvard, and I was hoping to start a master's at LSE. My professors endorsed me for a scholarship, but I thought I'd better leave it for those truly in need, so I deferred my place and am saving up for my tuition with odd jobs here and there. I'm enjoying my time at my gym. In a way, I'm living the dream; I can use the facilities for free to strengthen my constitution to stand up to the British weather. London is just *so* not SoCal."

They laughed as Hannah Robinson added, "And he interned at the UN last summer. Which division was it again?"

"UN-Habitat."

Felipe said, "I know the head of Urban Economy there. Poor Marco, tiring work for him. I still look the same refreshing me from Harvard, but he looks like a villain from *The Avengers*."

"I like *Spider Man* more," Brendon told the table.

"I'm looking forward to Zack Snyder's *Justice League*," Travis said excitedly. "I like DC heroes more than the Marvel ones. Many DC heroes also have to face their own mental problems and I think they are more relatable even for us spectators."

Felipe helped himself to a huge chunk of the shepherd's pie. He commented as he ate, "I have a friend whose daughter appeared as a hostage in the new *Justice League* film, and she cried after filming because Zacky made her scream fifty times so Wonder Woman would look more gallant. That's a life lesson for us. Wonder Woman on the big screen saves children, and Wonder Woman off the screen tortures them."

Patsy huffed, "Why do you always stuff your face, Felipe?"

"Haven't you heard that a growing youth has a wolf in his belly? And I'm eating my mother's portion for her. The good thing about being an eligible bachelor is that the whole household is fed if I eat well." He chewed carefully and remarked, "By the way, Patsy. This pie is salty enough to cause kidney failure in a cat. Did you loot a salt dealer or what?"

"Huh! My cooking is only for those who appreciate it and not for someone who cadges!"

Felipe turned his attention to Travis. "Let me ask you this, beefcake: what's the latest muscle-building crap among the yute?"

"Actually, there are quite a few: the keto diet is having a moment," Travis said. "And London as a city offers plenty of opportunities for ethnographical research. For instance, I just learned that Stamford Hill has the largest tight-knit Hasidic community in Europe. My undergrad thesis was on the kinship and social ties among the Hutterites fold."

"In Europe maybe, but no longer in the European Union."

"Won't make a difference to me: I still need to pay international fees, Brexit or not." Travis continued, "My internship at UN-Habitat was unpaid so later I moved on to another with stipends at the Global Environment Facility, the GEF. It's hard to save planet Earth when you can't afford to fill your belly."

"Speaking about Gef, Patsy, what does the case of the Talking Mongoose tell us about the news integrity of the residents of the Isle of Man? As I've always said," Felipe jibed, "the UN agencies should really have a productive roundtable with the International Labour Organisation on providing decent work and fair pay." He went to retrieve his card from his briefcase. "We have a few internship slots at Mercury's London office, so long as you can use Excel and know how to format a PPT, send me your CV, and I'll put in a good word for you." He handed Travis the card.

"I really appreciate this gesture." Travis took the card and swallowed noticeably. "Though I must say that the corporate culture there doesn't align with my values, so again, I better save this opportunity for someone worthy. It is easy to make a dime but much more difficult to make a difference."

"I think we have a great corporate culture there. Mercury was the Roman god of commerce and communication, and he was also the *messenger* of the gods. As John Buchan once said, capital has no conscience." Felipe shrugged. "But values can't fill your belly either." Having said so, he reached up and helped himself to another portion of the shepherd's pie.

"Enough is as good as a feast." Patsy moved the plate away from him and declared, "We shall save some for Cecil."

Sophie tried to diffuse the tension and had one of the pickled walnuts the couple had brought. "Umm. Which jar is the one you made?"

"Take a guess." Catherine smiled with expectation.

"This? It tastes almost like how Aunt Evelyn made them."

"But still not quite as piquant and figgy," Catherine said. "Maybe Mother used one or two secret ingredients that I don't remember."

"I remember how Mum once said Aunt Evelyn liked to innovate with piccalilli and wasabi when making pickles, so..." Sophie murmured.

"Uncle Feli, when you were in Japan this summer, did you eat a lot of sushi?" Brendon asked.

"Now, sushi is an over-marketed concept in London, but I had some authentic *basashi*. Do you know what that is?"

The boy considered with a hand under his chin. "I know a type of fish called 'basa'."

Travis said timidly, "I just love the sushi from Itsu, and I always wait for their fifty per cent off right before they close their stores. Sushi with plenty of wasabi and soy sauce is my soul food. Though sometimes it gets quite messy on my plate."

Felipe said, "I know someone who grows wasabi here. He tells me that only one per cent of the wasabi in the chain stores across the UK is natural. The rest is artificial or mustard."

"Oh, I didn't know that. You mean I have been eating chemical sushi all along?"

"It's a common industry practice." Felipe said, then told the boy, "And *basashi* is sushi made with raw horse meat–"

"Huh!" Patsy interrupted him. "Stop telling us any more of your abominable dining habits."

"Patsy, don't be so peevish. What Global Britain does not need is more lifestyle managers who pay no heed to first-world problems. If you have ever bought meat products from Tesco, you are likely to have tasted horse meat. As they say, you will never know what you might find in your Findus. But *basashi* is a delicacy in Japan, and I thought you were an embracer of food court multiculturalism?" Felipe dragged the pie plate back. "For your record, Patsy, in Peru, people don't *judge*, **coach**, or *tell* others how to enjoy the full-on splendour of fare."

Travis offered a placatory smile. "I guess this delicacy is not for me, then. I'm a pescatarian."

Patsy held onto the plate as her brows corrugated. "Why are you always tooting your own horn and ridiculously flexing your wealth with your motor mouth?!"

"You mean my kissing trap?"

"You've got thick skin, mister."

"Sure. And you just made it thicker."

Patsy let the pie go as she smiled cattily. "But you can't splash out anymore, isn't that right? Why have you been ousted from your corporate housing if you are running such a bumper business? You must have made a blooper to get the heave-ho."

"Patsy, you really do know how to gavel my nerves. Now, Brendon Boy, here's another life lesson for you. When things are going well, everybody's your friend. You see how you'll be bamboozled when you are down and out. People only remember the times when I cut the ribbon and not the times when I cut their enemies to ribbons. Even Patsy the Bennett goes for my jugular when I'm down." Felipe sighed. "I suppose you can call it a one-man collective action. I want them to realise that if they pay peanuts, they get monkeys, not me and my dastardly crime-as-a-service. I'm simply tired of waiting to step into dead men's brogues."

"So, you finally *admit* that you are the organ grinder's monkey."

"I am the organ grinder's second banana."

"Well..." Sophie cleared her throat and chimed in. "Got any plans for your break?"

"People say that we become lyrical when we suffer. But one good thing is that I no longer need to punch my ticket nor overload my bladder like stink." Felipe considered carefully. "Maybe travelling around the world? I've accumulated enough air miles to redeem a dozen free first-class long-haul flights. I'm also thinking about writing a book called *Canker in Eden*."

"You writing a book? Ho-ho! That guff will be laughed out of court."

"Not so much in a kangaroo court, Patsy. I'm considering writing a hanky-panky bonkbuster with lots of bonking and even more busting. And it will be an eucatastrophe."

"You perp–"

"Patsy! If you insist on your imprudent behaviour, I might just change my work-in-process to *The Denigrating Bennetts and the Flaws in Their Moral Precepts*. And I won't invite you to my new adobe to explore my tit book collection–"

"You are *incorrigible*–"

Just then, they heard small noises coming from the atrium. Chance instantly recognised the sounds of squeaky luggage wheels.

Merete Suntook was back.

CHAPTER 4

Half an hour later.

"What did she say?" Catherine asked Chance anxiously as she passed him his jacket.

"She denied it." He put on his scarf and half whispered, "Never saw a phone."

"Could she be lying?"

He shrugged. "Too early to tell."

They said goodbye to Sophie and Brendon as Felipe offered some of his homemade paletas to the boy. "Although Señora Suntook denied my goodwill, all aspiring entomologists like my paletas. Eat up, and we can play sparkles later."

"I wouldn't mind enlisting some help from Johnnie Walker to stand up to the British weather," Hannah said as she retrieved a plaid shawl from her flat and invited them for a second party. "Catherine, why don't you two join us as well? I believe in Scotland people call a glass of drink before parting 'deoch an doris', right?"

"We'll pass. We need to get back to Mr Darcy. He's grumpy that we didn't bring him here."

"Some say you shouldn't leave a cat or a small child alone at home," Travis suggested.

Felipe laughed. "And some say you shouldn't leave a grown-up man and a grown-up woman alone in a room–"

"Stop being *so* impudent!" Patsy shushed him. "Just stow it!"

"Big deal! What is it this time?"

She reprimanded him quietly, "Don't you see what you're doing? You are hinting that she's a cougar–"

"Oh, I don't mean to appear smart, but what's so wrong about being a cougar?" He cleared his throat and announced with levity, "Some say you shouldn't leave grown men and women alone in a room, but they do it all the time in abbeys." He summoned the boy: "Come on, Brendon, let's get our sparkles."

The pair vanished inside, and Patsy apologised to Hannah as she walked past her, "I'm really sorry–"

"Don't be. Which licentious horndog didn't tell one or two smutty jokes over a couple of drinks?" The recently widowed woman wrapped her shawl tightly over herself. "Let's get inside, Travis. And I can show you the couch you'll surf on tonight."

"That'd be great. I could really use a lie-down."

Later.

The couple left and waited with Patsy for Cecil's driver, Eammon. Soon the Bentley arrived, and the couple drove back in their SUV.

They met traffic, and Catherine mused from the passenger seat, "I once read an article about Jayden Peng and the NP Consortium. He didn't strike me as the kind of person who believes in aliens." Then something clicked in her. "Oh my! Felipe is worried that Sophie and Brendon might be in danger!"

Chance considered, "It is unlikely yet possible."

"What exactly did Mrs Suntook say?"

He sighed and told her what had happened. "Felipe introduced himself as her new neighbour and asked if she remembered what happened on the 19th. She said she did see Ikenua Joseph but didn't pay attention to him. Never saw his phone and never heard any ringtone. When Felipe pressed for more, she threatened to call security."

Catherine said, "I don't remember seeing any security in the building."

He explained, "Initially, the building was designed as an office block, and when the NP Group bought it, they converted the top floor into several penthouse suites, one for Jayden Peng's personal use and another for Joyce, his sister. When the penthouses were ready, NP Properties separated the building into two: there was one entrance on Kingsway for the office block and another on Kean Street for the tenants. Technically, you can call security from the office side."

Catherine nodded as Chance continued, "the office workers have a separate lift and key card system to ensure they don't infringe on the apartment dwellers. During the Financial Crisis, NP Properties sold three of the flats to a Saudi businessman, but he whinged about the morning noises."

"Right." She reflected on the times when she lived there. "The delivery trucks for the Delaunay would arrive from five onwards."

"Then those rooms remained unoccupied. The one that Hannah lives in was leased to Eddy's company, and the one that Merete Suntook lives in is under her husband's name."

"Walk me through what happened on the 19th again."

"Well." The lights changed, and he drove on. "From what I gathered from Sarnai and Ikenua Joseph, the chain of events happened like this: in the morning, Hannah went to a flotation tank session in

Vauxhall and later a rasul experience in Hendon, and she told Sarnai to use her spare key when she arrived. Ikenua arrived at a quarter to ten and he left at ten-thirtyish. Mrs Suntook came down at eleven-ten, and Sarnai and her friend went up a minute or so later, with Sarnai leaving five minutes after that. We have the CCTV footage from the lift to account for all the entries and exits after Joseph arrived."

"When did the call happen?"

"Eleven-o-three."

"And Mrs Suntook didn't hear anything?"

"No." They met traffic again, so he made a diversion.

Catherine considered, "Orla showed me a video today about cats playing *Fruit Ninja*. Do you think perhaps a gull might have picked up the call by accident? With its beak and the touch screen?"

"Actually–" he realised something and said instead, "A gull wouldn't tell a person to die."

"A budgerigar, maybe?"

"It's possible yet unlikely," he concluded. "The call went on for half a minute, and I don't think anyone would mistake a parrot for a human. Even in a drugged state."

"Hmm. Maybe you're right." As she chewed her nails, Catherine recalled, "Can't we go through all the numbers recorded on the mobile base stations close to Kean Street that day? Then we might know whose phones were around at that time."

"That would be a daunting task beyond our...my capabilities as a civilian. And it's not enough to know all the numbers, but to know whose number you are looking for."

"I see."

Her phone blipped, indicating that she had low battery. "Something occurred to me," Catherine mused. "On the day we flew to China, I had a morning shift at the flower academy. Patsy came to give me a power adapter, and Mrs Suntook was there to buy some flowers. They seemed to know each other."

***

They arrived home, as Catherine thought back on that day. "I couldn't tell if Patsy was surprised or shocked to see her, and just now, they acted as if they were strangers."

Chance put away his keys, and Catherine picked up her cat loaf curled beside the umbrella stand. "Doesn't the atrium have any CCTV cameras?"

"They had two mounted on the corners, but the reception had to remove them because the Saudi businessman said he didn't want too many eyes on his private life."

"But I remember seeing one near Hannah's kitchen window."

"It's a dummy, to act as a deterrent."

"I see." Catherine kissed her cat, touched his nose lightly, settled on her chaise longue, then scratched Mr Darcy's favourite spots behind his ears. "Pity that neither Hannah nor you had a smart doorbell." She quit her detective mode for the night and said as she enjoyed her furball's small warmth, "I always wonder if Mr Darcy might have tinkered with our smart doorbell. He always seems to welcome us at the door at the exact right time."

Chance sat beside her. "Who knows, maybe he's been hacking the FBI behind our backs?"

"Well, we can't have that, can we?" She joked, "I don't want to see him on the Feline Bureau of Investigation's top ten most wanted list." Then she shivered a little. "Raise the thermostat a notch, would you?"

"Of course." He turned up the house heating by a few degrees and brought back two cups of cocoa and a plush blanket for her. She thanked him and said, "Today, Melody got very interested when I told her that central heating is provided collectively in Northern China, and she said London should have that as well."

"That I'm not sure about. You'd need to have pre-installed pipeline networks." He sipped his cocoa slowly.

"Tell me more about it so I can tell her tomorrow." Catherine sat up with Mr Darcy lying in her lap. "Do people pay a flat fee?"

"It's calculated per unit area, and people might also qualify for certain social security benefits."

"But is it provided collectively? Do they start at the same time?"

"The exact starting date varies by province, and Inner Mongolia always has one of the earliest dates. When cold waves hit early, then they would start early." He considered, "And it's not compulsory to pay the fee. You can also opt out. I've heard of cases where, in a multi-storey building, if your flat is sandwiched between two or three fee-paying families, your flat would get warm as well."

"Ooow, sneaky." She then asked, "But how cold does it really get?"

"Well, you can take a cleaning cloth, dab it with some water, put it outside, wait for a few seconds, then it freezes up, and you can use it to slice bananas and cut apples."

"Oh. That's a very vivid image. Our basement can be cold as a dungeon in winter," Catherine reflected, "and sitting by the till isn't any better, given how frequently the door swooshes closed and open."

He was, to a degree, glad that she had brought up this topic of inconvenience. "How do you usually keep warm then?"

"Most often with a hot water bottle and a cup of tea. And Orla found a very appealing screensaver featuring a burning fireplace for us to look at."

"How about we buy a portable heater and bring it to your workplace?"

"Nah. The heat won't work too well with keeping the flowers fresh and looking their best." She sipped her drink slowly. "All the more reason I'm glad to have someone warming my toes after work."

"I can do more than that. How about a hot foot soak?" He went to boil the water and brought her back a steaming foot bath.

"Oh, this is heavenly." Catherine dipped her feet into the soak and watched him through her half-closed eyes. "Socks off, Mr Yang."

"Might it get crowded?"

"How can I expect you to warm my toes when yours are cold?"

He followed her suit and lowered his feet into the bath. Their toes splashed around, creating little waves.

"Now we just wait and bait to see if Mr Darcy will deign to get his paws wet."

"So, the task is to find a small-range device to keep you warm as toast at work. Let me look into it." Chance finished his cocoa as Catherine delighted herself with more wave-making. "My dad would tell me that when he was small, they lived in a hovel, and my grandad made a heatable brick bed, so when you cooked, some of the heat would warm the bed. But once, during the Chinese New Year, my grandma cooked so many dishes, and somehow the chimney got blocked, and the stovepipe exploded, and the bed collapsed."

"Oh, that's awful."

"But they managed to rebuild it in a day, so they didn't miss any celebrations."

"Nothing beats napping on a dry bed in the warm."

He collected their cups and they retired for the night. Catherine told him, "Today Brendon told me about a type of moth called the 'poplar kitten'." Then she asked him, "Do you think we make a good team?"

"Of course, we do."

"Team Poplar Kitten. It does have a nice ring to it."

Her cat meowed somewhere.

"It seems Mr Darcy opposes the idea. How about Team Poplar Ginger Kitten then? How's Yining, by the way? Did she receive the scripts for *Downton Abbey* I sent her?"

"Yep, and she's doing fine." He smiled. "She told me today that before coming to Somerset, she'd enjoyed a Subway sandwich from time to time, but now she has grown tired of sandwiches."

"That's a pity. I wonder if I should send Yining a brand-new collection of scripts instead of lending her mine. They have some marginalia. Maybe I'll get her a new collection as well." Mr Darcy stood by their bed, and Catherine hefted him up. "Oh. I wonder if Patsy fed him too well over the summer. Yining tells me there is an informal saying in China that nine out of ten ginger cats are heavy, and the remaining one will collapse your bed frame. Who knows, maybe a Flerken is hiding inside our furball."

Chance said: "I've set up a new cat tree in the parlour downstairs for him to better fulfil his curiosity. Though for now, Mr Darcy is more interested in its packaging box than the tree itself. I've also installed a childproof lock on the fridge. Just in case."

"He never tires of exploring, albeit sometimes it can get annoying." She suggested, "Maybe if you put the box away, he will get his paws on the tree?"

Then Chance remembered, "Yining told me that she joined her school's netball team, and they're playing a regional semi-final next Friday evening. She invited us to go. Would you like to?"

"Of course, why wouldn't I?"

"You said you no longer wanted to travel for a while."

"I can do overnight trips."

Catherine played with her cat for a while, then she asked him, "Do you trust me with your life?"

He settled down beside her. "Why ask?"

"I have been thinking about what Hannah said earlier. About allaying our fears and overcoming our worries." She hugged her knees. "I've always feared driving at night. But perhaps now it's time I overcame it."

***

The next day, he rode shotgun as Catherine drove to her early shift at the flower academy. Later, he met with Sarnai and Felipe in his apartment.

They talked at length about what might have happened on the morning of September the 19th.

"I never thought that I'd live through a Sherlock Holmes-like story. I've tried my best to help my friend to remember what happened on that day, and we found two things strange," Sarnai told them as she flipped open her pocket and took out a transparent zip bag. It contained a small, hollow metal tube the length of a staple. "Do you know what this is?"

Chance took up the bag and examined it. "Looks like a shoelace tip to me."

"It's an 'aglet'," she said owlishly. "I didn't know they have a word for things like this in English." She went on, "My friend found it that day when she cleaned the cleaning robot's dust box. We have a habit that if we see a button or screw, we store them in a ragbag in case they are needed at some point. However, this is strange because I've compared it with all of Mrs Robinson's shoes. She doesn't have this kind of aglet on her shoes." Sarnai explained, "When my boss did housework, once his employers framed him for stealing a pair of Oxfords. Since then, he recommended that we keep an eye on our clients' shoes and clothing."

"Might it belong to the late Mr Robinson?" Felipe asked.

"Maybe, but I gave the house a good hoovering only the day before. I thought maybe it belonged to Ikenua Joseph. Though I doubt it because he was only supposed to work in the atrium, but how come it ended up in the cleaning bot's dust box?"

"You said there was something else that was strange?"

"Yes. An electrical gremlin." She recalled, "When we came in that day, the cleaning robot was not on its charging station. I had set up a routine: it hoovers once daily in the mornings and returns to its charging place automatically. But on the 19th, it stopped by the sofa. Sometimes it stops if something is stuck between its wheels, but when I checked it, there was nothing there. I clicked its power button a few times and, in the end, I had to lift it up and put it back to its charging station."

Chance passed the aglet bag to Felipe, who then asked her, "Might it belong to Travis?"

"Who?"

"Travis Newman, her gym instructor."

"Oh, no. He never visited. That is, except last night." She went on, "There was a period in late August when Mrs Robinson was on her own. She hardly had any visitors except for me and the seagulls on her balcony."

"So, she had chaos?"

"Sorry?"

"The 'Can't Have Anyone Over Syndrome', aka 'CHAOS'."

"I guess you could say that."

"Thank you for this information." Felipe considered, "I propose we keep schtum about what happened, and in accordance with what we agreed earlier, so don't tell Mrs Robinson just yet."

"I won't breathe a word." Sarnai walked to the door and then turned. "By the way, I saw Mrs Suntook when I came to work. She was checking her mailbox in the lobby, and she tore a letter apart on the spot."

This caught Felipe's attention. "What kind of letter was it?"

"A small envelope with a printed address like a sticker."

"Perhaps a billet-doux from an old lover, then. Thank you again for your valuable information and for going through all this hell." Felipe assured her, "You mustn't feel bad about everything that has happened, because no good deed ever goes unpunished."

Later.

She finished her shift and decided to go to Borough Market for a bite. As soon as she exited the hospital's gate entrance, someone wolf whistled.

She turned back and crossed her arms. "What do *you* want?"

"Patsy, I thought you were done talking to me?"

She rolled her eyes profoundly.

Chance hurried to mediate before they started arguing again. "Nurse Bennett, we'd like to have a small chat if that's okay?" He pointed to a coffee house not far away. "It'll be very quick."

"Fine."

They went in, ordered, and she settled on a curved seat.

Felipe played with his fingers. "Patsy, I want to ask some questions about your testy friend."

"My friend?"

"Merete Suntook née Hurst."

She replied plainly, "She's not my friend."

"But you do seem acquainted."

Patsy had a sip of her chai latte. "We went to nursing school together. Only she didn't finish the course."

"And now you are consorting with an OBE, while she is the wife of a CMG. Didn't they teach you at school that independence ought to be valued?"

"What *do* you want?"

"Do I detect a trace of threat in your splenetic tone, Patsy? Very well. Let's stall no more. My buddy and I are investigating a possible impersonation."

"Impersonation?"

"Likely an imposter who instigated another to commit suicide." Felipe continued, "I've heard a lot about this Mrs Suntook lately, and she didn't strike me as the type of person one wants as a neighbour. We want to know if you can provide her with a character reference."

Patsy sighed deeply. "We lost touch years ago, but if there's one thing I know about Merete, she would *never* instigate **anyone** to die."

"Why not?"

"Her mother died of social abuse."

Felipe nodded meaningfully and took it all in his stride. "So, she resents junkies like you do."

Patsy felt her cup growing colder. "What exactly are you nosy parkers investigating?"

"Well, we—" Chance thought of a way to explain.

"It's fine. There are certain elements to the story that we can tell her," Felipe decided, and they spent the next few minutes detailing what had happened on that morning in Hannah Robinson's flat.

"It reminds me of the tragic case of Jacintha Saldanha." Patsy pondered for a while, then said, "Once we had a patient. She had recurring bruises, and we all thought she was a victim of domestic violence, but it turned out that she had Munchausen's syndrome. How can you be sure if this dad isn't hedging and making things up so he could shift some of his blame to others?"

Felipe responded, "There's no doubt about that, though the facts remain the same."

***

Patsy left, and Felipe looked at her unfinished latte. "You remember how once she said she saw someone tailing my car?"

"Yes."

"Gordon Sylvester told me he had the same problem over the summer: a Mondeo tailing him all over London like one dorgi chasing another's ass."

"Gordon Sylvester?" Chance recalled the man, one of the VPs for Mercury International, whom he had met once at a brown bag meeting.

"Sometimes I have my enemies' names inscribed on my shoe soles, and I feel so good walking in them...*stepping* on them," Felipe rumbled. "And I had his name inscribed on a pair of golf shoes. Guess where I wore them to?"

"You are not saying..."

"It seems that pillock wasn't content with only one gagging order. Hmmm. He must have found Gordon's name on his face when he shaved the next morning." Felipe finished his cup of java. "The big boss told me to lie low for a while, but don't worry, I've got people looking after you, Catherine, and her place. Discretion is the better part of valour."

Chance mulled over this as he took the Tube from London Bridge Station to Leicester Square Station. He walked carefully, wary of anyone tagging along with him. He noticed nothing out of place as he neared the residential block where Ikenua Joseph was doing a maintenance round that morning and had asked him to meet up there.

He quickly spotted the lone man's figure from across the junction. He crossed and greeted him.

"So, is that Merete woman back?" Ikenua pressed.

He countered with another question, "Mr Joseph, do you mind me asking a random question?" Chance didn't wait for his response. "What shoes were you wearing on the morning of the 19th?"

"A pair of work boots. The same pair I'm wearing now."

Chance looked down at the vamp; both shoelaces had their tips in place.

"There's another thing that I'd like to check," he said. "Do you still have your calling history printouts with you?"

"Here." Ikenua rummaged in his bag and took out the crumpled pile.

Chance took the pile, browsed through the records quickly, and pointed out, "You called your son that morning. No, wait: he called you first."

"Sometimes, he called for advice."

"And money," Chance added.

Ikenua sighed, "And money."

"Did he call for the former or the latter that morning?"

"You could say a bit of both."

"What did you tell him?"

"I told him what to do about his mood swings and I told him I was working, and I'd call him back once I was done. If I'm being honest, he was quite annoying at one point, so I hung up on him." Ikenua thought back. "I was in a rush that morning."

"I see."

"I remember putting my phone on vibration mode," Ikenua added. "Are we done here? I must get back inside to finish the rounds. I'm leaving tomorrow for Tanzania for Johnny's funeral. And poor Lindsay, she only got discharged from the ICU last night. But she still got a bad whiplash."

"Erm..." Chance decided. "Besides me and Sarnai, is there anyone else who knows what happened that morning?"

"Well...I've asked one of my mates to bring Sarnai's daughter to me. But he didn't know the reason behind it."

"How about Mrs Joseph?"

"There is *no* Mrs Joseph! If she had cared for our son, he would never have ended up the way he did!"

Chance simply said, "And do you think the same accusation might apply to yourself?"

The bereaved man softened his gaze. "I suppose you've got a point. I did dump Johnny in her lap. He needed a father figure who was not missing from most of his childhood and adulthood."

"I don't mean to condemn you or anyone." Chance shifted his weight to his heels. "I only want to grasp what happened that morning." He continued, "Suppose someone had found your phone and picked up your call. It goes against the grain to assume that they harboured ill intentions. For instance, they could ask who the phone's owner was, as Sarnai did."

"But this imposter told Johnny to 'fuck off and die'!"

"Again, you didn't hear that first-hand. It could be that Johnny was in such an agitated state that there was a misunderstanding, and whoever was on the receiving end got agitated–"

"Lindsay wasn't mainlining!"

"I'm not implying she was. If you can visit her, it might be prudent to ask her to recount what happened in detail. What kind of state was Johnny in?" Chance added, "Given the circumstances in which the accident happened, sometimes such a terrible shock is strong enough to alter people's perceptions."

"Fine! If this person was a good Samaritan, why was this call record deleted from my phone?"

"Possibly they heard the car crashing and got scared. I still think the police could help your case."

"I don't trust the police." Ikenua then demanded, "What would they do if they ever managed to find the imposter? What crime would they subject this person to?"

"I'm afraid that I'm not very familiar with the UK law."

"Johnny **died**! And I'm not letting this person off easily!"

A few passers-by caught this outburst, and Joseph calmed down. "Are we done rubbing minds here?"

"Nearly. Mr Joseph, if you want to find the identity of your so-called 'imposter', then I have a few suggestions to make." Chance told him his thoughts and inferences. "What do you think? Of course, I can't guarantee that any of this will go smoothly."

"Why are you helping me?"

"Well... Let's say that the landlord of that building is a friend, and he is not pleased with what has transpired in his property."

Later.

Chance chewed over his encounter with Ikenua Joseph as he toured the grocery stores in Chinatown. Then he went to meet Catherine at a parking area near Bedford Court. As he waited, he looked up the case of Jacintha Saldanha.

In 2012, Jacintha was working as a nurse at King Edward VII's Hospital in London. She fell for a prank call from an Australian radio programme when the emcees impersonated the Queen and the Prince of Wales and asked about Princess Kate's health conditions in her pregnancy. Jacintha Saldanha later committed suicide and the prank had led to a public outcry.

He pocketed his phone as he saw Catherine approaching; she was on her phone, conversing. "Right, do let me buy you a vanilla iced latte with oat milk if you are around. Orla tells me it's your favourite. Yep, many thanks again, bye."

She saw him and put her phone away. "It wasn't Mrs Suntook."

"I'm sorry?"

"Today at work," she explained as he stored his shopping in the trunk, "I thought if we can't prove Mrs Suntook took up that phone call, maybe there's a way to prove that she didn't."

"And?"

"Then Orla asked me how to mix lotus root powder properly, because when she tried, she made it all lumpy. I taught her to add some cold water first, mix it, then add hot water and microwave it. Where was I? Oh yes, that's when we began to chat about Mrs Suntook."

They sat in the car. "Orla said that Mrs Suntook is on our blacklist for upsetting one of our part-time assistants. The one who filled in for me during the summer."

"Olivier, right?"

"Mrs Suntook was one of our very first subscribers to sign up for our weekly bouquet plan, and a bouquet was delivered to her place on September 18th. After it was delivered, she called to complain as she thought the sweet Williams were not fresh enough. Olivier took the call, and she said she wanted to speak to his superior, but Melody wasn't in that day. The following morning, she called in again, and Melody pacified her. Their call went on for ten minutes."

"And this was around…?"

"I checked our incoming call records, starting from ten-fifty-eight. Melody had offered to give her another bouquet, so Mrs Suntook paid a visit to our shop shortly after. But when she saw Olivier, she had another row with him, and she spoke so harshly that she made him cry."

"I see."

"Anyway, that's why she's on our blacklist. But hopefully this clears her name. She might be a finicky, surly lady, but she didn't pick up that call." Catherine added, "I considered a scenario where she might have muted the microphone on her phone while listening to Melody and was goading Joseph's son at the same time. But Melody said Mrs Suntook hardly gave her any time to respond." Catherine confessed, "Orla told me about this a few days ago, but I was preoccupied with what had happened in that derelict seaside building, so it slipped my mind."

She stopped at a light and decided to change the topic. "So, Mr Yang, I see you've been shopping. What goodies did you get?"

"Some oldenlandia water, rice crackers, spicy peanuts, and a bag of hawthorn dolly mixtures. We can take Yining some when we go to her netball match."

"Good call. I can make us some pasta with beurre noisette for lunch."

They got back home, and Chance brought his laptop into the kitchen as Catherine prepared their lunch. He clicked open the video footage Felipe obtained for him and clocked it again in slow motion.

Mr Darcy finished his routine rounds on his cat tree and jumped onto the countertop with his tail curved like a question mark, looking intently at the screen.

Chance held the cat up and placed him on his lap. "H Darcy. Let's see if you can spot any *maoni*. Maoni means something fishy in Chinese." He played the video again, sifting through the major entries and exits. "Here is Ikenua Joseph arriving." Then he fast-forwarded the recording. "Here's Mrs Suntook leaving the building. And here's Sarnai with her friend."

He chatted with the cat as they watched the video back and forth, and Catherine observed them with amusement in her eyes. "Just remembering how our Meowriaty bit you, and now you are close as two coats of paint."

"Now we understand each other much better." He supported the cat as he stood on his hind legs. "Though I'd appreciate it if our Darcy stopped protruding his rear so close to my face."

She neared them. "Play it from the beginning for me, won't you?"

He did so, and their three pairs of earnest eyes were fixed on that lift.

"Hmm." A moment later, Catherine said, "Something's odd here."

"Yes?" He zoomed into the empty cab.

"Not with the video. I mean," she concluded, "it's the sound."

Her husband and cat turned to her. "The sound?"

"Usually, the 'Ground Floor' announcement should come simultaneously as the floor button lights up. You can see its reflection in the mirror." She pointed it out to him. "But here it is a little lagged."

"You're right." He marvelled at her astuteness.

"I noticed it that time when Eddy caught us making out in the lift." She considered some more. "Say, Mr Darcy wouldn't open the fridge if Pingu wasn't in there, right?"

"I guess so."

"Do you have the recordings for Hannah leaving the building?"

"I'm afraid not."

Catherine deduced, "If Hannah left that day by the lift, wouldn't Joseph have got directly in it? But he had to call it down from the ninth floor."

He nodded assent. "I will see if I can find the footage of her leaving."

***

Later.

She returned to the house, and as she dragged her tuckered-out body inside, she heard Sophie bawling, "It was not *me*, Father, who has engaged in such *cowardly* conduct!"

Patsy hesitated to announce her presence, then retreated and left.

CHAPTER 5

Four days later.

"Things are getting interesting," Felipe told them as soon as Sarnai and Chance entered his flat.

He showed them his phone. "Here's the complete video for the morning of the 19th." They saw Hannah using the lift around seven in the morning, a large gym bag on her shoulder.

Sarnai said, "I remember Mrs Robinson brought her own towels and housecoat when she went to her flotation tank session. She doesn't like using the public ones."

"Let's fast-forward." Felipe clicked a few times, and then the screen flashed a 'No Signal' warning. "After Hannah left, the camera inside that lift didn't catch anything between nine-twenty-six and nine-thirty."

He then showed them a photocopy of an A4 page. "The IT's maintenance log said they noticed the problem, but it was resolved by the time they sent people to check."

"Resolved? How?" Chance asked.

"Here's why it's interesting. Check out this video I got from the camera by the furniture store downstairs." Felipe found another video. They saw a cockeyed, distant street-view angle facing Kean Street towards the apartments' double glass gate.

The time stamp read '16/09/19 09:25:23', and they saw a DHL courier walking past the red brick wall with the clown-face graffiti, approaching the glass gate, swiping something on the card reader, and entering. He held a seemingly large box and had a snapback cap on his head. Due to the low resolution of the footage, they couldn't distinguish his physical features other than him being plump and tall.

"Any ideas who this might be?" Felipe asked Sarnai.

She hesitated, then shook her head. "No."

He wanted more. "But I see you have a thought?"

"Well." She reflected. "If Mrs Robinson bought something from Ocado, I always signed them off at the glass door. He used a key card, so maybe he was someone working for the front desk or the office building?"

"I asked them, and none of them knew who he was or why he was here."

"Maybe Mrs Suntook knows him?" Sarnai pondered.

"Let's put that possibility aside for now."

Chance then thought, "Although that looked like a heavy box, he didn't put it down when he took out his card, and he didn't drive."

Sarnai clapped her hands. "I know the DHL guy in charge of this area. He always drove and parked when delivering."

Chance watched the recording again, and he murmured, "I know that box."

"Yes?"

"The box that this courier was holding was the one that Sophie and Brendon used to collect my personal belongings. One of its corners was slightly crushed, so I remembered."

Sarnai drew closer. "I think I saw it in the refuse storage for some time. I thought Miss Sophie left it there after they moved here."

Felipe cleared his throat. "So, we have this person, who may or may not be a courier, entering the building. What do you make of that?"

"I'm not sure," she said incredulously. "It's not a big deal to find delivery persons in apartments."

"No, it's not uncommon to find delivery persons in apartments," Felipe concurred. "But it's quite uncommon to find couriers with evil intentions."

"What do you mean?" she asked with a hint of doubt.

Chance connected some dots. "Whoever he was, he might have used a jammer."

"A jammer?"

He explained, "It's a device malicious individuals use to disrupt CCTV cameras' signals. One possible reason why the lift's camera was out of signal."

She sat down on a nearby ottoman as shock flashed over her face. "Blow me, here was I thinking that we were living through a Sherlock Holmes story, but now it just became *Mission Impossible*."

Chance continued, "The camera inside the lift uses a wireless network, whereas the one that the furniture store has is cabled. Jammers tend to affect wireless devices within its proximity." He paced around. "You mentioned that Mrs Robinson's cleaning bot didn't return to its charging station that morning. It's possible that her Wi-Fi was temporarily affected as well."

"But why would anyone want to use a...a jammer?"

Felipe said, "We don't know for sure yet, but we know that what seems like a minor incident might in fact be organised crime."

"Crime? But *why*?!"

Felipe roamed across the room. "Who knows? Maybe this courier came to plant a time bomb somewhere on this floor?"

Sarnai sprang up. "Tell me you are joking!"

"I don't want to make your hair curl, but we are discussing a highly suspicious matter." He turned serious. "One time, the management of a subsidiary company caught a mysterious sickness, and I was sent to investigate. It turned out that one of our competitors had tampered with the office's air filter, so it was spreading harmful spores." Felipe continued, "There was another case when one of my superiors fell ill, and we eventually found someone had poisoned his hickory cutting board. They poisoned the middle layers so the chemicals would slowly seep into whatever fine brunoises his helpmate prepared."

"Ah!" Her waxy face turned ashen. "I must tell Mrs Robinson to change her chopping board! And we must call the police!"

"Why fritter the UK's taxpayers' money away when we can handle it ourselves?" Felipe said. "By the way, do you know that Westminster City Council is closing its entire CCTV network starting this month to cut costs? But don't worry," he assured her, "my buddy and I have had ample catch-as-catch-can experience dealing with these undesirable sitches and unwelcome guests."

***

Later.

"Then what happened?" Catherine asked him worriedly as he scraped and peeled a pair of Chinese green radishes.

"We discussed what that courier might be doing," Chance replied. "Do you remember when Mrs Parker's daughter was caught up in a sex-for-rent scam? The landlord might be after Felipe and me. Then we checked the key card records, and the imposter had used one of Hannah's cards. She reported it as lost only last week."

"But are we concluding he's an imposter so soon?"

Chance collected the peels and set the radishes aside. "In any case, his behaviour was highly suspicious. We had the video of him entering the building, but the furniture store's camera didn't catch him leaving."

"Maybe..." Catherine wondered, "maybe he hid on top of the lift and lurked around?"

"We checked its model and the elevator shaft configurations. The space there is too small to secrete a person. A possible scenario is that the person entered the building in disguise, did something, and left from the Kingsway entrance disguised as another person. All he needed to do was change his clothes, put the corrugated box in the refuse storage, and use the staircase," Chance continued as he prepared some batter with flour and water.

"Maybe he sneaked into the office side?"

"The lobby lift only stops on the ground floor and the ninth floor. The flat residents don't have access to the other floors."

"But if the residences and the office block have separate systems, how could the imposter escape from the Kingsway entrance?"

"There's a door in the emergency staircase where you can push a button on the wall and exit from there. But should a tenant want to enter the apartments from the Kingsway entrance, then they need to use their key card. For people working in the office side, their cards won't grant them access to the ninth floor. Maintenance staff can contact the front desk to go up." Chance sighed. "There is a slight complication now because the security system in the office block only keeps its building access records and CCTV footage for a fortnight, whereas in the apartments, they keep them for a month. And," he said, "I need you to ask Sophie, discreetly, where she and Brendon got that box. I want to ensure it was the same one the imposter used."

"I'll ask." Mr Darcy joined them and neared the bowl. Catherine picked up her cat. "What are you making, by the way?"

"Fried radish veggie balls." As he added some flour, he said, "A Chinese saying goes that in summer, people eat ginger and in autumn, green radishes." He set the bowl aside and took out a stainless steel grater. "And cooking does help to sort out my thoughts."

"Whoever this imposter may be, do you think he might have done it?" Catherine sighed. "That he might have sneaked into the apartments, did something dodgy and told Joseph's son to die in the process?"

"I don't know." Chance took a green radish and started grating it into the batter bowl. "The possibility is there."

He finished grating the radishes and made the veggie balls as Catherine heated the frying pan. Then they enjoyed their simple lunch with a cold meat platter and slices of cumin gouda.

"This is all nice and crunchy." She licked her finger as she sipped a glass of oldenlandia water. "Mr Yang, we must do something to burn off the calories this afternoon."

He smiled. "What do you propose?"

"Some mental work? We need some visual aids, so bear with me a sec," Catherine said and disappeared upstairs. She returned with a large flipchart pad, a box of markers, and a small jotter and declared, "Assemble, Team Poplar Ginger Kitten!"

Her furball vaulted onto her lap as she spread the flipchart and wrote a heading in the centre. "Let's figure out the tenants and their close networks. First, we have you, the ex-tenant of flat five, and based on Patsy's account, that nasty landlord may have tailed

Felipe's car and hence might be after you as well." She drew the nodes and connected them. "Then we have the current tenants of flat five, Sophie and Brendon."

"I don't think they are involved in this. They only moved in the following week after Ikenua lost his phone."

"Ah, my Watson. Once you eliminate the impossible, whatever remains, no matter how improbable, must be the truth." She wrote their names down. "Do you remember once I told you how Sophie lost her suitcase when we went on holiday to Phuket? She was doing some research for ESA at the time, and she was worried someone might have stolen her research output. Apparently, some people approached her supervisor beforehand. So, there's also a slim possibility there, given her recent stint at DLR."

He nodded slightly. "Very well."

"Then we have Mrs Suntook, who also seems to have some secrets. For example, she always wore satin gloves – maybe she doesn't want to leave her fingerprints around?"

"You did remind me," he reflected. "The other day, Felipe asked Patsy if she could vouch for Mrs Suntook. After learning her mother died of social abuse, he hinted that Mrs Suntook resents narcotics addicts as Patsy would. I'm not sure why or if that's the case."

Catherine hesitated as her cat napped on her lap. "When we picked up Mr Darcy from Cecil's place last time, I glanced at the mail pile they had on their tea table. I saw Patsy had a letter from Factor Eight," she said rather sadly. "It's an NGO advocating on behalf of the victims of the Contaminated Blood Scandal."

"She did mention her father had haemophilia. I remember the scandal was about haemophilic patients being infected with Hepatitis C and in some cases HIV."

"By a pharma product called Factor VIII that made use of plasma donations from high-risk populations in the US."

"This might explain why."

"At least we established that Mrs Suntook didn't pick up that call. Anyway, then we have Hannah, and I don't think anyone would have contentions with her. Then we are left with that Saudi businessman and Jayden Peng, who rarely go there." She finished the network mapping as her cat roused. "And now we shall consult our H Darcy, the criminal mastermind in residence, to see if he is willing to lend us his whisker-dom."

Catherine placed her cat on the flipchart, and Mr Darcy swung his tail and walked around. He sniffed at Hannah's name, then all the others, and started licking his hind leg on the spot.

"Well. That's not saying much," she concluded as they watched her furball grooming.

"Indeed."

"Why don't we go for a walk to burn off some more calories?" As she rubbed her abdomen, Catherine suggested, "We need to pick up your mohair coat from the dry cleaner."

"Of course."

They got ready, and Chance felt his phone buzzing in his pocket. "Let me take this. It's Sarnai."

"No prob. I'll take the rubbish out first."

He let the call through. "Yes, hello?"

"I didn't want to say anything before I got some confirmation," Sarnai said worriedly. "I asked my friend who works for DHL, and he checked for me that there was no parcel delivered to the apartments on the 19th."

"This further suggests we are dealing with a pre-planned sly move." Chance put on his shoes.

Sarnai sighed. "When you watched that CCTV video, didn't you find the man familiar?"

"Not really. Why?"

"Before he took out his key card to open the glass door, he first wiped his left hand on his left trouser pocket."

Chance re-checked the recording on his phone. "I didn't pay enough attention. You're right."

Sarnai sighed heavily and said, "I've seen Liam Killingback doing that many times."

***

The couple went for their walk, collected their laundry from the dry cleaner, then returned.

"How naive we were." Catherine looked at the flipchart they had completed an hour ago. "To think no one would have contentions with Hannah."

Chance reviewed the video again. "But this person doesn't look like him: Liam is leaner and taller."

"Do you know how tall Churchill was?"

"No. Why?"

"He was five foot seven, and yet the actors who have portrayed him were of varying heights, with Timothy Spall being a taller one. But when you watch him playing Churchill, you don't feel that he's too out of character." Catherine sighed. "There are theatrical effects and props that can make people appear different."

"Perhaps you are right." He considered the possibilities.

What did they know about Liam Killingback besides him being Eddy Robinson's long-lost twin brother and a badly off pornographic actor? They had only seen him a handful of times and talked with him on even fewer occasions.

"Hannah would take this so badly." Catherine paced around. "Mr Darcy was right, after all." She took up her marker, added Liam's name beside Hannah, and circled it in Day-Glo red. "Now I don't know if we should even trust him on his account of how Eddy had apoplexy. If Liam sought him out for a quick buck, then..." she trailed off.

"When he visited Brussels, Eddy did withdraw cash frequently."

"We don't have any CCTV footage of what happened in that hotel lobby, and now we only have Liam's word. Maybe they had a row that triggered Eddy's stroke?"

"It's a possibility."

"And you said Sarnai told you once she saw him going through Eddy's things?"

"Yes."

"You're right." She sat down and murmured, "danger could be next door."

He let out a breath he had been holding. "I'm starting to feel everything is exceeding our capabilities as civilians."

"I thought pursuing the answers would be the right thing to do, but now I'm not even sure if I want to know them."

They fell silent for a while, then Catherine thought, "Do you happen to know Mrs Yoo's number?"

"Mrs Yoo?" He sounded surprised. "No, why?"

"Oh, nothing; I just wanted to ask about one of her recipes." She shrugged and decided to keep her own counsel. "Perhaps I will ask her next time we are in town."

Next morning.

He drove Catherine to her early shift at the floral academy, then steered his way towards Drury Lane.

The lane was teeming with crocodiles of primary school pupils and their respective parents and frazzled au pairs, and he waited five minutes to clear the hundred-metre-long block.

He parked his car near Aram, the modern furniture store, and noticed a large crowd had gathered around the usually quiet corner on Kean Street.

He got out and asked a bystander who was smoking by the wall with the clown graffiti what was happening.

"The fire alarm went off, so we've all evacuated the building." She puffed. "Today's not Wednesday, so it shouldn't be a drill, and a colleague saw some smoke, so we thought it was pretty serious."

Someone else commented, "Let's hope what happened with the Holborn fire won't be repeated."

"You mean you don't want some more paid leave?" the lady scoffed.

A moment later, Chance saw Sarnai and Felipe emerging from the apartment lobby, the latter coughing and tearing up.

"Everything is under control." Sarnai dragged him aside and whispered, "Mr Kazama proposed that we stage a fake alarm to check some things."

"What's wrong with him?" He looked at Felipe, who cried into a handkerchief Sarnai gave him.

"We placed some foggers, and he escaped too late," she told him. "I might not know how to use a jammer, but I do know how to use a fogger to drive out the bugbears."

Soon the episode was over, and the office workers returned to their side of the building.

"Let's stay here so we can enjoy some fresh air. And you never know what skills might come in handy when the occasion demands." Felipe coughed again. "It is my belief that everybody can be amateur detectives." He added, "Last night, I had the opportunity to review some of Liam Killingback's notable works, and indeed he wiped his left hand on his loose trousers in various scenes. For example, in a breastaurant, a fake cab, and even when flying in the mile–"

Chance stopped him. "We get the idea."

"So, I'm unofficially announcing that he is one to watch."

"Mrs Robinson told me that he is visiting next weekend so she could introduce him to her sister and niece. I feel it will turn out to be a disaster." Sarnai rubbed her hands in the cold air. "And she told me not to tell her sister what he does."

"Well, there are worse occupations and sorrier duties."

Sarnai sighed. "I tried to remember how he carried himself when he visited. Then I remembered he once asked me whether Mr Robinson liked cheese pizza."

Felipe tilted his brow. "Isn't that a revealing question?"

"Then this morning, I happened to read about the term on my bus here. Do you think that Mr Robinson was a...pervert?" She left her question unfinished and added, "But it can't be, right? I have overheard Mr Robinson saying many times that he didn't like children and didn't want any."

"To wit, not all teachers became a teacher because they wanted to engender the next generation of changemakers. Sometimes they have other evil intentions." Felipe recalled, "Hannah once said her husband had saved her sister's little girl at a swim meet. Who knows, maybe he made her drown so he could cop a feel–"

Felipe stopped as they saw Merete Suntook coming out of the lobby. She seemed discombobulated. The three of them watched as she hurried towards Kemble Street.

"We still need to figure out what secrets she's hiding," Felipe grinned. "And there's no time like the present. Now that you've learnt how to set up a booby trap, do you want to bring your detective skills to another level by tailing the suspicious?" he asked Sarnai.

"Not really. I still have work to do."

"Leave it to us then."

They bade her a quick goodbye and followed Mrs Suntook up Kingsway, where she spent some time at the entrance of Aldwych Post Office, hesitating and finally withdrawing some cash from a hole in the wall. Then, she walked further north and went inside a cafe on Southampton Row.

Chance and Felipe went in and settled at a corner table where they could see her but not the other way around.

They saw her ordering an Irish coffee, and a waiter came and went away. Then Merete Suntook spent the next half an hour sitting there alone.

Felipe yawned and yawned again.

"I don't see how this unconscionable waiting is useful," Chance said with a frown.

"Patience, amigo mío." Felipe gulped down his third cup of espresso. "And we are helping the local food and beverage industry. By the way, I've managed to keep chaos at bay by finding my pursuers and settling my hash with them, so all is in Bristol fashion again." He chuckled. "Really, the lies people tell these days. According to the nephews, his uncle told them that one day, two thugs broke into his flat and duffed him up, conveniently omitting Gladys and her circumstances."

Chance nodded wearily. "At least that's that done."

"They admitted tailing my Aston Martin over the summer, but they said they had nothing to do with what happened on the 19th."

"Do we know Liam's whereabouts on that day?"

"Funnily, one of his tweets announced that he was in Japan for the entirety of September for a production." Felipe showed him his phone. "However, he might not have been there all the time."

Chance looked at the screen: a tweet accompanied by a short text: 'Spotted a Smoking Gun. If you know him, good for you; if not, no harm done.' Liam Killingback was pictured smoking and taking a selfie with his fan.

Chance noted the time; the post was dated September 12th.

"Of course, the post could have lagged behind Liam's presence in London, so I've been doing some social media intelligence." Felipe rubbed his pouchy, red-rimmed eyes. Chance was reassured that he hadn't spent all his time perusing Liam Killingback's notable works last night.

Felipe swiped his screen and clicked open a webpage. It was a customer review on Tripadvisor posted on September 12th. Accompanied by a photo taken outside a famous bakery in Soho, Liam's hand could be seen on its smudgy edge.

"So, if you have time, try to suss out if he's been seen around the apartments. This falls into your area of expertise."

Yes, sitting in front of a monitor for hours and hours and looking for traces of discordance in lengthy CCTV footage was something Chance was good at. Or at least, accustomed to.

"And guess what we found just now?" Felipe took back his phone and clicked a few times. There was another photo, of a pebble-shaped object with jiggered wires projecting out. "Take a butcher's. Just now I swept the apartments and found this bug."

"Where was it?"

"Inside one of the terracotta pots in the atrium. Sarnai says she may or may not have brought this flowerpot out from Hannah's bedroom for some sunshine. She can't recall. This leaves us two options: one, the bugger planted the bug in the atrium; two, the bugger planted it in Hannah's flat."

Chance considered the possibilities. "Then whoever we are dealing with, he might have heard us through this bug that day when Sarnai and I confronted Ikenua Joseph."

"Haven't dealt with a cunning chaos creator for a while."

"What should we do?"

"We just need to play it by ear and shuffle our cards differently."

A moment later, Mrs Suntook paid her bill, and they followed her. This time, she went into a nearby Ryman stationery store and bought one large plain envelope and some stamps. Then she returned to the coffeehouse.

"I should get going," Chance said.

"Just one more hour. If nothing happens, then it's our hard luck." Felipe ordered another cappuccino. "By the way, today's Thursday, isn't it?"

"Yes."

"On Thursday, Patsy works the night shift." He decided. "Let me call her while you keep guard."

***

They sat there for twenty minutes watching Merete Suntook sitting there alone. She didn't do anything with the envelope she had bought other than stare at it listlessly.

Felipe passed Chance a small, unmarked bottle of spray. "You know the drill."

"Is this necessary? It always gets messy afterwards."

"Some people deserve a Scotch, and some others deserve to get scotched. Remember, we get paid to make it happen."

Finally, Chance pocketed the item and said, "I really should go. Still need to get ready for our trip to Somerset."

"I've almost forgotten you and Catherine are visiting your friend's daughter tomorrow. Got any plans for the weekend?"

"Yining is a *Downton Abbey* fan, so we'll go to Highclere Castle first and then spend a day in London."

They saw Patsy entering, and she walked brusquely to their table. "What is **happening**?"

"Patsy? Ooft, Patsy?! We are in good hands! Now my day is all sunshine!" Felipe whined as he collapsed on his seat and reached for her. "Save me from drowning in a caffeine overload! Save me from *this* classic cycle of **never-ending** despair!"

She brushed away his hand brutally. "What are you doing here?"

He straightened his posture slowly like a sloth. "We are observing who might be undercover aliens. Today it happened that our subject is Merete Suntook née Hurst."

"You have got to be **joking**!" Patsy crossed her arms. "Didn't you say she didn't do it? Can't you stop annoying me?"

"By the way," Felipe sent her a gleaming smile, "should I feel happy that you haven't thrown that burner away? Did you daydream of anyone booty calling you in the dead of night?"

"I'm utterly brassed off," she said tersely. "I'm leaving now!"

"By Jiminy! Let me feast my eyes on you for a minute longer!"

"Don't make me hate you *more* than I do already!"

He dragged her down. "Don't let her see you!"

Chance cleared his throat and offered Patsy a glass of water. "I'm sorry we have to drag you into this."

"Take a pew, will you?" Felipe offered. "We think there is a high possibility that someone is blackmailing your old-time nursing school friend."

"Someone is blackmailing Merete?"

Felipe continued, "There are two types of blackmailers: ethical and not-so-ethical. The ethical ones like me will stop once they have what they want; the not-so-ethical, if you give them an inch, they will want another foot."

"That's rich." An unknown anger coursed through her. "And here you have the *gall* to call yourself an 'ethical blackmailer'."

"Perhaps you'd be so kind as to exercise some consideration?"

She sighed. "I can't believe I'm doing this."

Felipe then said to Chance, "Might I beg a favour of a private word with the lady?"

"Erm...of course."

He went to use the washroom, and the waiter had just cleaned their table when he returned.

Chance looked out and saw Merete Suntook coming out of the Ryman store across the road. A few seconds later, Patsy went in.

Then he saw Felipe tailing Mrs Suntook again, and he hesitated as he waited for a light and crossed the road. Felipe made a gesture, and Chance understood what he wanted. Chance went inside the stationery store, which also had a Post Office counter.

He heard Patsy speaking to one of the clerks in front of the counter. "I'm terribly sorry. I just remembered I'd forgotten to sign a part in the letter I just posted."

"Well. It happens." The man went inside the counter and reached his hand into the mailbox. "Which one was it?"

"That plain ecru one with a first-class stamp. FAO Paul Hogan."

The man fished in the mailbox, "This one?"

"Yes, thank you." Patsy took the envelope. "I'll be quick."

Chance walked by her, half shielding her movements from the clerk as Patsy took a quick photo of the front of the letter. It was addressed to a PO box in Woodford Green.

"I can't believe I'm doing this," she muttered as much to herself as to him as she tilted a corner of the newly glued seal with her gloved finger.

Patsy took caution with the seal and inhaled deeply. "Do you do these things often?"

"I'm sorry?"

"You used to work with Felipe, right? Did you always do things that edged on illegal?"

"Sometimes. Not always."

Eventually, the glue broke off, and she opened the envelope. Inside was a stack of cash amounting to one thousand pounds.

"Nurse Bennett," Chance asked as he took out that small spray Felipe gave him earlier. "Do you mind if I borrow your gloves very quickly?"

CHAPTER 6

They walked back to Kean Street, and Felipe waited on a chair outside the counter at the Delaunay.

He was on his phone talking. "Right, Chiz-chan, I won't deprive you of your sleep any further. Let me treat you to some handmade soba should our paths cross."

Felipe saw them, put away his phone, and commented, "Now, one grand is a poxy king's ransom that I wouldn't entrust to the Royal Snail Mail."

Patsy took umbrage at his remarks.

"I followed her to a Waitrose, did some shopping there myself, and now she's back to her nest safe and sound. I have a prior engagement at the Harvard Club Bar, so I think we shall dismiss for today." He stood and bowed. "Patsy, thank you again for your generous help. Now we have settled that you are only a tea leaf who stole Cecil's heart, but you can steal so much more with a smile! Woot woot!"

She said nothing but only shot him a withering look.

They parted, and Chance collected his car. Then he saw Patsy heading towards the bus stop on the Strand.

He pulled over. "Nurse Bennett, may I drive you home?"

She got into the passenger seat and secured her seatbelt.

They conversed very little, but as they neared Holland Park, his passenger finally said stiltedly, "Would you care for a cup of tea?"

"Why not?"

He parked, and they went in; soon, the tea was ready. Patsy put down a tray with a Brown Betty. "Shall I be mother? Catherine says you like to take your tea with a pinch of salt?"

"Not all teas, only black tea. And only when I feel like it." Chance hesitated. "Sorry about your gloves. It didn't turn out the way I had expected. I will buy you a new pair."

"Don't bother."

They took time with their tea, and she waited for him to prompt her, but much to her consternation, he didn't. In the end, she asked, "How did you end up working with him?"

"Well, I was headhunted. A Shanghai company acquired a gaming start-up in Cambridge, and I saw through the transaction for a part. Then I was headhunted by Mercury. They had a client in Japan who wanted to go through a similar acquisition."

"I see."

They fell silent once again. Chance waited a moment. "Nurse Bennett. I hope you are not offended if I tell you that you remind me of my grandmother."

"Your grandma?"

"She was a traditional healer and worked as a 'barefoot doctor', as you would call it. She knew a lot of recipes for homemade remedies. In winter, we would keep our orange peels so she could make cold syrup with them."

He recounted, "Once, as a boy, my grandpa worked in the fields and accidentally chopped off the tip of his index finger with a ball pein hammer. My grandmother insisted that he go to a hospital, but he said he would be fine if she could get him some burnt incense ash from a nearby temple so he could cauterise his wound."

"Oh, I hope he ended up okay?"

"He caved into my grandma's request, and as we rushed to the nearest clinic, I saw this sad, frail, lost expression on her face. The very same worried expression you are sporting on your face now. If I may ask, why did you cave in earlier?"

"Well." She put her cup back onto its saucer. "Felipe has certain... knowledge of me that I don't want others to know." Patsy wrung her hands. "Perhaps it won't matter so much now that they know." She confessed, "I covered up for a colleague when Cecil lost his wallet last December."

"I see."

"There's more to it. I passed his card details to someone."

He only waited.

"When I was small, my father had fallen very ill following a patient safety incident. Our family and many others sought a way to have our voices heard to no avail. Yet one day came this...this ambulance chaser who said we should file for tort. He promised us many things but delivered nothing. He used to work at Cecil's Chamber."

Chance waited some more.

"So, when I saw Cecil's card and work ID, something came over me." She shook her head. "No, that's a lie. Nothing came over me. I just made a silly decision. Cecil is very kind-hearted, and I was only being invidious, but what's done can't be undone." She hung her head. "There, I feel so much better now that I told you. If you want to tell Catherine, go ahead."

He thought. "How much does Cecil know?"

"He knew that I covered up for a colleague, but not the other half of the story."

Chance considered. "I think he knows."

She breathed, "I think he knows that I know he knew."

"That just came out like a tongue twister."

She smiled a little. "Either way, my secret is out."

He offered tactfully, "Your secret is safe with me."

This angered her. "I don't need your sympathy!"

She watched as he blinked slowly. Finally, he said. "Felipe has... certain knowledge of me that I would never want Catherine to know."

"So, was that why you ended up bending to his will?"

"In a way, yes." He clapped his hands. "I think we can agree that our secrets are safe with each other?"

"Perhaps." She relaxed gradually as she refilled their cups. "I'll talk to Cecil tonight before my shift."

A minute later, he asked: "Nurse Bennett, would you permit me one more question?"

"Yes?"

"What did Felipe ask in exchange for keeping quiet?"

"Well, being a nurse, you get to meet people of all trades," she answered. "He gave me a burner and texted me a Bitcoin wallet address, and I gave him a postcode. But now I regret that I made a bigger mistake in doing so, and I can't always kick it into the long grass." Patsy took up her phone and showed him an article. "Do you know about this fire?"

Chance took it over and checked; it was a story about a fire caused by a faulty router that had severely injured a teen that June.

"I might," he said as he read on. The victim's family had set up an online auction of the boy's *Harry Potter* collectables in aid of fundraising.

"I can't constantly dwell on what happened," Patsy sighed, "but I want to know **why**."

"Well," Chance slowly responded. "It all began this May, when Mercury held a leadership boot camp for some sixth form students in Cumberland Lodge."

He continued with his account, and soon their tea grew cold.

***

Meanwhile.

"That will be all."

"Thank you."

Catherine thanked the staff at King's Modern Language Centre, collected the receipt for her beginner's Mandarin evening class, and decided to meet up with Sophie at Chapters for a quick lunch.

The place was busy on a teaching day with its quick meal options, and they eventually found two opposing seats.

"How are things going?" her friend asked as she tore open a sandwich's packaging.

"Good, good. Yourself?"

Sophie shrugged. "A-okay."

"How's the school search?"

"Not as smooth as I hoped," she said as she picked out the tomato skin from her BLT. "I'm not sending Brendon to any boarding schools no matter how much Father insists. Not even Bedales."

"No, we wouldn't want that." Catherine pictured the boy sulking in a house. She feared he would never fit in at a boarding school.

Her friend sighed. "But the circumstances are against me to continue home-schooling. My work, for one, demands a lot more. Maybe the best option for now is to use the staff childcare benefits."

"I don't mind minding Brendon from time to time. I'm sure Patsy wouldn't mind either."

"I don't want to put her out too much. You know that she doesn't trouble others with her problems," Sophie said. "I feel Father and Patsy...their relationship is already under strain, and I'm afraid it was my fault."

"How come?"

"Last week, I had a row with him back at the house. I said some things to him, and I think she overheard us. I saw her leaving from the upstairs study window."

"Oh. What did you say?"

"How he shouldn't...never mind." She lifted the lid off her coffee cup.

Catherine wanted to know more. "Sometimes I wish you could tell me what's troubling you like you used to. Are we not best friends anymore?"

"We are, and this much I can say: Father is not the person you take him for."

Catherine found the reply had the same hollow ring over the years. "But I don't understand. Don't you remember how thrilled you were when Cecil got you Anthony Head's autograph?"

"I do remember how thrilled *you* were when Mick got you your first Anthony Hopkins autograph. I used to love Buffy and Giles, but not since I watched him as the PM in *Little Britain*."

"Please, stop deflecting." She was frustrated.

Sophie chuffed a laugh. "Little catling, now you ought to know that there is more to life than collecting celebrities' autographs. We can't take everything as read."

"Not funny," Catherine pouted.

Sophie added, "Though Anthony Head gave up part of his career to spend more time with his family, that was commendable."

"And Cecil gave up the opportunity to work in The Hague."

"That was different." Sophie added, "Father was making up for some other past...laments." She said, "Just remembering how we joked about landing a top lad named 'Anthony'. How are you finding domesticity?"

"I'm enjoying it immensely."

"And how was your check-up?"

"Oh, nothing worrisome except for a few bowel complaints." She brought their topic back on track, saying, "Really, Phia, I'd like to help if there is anything I can do. I feel you are keeping a lot to yourself."

Sophie considered. "Perhaps. Let me tell you a story. Once upon a time, there was a lucky little girl. She had parents who loved her, and she had gone to the best schools; she was tutored by the best in her field. Then came a time when she went on a trip with her peers and supervisor. She discovered that, as her renowned supervisor showcased his research to industry experts in the daytime, at night, he domineered a toxic relationship with one of her friends. She only learned everything when her roommate had a severe mental breakdown in their shared quarters. That was when our girl decided to grow up."

"Are you saying..." Catherine suddenly remembered how, after attending a conference in Rio de Janeiro, Sophie had withdrawn her PhD application at Imperial and chose to study at TUM instead.

"My roommate tried to have him removed, and it didn't end well. Sometimes it goes against the grain to tell the truth. It wasn't until years later that I learnt a concept called 'testimonial smothering'; if the whistleblower thinks others won't accept her account or if she thinks telling the truth might expose her to more risks, she might remain quiet about everything. Cathy, we're quite lucky because we have been shielded from the ugly side of humanity. Just because people wear bowler hats or have titles doesn't mean they are, quote civilised unquote. For some, living is about wielding power, however grisly the means may be." Sophie thought quickly. "Are you certain you won't mind having Brendon around from time to time?"

"Of course not."

"What about your Mr Yang? Might he object to a third wheel?"

She smiled. "I don't think so, and I can convince him. We already have Yining under our wing anyway."

"Right." Her friend mused. "You are going to Somerset tomorrow. Is it possible for Brendon to tag along? I have a hundred and one grant applications to do, and I hope I can draft them in one go over the weekend."

"Of course, no problem. What time should we pick him up tomorrow?"

"Nine. No, better make it nine-thirty."

"Righto."

"He still objects to going to school. I think if he sees more of the environment, then perhaps he might become more interested."

Catherine nodded. "Perhaps Yining can give us a brief tour over her lunch break."

Then Sophie observed, "Cathy, you have changed."

"How so?"

"I can't pin it down in words, but you are different in a positive way."

"I'll take it as a compliment, then."

"I think that Mr Yang of yours has much to take credit for. My bouquets to him and his pleasant disposition."

Catherine's cheeks were suffused with pink. "He'll take it as a compliment, then."

Her friend observed eagerly, "Though I feel you two are withholding something. What is it? Spit it out *now*."

"It's nothing, really," she said hurriedly. "It's just that I developed a liking for salted duck tongues during our summer travels."

"Very chewy, I suppose?"

"And very savoury indeed."

Catherine found another topic. "By the way, Phia, I have a somewhat random question. Do you remember that cardboard box in which you and Brendon gathered my hubby's things for him?"

"Uh-huh. What about it?"

"Where did you get it?"

"We took it from the refuse storage, if I remember correctly. Though I'm not sure where it came from. It could be that when the removers came to collect your butler's desk, they left it there."

"I see." Catherine chewed over this information.

"Oops," Sophie checked her phone, "my office hours are coming up. I will get going and get Brendon ready for your escapade tomorrow."

***

Catherine finished her chicken salad alone and strolled out of the student-packed Strand campus. Soon it started to rain. As she ambled towards Covent Garden, a voice stopped her.

"G'day! Where are you heading?"

She turned, and Hannah Robinson waved at her from the other side of the road.

She navigated through the busy streetscape. "Hi, Hannah. I was just planning to go to Waterstones."

"Always a bookworm? My sister Wren is a bookworm as well. She loved to crack a book as a small girl and now she is a published author and that's right up her alley. Did I tell you she and her girl Bella are visiting tomorrow?"

"Yes, you did. You must be looking forward to it."

"Have you had lunch?" She pointed to the Kimchee To Go nearby. "How about a quick bite while we wait this rain out?"

Somehow Catherine felt obligated to spend more time with the recently widowed woman. "I've already eaten but wouldn't mind a yuzu tea. What has your sister had published?"

"Novelettes, and columns on how to make the perfect Rødgrød. I never know if I pronounce that correctly."

They went in, ordered, and waited for their food.

"So, how are you getting on these days? I don't see you much since Chance moved out."

"You can always find me at the flower academy." She quickly corrected herself, "That is, on Monday, Wednesday, and Saturday."

"How nice. I'll pop into your store this Saturday for some blooms."

"Oh, I won't be in this weekend. I'm heading to Somerset."

"How nice! What's happening in Somerset?"

"A friend's daughter is doing an exchange there, and we will attend her netball match tomorrow night. Then we will bring her back to London for some sightseeing and introduce Mr Darcy to her."

"How intriguing. Why don't you bring her to Kean Street, and we can organise something? A rooftop barbecue in the open-air atrium, maybe?"

"Oh, I'm not sure about that."

For a moment, Catherine wanted to tell her everything that had happened, but then she shushed her inner self.

"Bella will be over the moon, and I'm sure Brendon would benefit by spending more time with his peers."

"Perhaps you are right, but..."

"No 'buts'." Hannah ate as she said, "I'm returning to the States soon, so let's have some more fun before then."

"Are you relocating permanently?"

"Yes; the lease is ending, and I packed my traps already. It was nice for Eddy's company to allow me to stay there for these months. So, I've decided to have my sister and her girl over to enjoy the view. Then I will go home with them. Perhaps one can never get tired of London, but it is nice to have a change of scenery."

Catherine realised that she hadn't heard Hannah mentioning her late husband's name since they returned from China.

She risked a question. "Have you kept in contact with Liam?"

"He messages me from time to time. I asked him to come over, hoping to introduce him to my sister." She put down her plastic fork. "Liam is a different person than Eddy."

Catherine only waited.

"Sometime after Eddy passed away, I found he had a bank vault at Coutts, so I went there to check it. I went through some wearisome procedures and finally had access to its contents. Inside were some valuables and a key to a gym locker that held a hard disk." She paused and admitted reluctantly, "Its contents made me want to gouge my eyes out."

Hannah Robinson continued, "For all these years, my life revolved around Eddy, and now I have decided to live for myself. I thought I had given Eddy enough and I had given him what he needed, but I was mistaken. Liam may have a blameworthy profession, but..."

Catherine risked again, "If anything is worrying you, please let me help."

Hannah contemplated. "I so wish to tell you, but it behoves me to let everyone remember Eddy as the man he was. What are you going to do?" She sighed and shrugged. "It's useless to divulge his seedy affairs when he's dead."

Someone came into Catherine's peripheral vision, and she saw Travis Newman approaching Hannah, who had her back to him. He noticed her curious gaze and put his finger on his lips, telling her not to say anything.

He stole up on her with quick steps like a fox and covered her eyes from behind. "Guess who?"

"Oh, God!" Hannah soothed her chest with her hand. "Travis, you gave me such a fret! You hellion!"

"Sorry." He sat beside her. "I saw you through the display window and your brows knotting. I just wanted to remind you that we need to have a promotion mindset wherever we are. Treat all your troubles and worries as opportunities to learn."

"I'm glad I hadn't thrown my tray away," Hannah grouched softly.

"You did look like an absolute fright."

"You've met Catherine."

"Hi," she said.

"Hey, Catherine, how are you doing today?"

"Pretty well."

"Good to know. If you have time this afternoon, would you like to have a free meditation session?" He passed her a leaflet. "Your friend Felipe has already signed up for my class."

"That's good to hear, but I'm afraid I have a few tasks to attend to this afternoon."

"By the way, Travis, do you think you can get me another jar of that honey you got me?" Hannah explained, "Travis gave me this wonderful jar of honey, and I feel so refreshed after drinking it every day. I feel I'm living in an entirely different world."

"My favourite thing is to spread it on toast. No problem; I will see what I can do."

"And I *insist* on paying this time."

"If you say so." He told Catherine, "A highly revered Nepalese medicine doctor sources this unique honey, and they are not keenly priced. He's a maven of *sowa rigpa* – traditional Tibetan medicine."

"I see."

Hannah said, "By now, money is no longer my concern. All I want to do is to enjoy the moment. A few k won't break the bank."

"That's the spirit." Travis then looked at Catherine and asked, "Cathy, I hope you don't mind me calling you 'Cathy'?"

"No, not really."

"How's your day?"

"Fair dos. You?"

"Spent this morning sightjogging along the Thames." He added, "Cathy, I hope you don't mind me asking you a question? What do you do when you're in a funk?"

"Well. I make my kitchen spick and span, attend to neglected chores in my garden, and sometimes uninstall nagware on my laptop."

"That's a unique approach." He said, "I'm pulling together a list of things people can do to maintain their mental well-being for Room 13; it's a counselling and mental health service at Harvard. There are so many creative approaches and harmless indulgences, such as bell-ringing, tree-climbing, spelunking, and retail therapy, that work wonders."

"There was a time last winter when a Southwark church's bell kept ringing twenty-four-seven. I dare say that's not the best way to relieve one's stress," Hannah recalled.

"There are always moments when we feel we are small-timers and we might resort to escapism. Moments that knock the stuffing out of us. It is in moments like this that we need to hone in and take back control. Some people also refer to mindfulness as neurolinguistic programming." Travis considered as he deepened his intense gaze. "Have you had moments when you are flower arranging, say, when something or someone spites you so, then you snap off a scion a little bit harsher than you would like to?"

"I can't say that it has never occurred. Though the truth is their thorns hurt me much more often. Some stats says that ninety per cent of florists have dermatitis."

"Bees are a type of florist of nature," Travis reflected. "Only they are non-profit." He continued, "I'm in two minds whether to take a vacation early next year and learn how to do beekeeping in the West Mediterranean region in Turkey."

"That sounds wonderful!" Hannah exclaimed. "Can I visit you? I've been thinking of taking a trip in Continental Europe."

"Of course, you can. I'd be more than glad to have a travel buddy. But let me work out the details and logistics first." Travis checked his G-Shock watch as he told them, "I better go; I still need to grab a lunch sushi box from Wasabi. And Cathy, if you have any meditation or nutrition needs, you can always find me at the gym."

"Right."

He fished in his gym bag. "I thought I had it on me." He gave her a sealed, translucent Perspex vial the size of a tea bag, with some brownish liquid in it. "Try this honey whenever you feel down."

"Thanks." She pocketed the item.

"It really works," Hannah Robinson vouched.

"Got a class starting soon, so I'll set off."

"Be sure you won't scare me silly with your hijinks like that again!" Hannah added as he left.

"I promise I won't do it again. But I can't promise that I'll keep that promise!"

She turned back and shook her head. "Such a childish cut-up."

Catherine offered a simple smile in reply.

***

Half an hour later.

Catherine went to the Waterstones in Covent Garden as she wondered just what about Eddy's last legacy had made Hannah want to gouge her eyes out and yet decide to keep mum.

Would it matter if we knew? Would it matter if we didn't?

Ka-ching! The sound of the bookstore's till operating startled her slightly.

"Here's your receipt." A young attendant handed her a slip of paper and her purchase.

"Thank you." She pocketed her coin case and stacked the books she'd bought for Yining to keep: the complete scripts of *Downton Abbey* Season 1 and 2, as well as a copy of *The Remains of the Day*, one of her favourites, which she hoped the girl would enjoy as well.

The rain dwindled to a drizzle, and Catherine caught a cab home. As they passed Cecil's place, she saw Chance's car parked in front.

She returned, put away her purchase, and settled on her lounge chair, muffled in a blanket, with Mr Darcy snuggled on her knees.

Catherine brooded over the changes that had happened since her summer holiday. Her happy memories were adumbrated by losses and deaths.

A sense of lassitude was stealing over her, and she lay there idle, absorbed in her thoughts, and caressing her cat without an aim.

Then she heard some faint noises, only to find her phone buzzing.

It was An, Chance's cousin, dialling in for a video call.

Catherine calculated the time difference as she let the call through; it was already night-time in China.

The video opened, and she saw a vast expanse of darkness and heard waves breaking by the esplanade.

"Sorry, Catherine. Do you have a moment?"

"Of course."

"I want to talk to someone, but my brother seems busy."

"You can call me whenever you want," she offered. "How is everything?"

"Things have changed," the girl told her agitatedly. "Those derelict buildings are gone. Detonated last week."

"I see."

"With them gone, the Golden Bridge Group is inclining to conclude what happened there as an accident, but the police are still investigating," An explained. "Rumour ran rife that they had found a partial fingerprint on Jin-goon Kim's belt, and they are now after a primary suspect."

Catherine swallowed. "Have you heard back from..."

"He contacted me a few days ago. He's now in Seoul, working for a canteen under a church branch," An said. "He asked me to lend him some money."

Catherine only waited.

"Reverend Shin is celebrating his sixtieth birthday later this month, and his followers can show their devotion by buying tickets to his birthday party. Each ticket sells for a hundred million *won*."

"That sounds like an astronomical figure."

"About six thousand pounds. He said it's an opportunity to get closer..."

"Did you lend him the tranche?"

"He roped me in. I did some research, and Reverend Shin is powerful now. He's friends with politicians, *chaebol* owners, and even idol group managers. The security there will be tight," An said, aggrieved. "Oh, Catherine, I've already *lost* a friend, and I don't want to **lose** another."

"An, I'm sorry to hear this."

"So, I have decided that I *will* go to Seoul, and I **will** bring him back, and we *will* face whatever we need to face."

"I kept on thinking how things might have turned out differently," Catherine reminisced. "And I think we still need some answers. Do you happen to know Mrs Yoo's number?"

"Mrs Yoo? Yes, why?"

"There is something that I want to check quickly. Can you read me her number?"

"Hold on." A moment later, the girl recounted the digits one by one to her in her still nasal tone.

Catherine's suspicion had been confirmed, and she said, "I have something to ask Mrs Yoo. Do you think you can call her now?"

***

A moment later, Chance was back.

He came in, shook off his down vest, and checked his phone.

"An called. Allow me a moment to call her back."

"There's no need." She told him what had transpired. "She's gone back home."

"I see. Then I'll leave a message."

"I saw you at Cecil's place."

"I had tea with Patsy." He typed a message on his phone. "I told her that she reminds me of my grandmother."

"Good-oh. Mr Yang, I doubt if that's the best compliment a lady wants to hear."

"She didn't take offence."

Chance put away his phone, rolled up his raglan shirt sleeves, trying to school his emotions after Patsy's account and how she might have unknowingly abetted the arson that concerned Wilfred Perry.

She told him Sophie's confirmation – that they had taken the cardboard box from the refuse storage to collect his things.

"I'm glad I didn't throw it away."

"How's Patsy?" Catherine asked, hugging her cat closer.

"She's a bit worried."

"I had lunch earlier with Sophie, and she said that things are strained between Patsy and Cecil."

He offered her what he could, "Last week, Patsy overheard Sophie arguing with her father, and she thought that some of Sophie's scathing remarks were directed at her."

"Oh? What did she say?"

"I'm not sure, but Patsy said she heard Sophie referring to her as a 'coward'."

"A coward? But why?" Catherine sat up urgently. "No, something's terribly wrong here. Sophie told me that she had a row with Cecil and was worried Patsy overheard her because she had said some awful things about her father. Then why would Patsy think that her remarks were directed at her?"

"I'm not sure," he lied impassively.

"I must call Sophie and explain this misunderstanding at once." Catherine took up her cell, but he stopped her.

"How about a text first? She could be in her lab now."

"Right; a message then."

She typed up a succinct text and settled back on her lounge chair again. "After lunch with Sophie, I ran into Hannah, so we stopped for a quick bite at Kimchee. She told me some things..."

He only waited.

"She found Eddy had kept a safe deposit box with a key to a gym locker, and inside was a hard disk whose contents made her want to 'gouge her eyes out'."

He considered a moment and told her what Sarnai told him and Felipe in the morning; that Liam Killingback had asked the cleaner if she knew Eddy liked 'cheese pizza'.

Catherine's eyes widened. "Do you think?"

"Liam seems to be withholding some information about Eddy. But it is too early to conclude anything." He thought. "With these things, people leave traces even if they are trying to stay anonymous. I didn't find anything suggestive when I tracked Eddy's digital footprint in April."

"Or he might have hidden them really well." She hugged her knees and buried her scrunched-up face in between. "It was Mrs Yoo."

"Sorry?"

"Mrs Yoo sold Lin Min Huan out," Catherine explained. "That day when we were at his fried chicken deli, Mrs Yoo came into work, and that's when I connected the dots. She excused herself because they received a delivery order. I glanced at the order printout and noticed the last four digits of the orderer's phone number. I asked An if she knew Mrs Yoo's number, and I compared it with what I remembered. They were the same four digits."

He sat down beside her.

"We called Mrs Yoo, and she admitted it. Most people in that neighbourhood had heard about Jin-ae's accident, so Mrs Yoo suspected Lin Min Huan might have had a role in the three deaths. The morning after Ghost Night, she went to work and found their kitchen untidy. She cleaned up the glass shards, and she didn't tell the police anything. But still, she didn't know what to do. She didn't believe Lin Min Huan would do something so cruel, but on the other hand, her daughter was studying at an international school so she could use some money. She had overheard us that morning and had tipped off Pae's husband. She is the missing link as to why that fraudster disappeared."

"I'm not in a position to disapprove of what she did," her partner responded glumly.

"*We* are not."

Catherine spread her blanket over his torso. "When my parents had their car accident, for a while, I was scared. I wondered if they were arguing and Father had lost his attention. So, I asked many witnesses around the scene and passers-by if they saw anything unusual, but they all blamed that drunken driver. So, I thought, why did it have to be me? Jin-goon Kim must have felt the same. Ikenua Joseph must feel the same. Why did it have to be them? Why did it have to be their family?"

"Catherine." He offered his arms.

She looked up and gave him a teary smile. "Sorry for being so emotional today."

"These are your honest feelings, and they are understandable." He cuddled with her and the cat.

"And you appreciate them?"

"Yes."

"And Mr Darcy?"

"I'm sure he appreciates them as well." They listened as the creature purred. "I've heard that cats purr to help lower our stress levels."

She smiled. "Which he does so brilliantly."

Chance barked a small laugh. "He is a *lad o' pairts* with many latent talents."

"Indeed."

He took up one of Mr Darcy's front paws. "Perhaps you don't know, but I learned from my aunt to read palms." He pointed out to her. "This spot here means that our Darcy was destined to meet a very generous benefactor when he was nine weeks old."

She swatted him lightly. "Cheeky tiger. You can always make me laugh."

Then they sat there listening to her cat purring and the lashing down outside for a long time.

It wasn't until after dinner that Sophie called her back.

"Got your message." Her friend added quickly, "I've spoken to Patsy, and we are both happy that the misunderstanding is over."

"Glad to hear it." Catherine heard some faint whimpering in the background that might have been from Brendon.

"Sorry, Cathy, Brendon can't tag along with you tomorrow anymore."

"Oh, why not? We don't mind, really."

"It's...well, I better go. Thanks for offering anyway. He's upset because his Twiggy died."

"I'm sorry to hear that."

Catherine suddenly remembered something. "Phia, do you mind me asking you another random question?"

"Fire away."

"Do you remember when Cecil took us to Phuket, and you lost your suitcase and laptop?"

"Uh-huh."

"And you said that some suspicious Iranians had emailed you beforehand. Have you had similar encounters this year or so? Or at DLR?"

"Oh, that." Catherine heard her friend zipping up a coat. "It wouldn't matter so much if I tell you now. There weren't any 'suspicious Iranians'." Sophie laughed weakly. "Someone wanted to edge me out and I was framed as being complicit in international business espionage for wanting to speak the truth."

"Framed?" This rendered Catherine wordless.

"Yep." She heard a door closing. "Really, Cathy, I don't know if I could go through all that hell if Father didn't know the law so well. Your uncle correctly said academics are like the mafia, and non-conformers can be ostracised."

"Do you think whoever did it might come back to you in other ways then?"

"That I doubt. He's dead for good. Listen, I need to get to the dry cleaners, and they close in two minutes. Talk to you soon."

"Sure."

Catherine ended their call, feeling lost again.

CHAPTER 7

OCTOBER 14TH, FRIDAY.

Patsy finished her night shift, feeling refreshed.

Her secrets were out, and she felt she had finally escaped the feelings of suffocation. Now, no one could hold them against her anymore.

Not even Lady Justice at the Old Bailey.

Walking past Waterloo Bridge, Patsy recalled the happenings last night. Sophie's call was surprising, proving her assumptions wrong once again.

But...

She remembered the heated conversation she had eavesdropped on. If she wasn't the 'coward' to whom Sophie referred, who was it?

Cecil?

She thought about her partner, who led an upright career and life.

Or...Brendon's father?

Patsy thought about this absent figure she had neither met nor heard much of as she approached Kean Street. She had decided to visit the young mother and son in the early morning on a whim.

I could make some waffles...or would Brendon prefer pancakes?

She pressed the intercom button for flat number five, and the glass gate opened quietly. She got upstairs, and the door to Sophie's flat was ajar.

"Morning." She entered and declared her presence, "Just thought that I'd drop in and–"

Then she saw Felipe Kazama sitting on the sofa with his legs crossed and Brendon by the breakfast table, perching on a tall chair in his pyjamas, misty-eyed and sulking.

"Patsy, you look dazed and confused," Felipe said as he popped a blueberry into his mouth. "I see the deleterious effect of steamrolling Brexit already. Blueberries rose to three-fifty; they used to be two. What a social fig leaf!"

"Finally drawing in your horns, I see," she mocked. "Where's Sophie?"

"She went to her office to catch up on her tedious backlog, so I proffered myself for babysitting." He picked up another blueberry with his thin, long fingers. "Really, every house should have a kid-free zone. That would prevent so many conniptions and domestic incidents."

Brendon exclaimed, "I'm not a *baby* anymore!"

She observed the upset child with tear marks on his face. "Oh, Brendon, what happened?"

"My Twiggy died."

"Now," Felipe ordered, "stop your hissy fit, pesky Peter Grievous–"

"But my Twiggy died!"

"And whose fault was it?"

"I, I..."

Felipe stood up and walked beside him. "Did I or didn't I tell you to close all windows and doors yesterday morning?"

The obstreperous boy lost his bravado. "You did."

"And did you or didn't you promise me that you had them all shut?"

"I...I did."

"Then I can hardly see anyone else who is to blame."

"But my Twiggy needs fresh air! Or he might feel lonely and bored out of his mind and...suffocated!"

"Ha! I know the truth now. You wanted to test if your Twiggy could survive a fogger like how people tested if a wagonload of monkeys could survive gas attacks–"

"Boohoo! I *did* not!" He blew Felipe a raspberry.

"Diddums!"

"I **HATE** you!" the boy cried. "I wish Mum had asked Mrs Robinson...or...or Travis! Anyone but *YOU*!"

Patsy comforted the boy. "Come on, Brendon, why don't you wash your face, and I can make you some yummy breakfast? We can ask Grandpa to get you another Twiggy–"

The boy turned away pettishly. "There won't be any *other* Twiggy! My Twiggy was **unique**!"

"Patsy, work with me here. I'm trying to instil principles and honesty in him."

"Not with all your intimidating chutzpah." She walked around and shielded the boy.

"Fine! Today, he lies through his teeth about his Twiggy; ten years from now, he could be tried for treason! That's the four stages of cruelty!"

"You *always* exaggerate–"

They heard some soft knocking and watched as Hannah Robinson came in. "Ah. Here you are, loves. Everything okay? I heard some shouting."

"All is ring-a-ding," Felipe greeted her. "We are just having some productive disagreement and divergent thinking. But we will, as they say, agree to disagree."

"My sister and her daughter are visiting tomorrow, and I'm organising a rooftop barbecue tomorrow for lunch. All are welcome!" She told the puling boy, "Don't be in a snit, Brendon. My sister's daughter Rosabella is all sweetness and light. I'm sure you two would get along wonderfully."

The boy asked through his sobs, "Is she...into insects...then?"

"She might be. I haven't seen her for some time, so who knows?"

"In that case," Felipe offered, "perhaps I will get us some fresh oysters and mussels tomorrow morning from Billingsgate. And we can recreate our own little 'Burger and Lobster' experience. Just leave *mise en place* to me."

"That's so kind of you!" She recalled, "Bella has a wheat allergy, so I will get her some wheat-free and gluten-free buns."

Patsy smiled. "Can I help you with some home-baked ones?"

"Absolutely! Ask Barrister Stone to join us as well!" Then Hannah hesitated as she rubbed her hands nervously. "I've asked Liam to come, and I'd prefer that my sister stays...umm...unaware of his occupation, so just do me a favour there."

"Rest assured! She won't hear a word from us!" Then Felipe said, "By the way, do you need transport from Heathrow? My company has a seven-seat car that I can still book."

"Oh, we won't trouble you. We are taking the Tube to Covent Garden Station, and Travis says he'll take a day off and wait for us there to help with their luggage."

Felipe escorted her out. "By the way, I want to ask you about your flotation tank experience..."

***

Later.

By the time Felipe was back, Patsy had coaxed the morose boy to wash his face and change into more appropriate day wear.

She made him some coddled eggs with chipolata and slices of Miss Muffet cheese and a glass of Horlicks. She handed him the warm plate, saying, "Aunt Pat can't help you revive your Twiggy, but I can help you lay him to rest. What do you think?"

"I've already buried him in the atrium." The boy picked up his sausage with his knife. "Aunt Pat, why don't you like caterpillars?"

"Oh." She sat on the chair opposite his. "When I was little, my father was ill, so my mum had to take care of him. For a while, they sent me to live with my aunt in York, and the people in my class weren't the nicest. They put caterpillars on my desk and in my bag."

The boy listened. "But don't you find bugs cute?"

"People have very different definitions for cuteness, then."

"But why would people say 'cute as a bug's ear', then?"

"Well. I do like horses and goslings. My uncle liked betting on horses, and sometimes he'd bring me to the stables to guess which gelding might win."

"Speaking of horses," Felipe said, "I once stayed in a building that had once been a royal stable that housed the so-called most famous racehorse of all time, Eclipse. People say that eighty per cent of all English thoroughbreds have his DNA in their pedigree. But what is funny is that English thoroughbreds come from Arabian horses, so there is nothing 'English' or 'thoroughbred' about them."

"Uncle Feli, do you know that horse flies are very speedy fliers and have something called 'labellum' at the tip of their proboscis?" the boy told them. "And a honeybee's heart can beat around three hundred times a minute. And that sometimes, when people have coffee allergies, they aren't really allergic to the coffee but the remnants of cockroaches. And Travis told me that there is a professor called Carroll M. Williams who conducted some experiments at Harvard where he joined eight brainless diapausing pupae—"

Patsy grimaced as Felipe said, "I have heard of him, and with such a keen interest in insects like his, let's hope that he has become a shit-hot source of food for worms. Now, Brendon, instead of giving us more studies on how to break a butterfly on a wheel, here is a math question for you. If Chicken McNuggets come in packs of 6, 9, and 20, what's the largest number of McNuggets that you can't buy?"

"Hrm... I'm not so sure. I think I'll need some time to find out."

"Alright, another then." Felipe slouched against the countertop. "My company has a perk that if there is a book you want to read, you send its ISBN to an email address, and they will deliver it to your home. Every employee has an annual allowance for six books, so my three years at Mercury entitles me to how many books?"

"Eighteen," the boy calculated in a trice.

"That's the stuff. I have decided to make use of this neglected perk. Can you help me put together a reading list? You can put in any books that you want to read."

Brendon considered for a moment. "Fine. I do have some books that I want."

After breakfast, they gathered around Sophie's desktop. Patsy watched as the boy hunted and pecked the keyboard as he found a few illustrated checklists from Lynx Nature Books that he wanted and another by John James Audubon and noted their details in a Word document.

"What books do you want to read?" he asked Felipe.

"Classics, of course. We can start with *Lady Chatterley's Lover*."

"Oof." Patsy gave an appalled look. "Why am I not surprised."

"Right. Is it 'Lady Chatterly' or..." The boy found its ISBN as the search engine automatically suggested its title. "What else?"

"Lemme see... *Homer Economicus*. And then you can put down *Lolita*, for I've heard it's a good read."

Patsy retorted, "No *sensible* adult would find *Lolita* a **'good'** book."

"Tut-tut." He wagged a finger at her. "Penelope Fitzgerald would disagree with you."

She only looked at him.

"Why, Patsy, do you think we, the uncultivated, only know how to show our barbarian ways?" He added, "Oh, and Brendon, here's another book I want to read called *Busty, Slag and Nob End*. And another called *On Bullshit*."

He directed the boy to note a few other books, thus completing the list. "Let's click 'save'. Now, Brendon, as you might know, Uncle Feli is currently plum job searching. I submitted a few applications, but never heard back. Do you want to look at my resume to see where things went wrong?"

"Sure."

He jacked his phone into the Wi-Fi, connected to the wireless printer and printed the document out. "Here it is. Tell me what you think."

The boy read it out aloud. "Felipe Kazama Infante, CAMS...is it 'Cams' or 'C-A-M-S'?"

"Carry on."

"Felipe Kazama Infante, CAMS, CFA, CGSS, CIPM, CIPP, CISA, CISM, CMI, FRSA, F-RSS, MSC, MBA, PMP," the boy said in a long breath, "is an experienced M&A professional. He is a marquee, deedy team player and an incurably curious force of nature who thrives in multicultural, bleeding-edge environments. A completer finisher as defined by the Belbin Team Roles who can deliver under pressure and within deadlines using his unique abductive approach. Also, a determined cutter, he has co-authored several articles for *The Deal* on M&A and global IPOs. Felipe enjoys rock climbing, skiing, advanced nitrox scuba diving, and indoor succulent growing. His credo is 'be the business and the rage'. Note, this profile may constitute consultant advertising and over-selling."

Patsy said coldly as the boy put the page down, "No wonder they rejected you. For two pins I'd do the same if I saw a resume with the first line looking like a waspish cat had bopped around on your keyboard."

"Patsy, the attempt to sum up my stellar career in two minutes is insulting. And don't be so narrow-minded. An old friend I ran into yesterday at the Harvard Club Bar read the same thing and promised me a very enticing offer as a VP for North America at his company. Everybody knows that I'm a bang-up tailwind and a pyrotechnic go-getter. Brendon, we can perfect my resume later. I just remembered that last night, when I regarded the moon, I got inspired and composed a very little nice *haiku*. Do you want to hear it?"

"Sure." The boy did not sound interested at all.

Felipe cleared his throat and recited, "Rut season begins; for a very late bloomer; I will Farewill."

Patsy scorned. "These mawkish lines can hardly count as a 'haiku'!"

"Ay! You're just the perfect model of rectitude, aren't you, prissy Patsy? Does it not call the scenery of nature to mind? And does it not allude to the transience of life? Believe it or not, there are even haikus on horse shit." He then said, "By the way, Brendon, I downloaded a highly actionable computer game earlier. What do you say? Do you want to check out my digs?"

The boy became interested. "What is it about?"

"How about you watch *Peppa Pig* with Aunt Pat instead?"

"It's a niche mod of *Counter-Strike* called 'Counter Cormoran Strike', where you play the role of a sharpshooter Afghani insurgent, trying to protect your family from abusive British militants."

Patsy finally flared up, "Just *what* is the **matter** with you? Exposing a child of his age to inappropriate reading and imbuing him with dippy thoughts–"

"Hear, hear. So says the post-colonial colonial apologist. Patsy, haven't you heard that play is the highest form of research and game is the new rock and roll?" He looked at her. "Don't you deem it essential to learn that the Universe does not revolve around Global Behind IRL? What is so wrong about me teaching him cross-cultural competencies and a global problem-solving mindset? What is so wrong about me teaching him the truths of life? Cormoran Strike may have lost a leg, and yet the people in Afghanistan lost their lives! A complaisant person gets wedgied, and a meek horse gets gelded. By the way, Brendon, did you know that the creator of *Wonder Woman* had a very keen interest in bond–"

"Bonding with others!" she hurled back. "Pft! That's it! We're **done** talking to you!" She ushered the boy away. "Come on, Brendon, why don't you show me where you buried your Twiggy? Let's stay away from this git and his yackety-yakking!"

"Patsy! Language, please!"

She ignored him as she brought the boy to the atrium. She desperately needed some fresh air.

He led her to a corner of a terracotta pot with a newly added soil heap and a small cross made of twigs. "My Twiggy sleeps in here."

"I'm sure he will have a peaceful and restful sleep." She took up the trowel nearby and added some soil.

"Aunt Pat, it is not that I don't want a cute puppy or a kitten. But they take much more time to care for, and you can't bring them and move house so easily."

She asked him, "Why don't we try to find some other insects in the atrium?"

Then came Felipe's voice from behind: "I wouldn't try if I were you."

They ignored him again and began their task as they looked high and low among the leaves, branches, and the mulch beneath. Then she asked the boy, "Brendon, Aunt Pat wants to ask you a question, but you are not obliged to answer it."

"What is it?"

"Do you miss your father?"

"Patsy," Felipe's voice came again, "I wouldn't go down that road if I were you."

"But you aren't me," she returned coldly and resumed insect searching, flipping stones and fallen leaves here and there. "Brendon, you don't have to tell me if you don't want to."

The boy thought. "It's hard to say if you miss someone if you have never met him."

"You have never met him?"

He shrugged. "Mum says he's working in a very, very far-away place. So, either, he is dead or he's on the ISS."

They carried on sullenly for a moment, and the boy asked her, "Aunt Pat, do you think I should go to school?"

"Well. Sometimes I didn't enjoy school, but I liked going to school most of the time. To become an entomologist, you should need special training, just like I attended nursing school to become a nurse. And how your grandpa had his training to become a barrister."

"But how can I be sure I will enjoy school when I have never attended any?"

"That's why it's important to you and your mum to visit schools, to get to know the learning environment before you decide, and to hear what past and current students have to say about their schools."

"Did you always want to become a nurse?"

She took a deep breath. "Yes, I did."

"And you don't regret going to nursing school? What if I had my special entomology training but ended up having second thoughts?"

"Well, you can change tracks. Like your Uncle Mick: he trained as a dentist yet he became a choreographer. Most fields require a good foundation in STEM subjects and reading, writing and speaking. If you grasp that knowledge well, it should equip you with the necessary learning skills to take on new challenges. Twenty-first-century workplaces are hiring for attitudes and training for skills."

The boy considered. "But tuition is expensive. Just yesterday, I heard Travis talking to Mrs Robinson, asking her if she could lend him some money so he could pay the deposit for his course." Brendon continued, "Gerald Durrell didn't really go to school, but he was always in his element and still had a career as a zoologist."

"Funny that you brought that up, Brendon." Felipe cut in, "I have a friend whose boy studies food science at university, and he mugged up on the diagram of household toast and paid nine thousand quid a year for his degree. I never dined with Gerald Durrell or played golf with him, but I dare say that he certainly enjoyed some of his white privilege."

Patsy cut him short. "If you ask people who live in POLAR4 quintile one areas, they don't find any white privilege."

The boy reflected again, "And why would I even go to a boring, ordinary school when I might get into Hogwarts? Aunt Pat, do you think Hogwarts will want me?"

"Well..."

"It doesn't matter if Hogwarts wants you, Brendon," Felipe stated. "Hogwarts doesn't *deserve* you. There is nothing ordinary in any job. Your Aunt Pat and her colleagues are putting in hour after hour of work for their patients, and your mother and her colleagues have put in hundreds, if not thousands, of hours to ensure their payload launches succeed. Not to mention that it is highly unhealthy to eat in a thousand-candle-lit environment. It'll get your nose all sooty and snotty."

"But I want a werewolf for a teacher!"

Felipe laughed shrilly. "You want a werewolf for a teacher, and she wants a vampire for a boyfriend; it won't be long before people want a mass murderer for a mentor or, even worse, a dictator for a dinner companion."

Patsy huffed, "No one in their *right* mind would want to have a dictator for a dinner companion!"

"Are you speaking for yourself, Patsy, or Margaret Thatcher and her pal Pinochet?" He looked at her askance. "The problem with the business of selling dreams is that when that dreamy bubble pops, you are only left with hot tears, cold sweat, or some other bodily fluids."

"Really! You can turn any good conversation into something nasty!"

"As I said, young screenagers today don't need more stories of magic. They need helpful stories on *reality*."

"I've learnt plenty of helpful things reading *Harry Potter*!" Brendon announced. "Like...like snogging!"

They both smiled. Patsy had expected the boy to say something about 'teamwork' or 'friendship'.

"Ah. That's a fair comment, Brendon boy," Felipe said. "All human thinking stems from base instincts – be it *Harry Potter* or *Magna Carta*."

"Certainly not *everything*!" Patsy countered.

He half leered, "A friend who works in entertainment tells me that British medical students prefer *Grey's Anatomy* over *Scrubs* because the former features more shagging. Are they saints or sinners?"

The boy considered some more. "Uncle Feli, did you always want to become a consultant?"

"If I tell you that I wanted to become an accoucheur or an ob-gyn doctor–"

"Ha! Felipe, you are revealing your true nature! You only wanted to because you want to see people's front bottoms!"

"Patsy, why can't you believe I have had a holistic experience influencing my perspective and selfhood regarding my future career choice when I was a boy? So, don't say that I'm unfeeling." He cleared his throat. "To answer your question, Brendon. No, I didn't always want to become a consultant. I only did so because it's a lot of moola for a lot of jam."

"It's always money for you, you gannet. Money isn't the be-all and end-all. Living is not all about creature comforts." Patsy spoke with an injured tone. "I spend money to create the world I want, whereas you barracudas spend money to frig about commodified leisure."

"There is a reason **why** your royal riff-raff all drive Audis. Money is like manure, Patsy. Twenty-first-century workplaces taught me that choosing is more important than paying efforts. It helped me stand in good stead. I'm rich enough to buy half of Derbyshire and the lock, stock, and barrel of the other half as well."

"You are corrupting the boy!"

"There are only two sure-fire ways of winning respect in the world today: having the power to **help** others or having the power to **hurt** others."

The boy urged them. "*Please*, you two, just stop arguing!"

"Alright. Ceasefire for now." He considered. "Patsy, I bet that you can't find any bug within the next five minutes. If you do, I will willingly donate ten thousand quid to caritas."

"Fine." She took the challenge and rolled up her cardigan sleeves. "I'm doing this for a cause."

A moment later, she exclaimed with a degree of frustration, "I can't believe it! Not even a woodlouse!"

Felipe used the same jeering voice, "The answer is easy. Patsy, they have voted to leave–"

"Holy mackerel! What have we here?" She feigned her surprise. "Brendon, you know what I found? I have found the largest *squander*-bug."

Just then, they saw a giant ant finding its way on the stone pavement. She gestured for Brendon to come closer, and they followed it excitedly.

"Aunt Pat, will you keep watch? I'm going to grab my pooter!"

"Be quick!"

She saw the door in front opening in her half-crouched state, and a pair of slipper-shod feet appeared before her.

"Care for a cuppa, Trish?"

She heard a familiar voice and looked up. Merete Suntook looked down at her with frigid hauteur.

***

A moment later.

They each had a cup of Yorkshire Gold, speaking little.

"More biscuits?"

"I'm fine."

Patsy watched as her former friend bustled around in the kitchen, opening a pack of Hobnobs with her satin-gloved fingers. She had another sip and finally spoke. "Merete, for all these years, I've wanted to apologise for the things I said."

"No, Pat. It was not your fault. Not by a long chalk." Merete Suntook settled down and offered her a thin smile, her gloved fingers drumming restlessly on the polished worktop. "I had my own reasons when I dropped out. Shall we say...due to deeper layered reasons? But I appreciate your words, and I want you to know that I have been fighting in my own way. You know it's the truth. I did not invite you here to unpick our chequered past."

"Only to recall our nights frittered away together when we had patients' medical routines down pat over plonk?"

"That's right. And sassing our teachers and matrons, of course."

"Ah." Felipe invited himself in. "Señora Suntook, you haven't had the opportunity to taste my homemade beersicles, given how we parted in discord the other night. Why don't I bring some now?"

"Fair go! I'd prefer no one interrupts when I'm having a *private* chat," Merete Suntook raised a suspicious brow and told him churlishly.

Felipe gestured. "But don't you see you have made Patsy sad?"

She returned him a soulful glance. "I do **not** like you, mister."

"That makes two of us, so stop queening over the world."

Patsy sighed. "Why are you *even* here? You should be minding Brendon–"

"He's with Sarnai, learning some important life lessons, including removing stubborn pit stains on gym outfits. And I still have some questions I want to ask your friend, so why don't we chat like adults?"

"Look–" the other party laid her hands open– "I've told you I know nothing about that plumber who lost his phone. What matter–"

"*No.*" Felipe joined them by the countertop and gave a sickly-sweet smile. "I want to ask why you made Patsy sad."

The two of them exchanged an incredulous look. "This is *none* of your business, so stop stickybeaking."

"Ah, but I love role-playing, and I love playing Dick Tracy." He grabbed a stool and settled on top comfortably. "You never know what catfight might arise when two old friends meet again."

Merete Suntook considered, "I have no intentions of making Trisha sad. I only told her how much comfort I have found whenever I recall our time together at nursing school."

"I'm all ears," Felipe said and waited.

Patsy stared at her unpolished nails, then picked out a hidden dirty particle. She told him, "You know how my father fell victim to an NHS patient safety incident, and Merete's mother suffered the same consequences. We went to nursing school hoping to change things."

Merete Suntook continued, "And sometimes we did more than that. Sometimes we went to protest. We went after those responsible in our own ways."

Patsy recalled and smiled feebly. "Remember how we broke that bungling ombudsman's dormer window?"

"How can I possibly forget?" her former classmate said. "That's why I'm adamant about having good security around my house." She jutted out her chin. "And as cliched as it might sound, I fell in love with one of the sons of our enemy. Then I left my course unfinished and decided to go with him to Australia."

"I said some awful things when you told me you were leaving," Patsy reminisced. "Hopefully, that's all behind us."

Her friend concurred. "Let bygones be bygones."

Felipe clapped for a few short seconds. "It's always nice seeing former friends making up."

"Door's that way."

"Not so soon, please." Felipe looked around. "That's a nice wood boomerang for home deco, and is that doodad a paisley pattern?"

"Really, what more do you want?"

"Since you kindly brought it up, why don't we chat about that plumber and his lost phone?"

"I've nothing more to tell you."

"Favours for favours, Señora Suntook." Felipe added mysteriously, "I can keep 'Paul Hogan' quiet."

Merete Suntook blinked. "How..."

"Nothing to be ashamed of. Did you know that blackmail and harassment are the top two reported crimes in the Square Mile? Not mentioning what's lurking below the tip of the iceberg."

"How did you know about Paul Hogan?"

"I believe your friend Trish can enlighten you."

Patsy watched her friend frown and glared at him. "Don't you dare–"

Felipe shrugged. "Fine, I'll take the bludgeon." He took a folded, laminated sheet from his shirt pocket and rolled it open on the countertop. "A couple of days ago, I found these in the communal bin after Sarnai told me she saw you tearing an envelope apart. Please remember from now on that the *only* way to get rid of written evidence is by burning it."

Patsy leaned over. There were several torn pieces glued up, and the page looked like a ransom letter featured in noir films: it was made up of cut-out letters from various print materials. The page leapt to her eye and read:

£1k cash address below
leave town asap

Patsy traced the address; it was the same PO box in Woodford Green that she saw on the envelope only yesterday.

Felipe said aside, "You leave this to me, and I assure you, you won't be troubled again."

"Keep him quiet, how?"

"That would be telling. Maybe I can invite him to swim in a pool infested with crocodiles?"

Patsy shot him a furious glance. "What are you suggesting?"

"Don't be so chary, Patsy." He nudged again. "All your friend needs to do is to answer a few simple and quick questions."

Merete Suntook nodded wearily. "I suppose there's no harm. What do you want to ask?"

Felipe said, "Do you remember any unwonted happenings on the morning of September 19th?"

"September 19th..." She checked as she opened her diary organiser. "That morning, I called a local florist because they made a bouquet that was not to my taste. The owner offered to have it remade, so I went there."

"But I think there was more than that," Felipe deduced. "Something must have triggered your grumping other than a bunch of nicely cut blooms."

Merete hesitated, then finally conquered her inner turmoil. "Fine. I'll tell you." She explained, "Some people are holding something I said off the record against me and my family to bilk us. I tried to settle with them on my own."

"How much did they ask?"

"Ten thousand dollars payable in a CommBank cheque." She added, "I got an ultimatum on that Monday, the morning of September 19th, and they told me to deliver what they had asked within a week. It set me on edge."

"And did you cave in?"

She gave a reluctant nod.

"Did they continue afterwards?" Patsy inquired.

"They promised never to reach out again, until I received this note, this time asking for a thousand pounds in cash." Merete opened her hands. "I don't know if they had internal disagreements or...if they regretted not asking for more. They said they would use the money to further their cause. Despite it being a manky cause I don't support, this time, it is blatant blackmailing."

Felipe listened intently. "The timing is the key to everything. Are you sure you remember nothing unusual about the morning of September 19th? Anything might do."

"Well, I got their ultimatum, and I wanted some air, so I was out on my balcony when I called the florist. I remember there was some sort of event at St Clement Danes Primary School, as the students had gathered on their rooftop. A photographer flashed his camera at me quite annoyingly. After that, I came back inside."

"Any more details?"

"More details? No dog barked that morning."

This caught his interest. "No dog barked?"

"For some time over the summer, I could hear a dog barking in the mornings, and it really set my teeth on edge." She blinked. "But come to think of it, I haven't heard it since I came back in October."

"And what kind of barking was it?" Felipe mimicked, "Was it '*ah uh ah uh~*', or '*ar rooff~*', or '*arf~*'?"

"I suppose it's more like a good old 'woof'."

"And you heard it for some time?"

"Yes. If you know whose it was, then I have some serious complaints to make. This place is supposed to be a pet-*free* residence." She concluded, "My call with the florist ended, and I went to the refuse storage to throw away that poorly made bouquet. That's when I saw that plumber. Then I went to have my bouquet remade."

Felipe nodded slowly. "You saw him at the refuse storage? What was he like?"

"I don't know. I paid him little attention."

"What else do you remember about him?"

"Nothing. He had his back to me." She hesitated. "He was flattening a large cardboard box, and it wouldn't fit into the bin."

"Señora Suntook, I want you to close your eyes and *focus*. You were in that refuse storage, and you saw this man flattening a box. What else did you notice?"

"Well... Umm... The tip of his thumb was quite dirty." She gulped. "I couldn't see his hand, only his thumb grabbing onto the edge of that flattened box."

"What kind of 'dirty'?"

"Like...like he had stuck it in soil or mud... Like how sometimes we plunge our fingers into a pot plant to see if it needs more moisture."

"Not greasy and oily like a mechanic?"

"No."

"You may open your eyes now, Señora Suntook." Felipe stood up and looked around. "Do you have an ironing board that I can borrow?"

"No."

"Your TV then?"

"What do you want my TV for?"

Felipe walked around the large LED screen and unplugged its cables. "Shall we pretend this was the flattened box that you saw?" He heaved the item up. "And how was the plumber facing you?"

"Your shoulder should be more slanting."

He moved as she instructed.

"Your face should be away from me."

"Like this, then. Now, please position yourself at the distance from which you saw him the other day."

As they walked further apart, Patsy watched them, and Merete said, "This should be right."

"How did he hold the box?"

"On the bottom. He held it from the bottom edges."

Felipe did the same, and Patsy saw his thumb pressing into the LED screen.

"Yes, just like that."

"What happened to his other hand?"

"I don't know." Merete Suntook tried to recall. "It wasn't a bare thumb. He had a glove on."

"Thank you." Felipe put the TV down and rearranged its cables. "Your assistance has been extremely helpful. From your description, we learned that he might have left his thumbmark on that box. Fortunately, my buddy is a hoarder of helpful household items, and he still has that box with him."

They returned to the counter and Felipe said, "Do you recall if the man you saw in the refuse storage had a vest on?"

"He *may* have had a vest on."

"Was it," Felipe said, "by any chance, a rush order courier's vest?"

"Maybe. Brown or yellow. I don't recall."

"When you went out, did you have to call the lift up?"

"I don't remember, honestly." Merete Suntook closed her eyes again and opened them after pausing for a few seconds. "I do remember the lift had a very strong sweaty stench."

"You see," Felipe explained, "CCTV shows that that plumber, aka the owner of that lost phone, came in at a quarter to ten and left at ten-thirtyish. When did you call your florist?"

"I can look it up if you wish to know." She took up her phone and browsed her calling history. "I called the shop at...ten-fifty-eight." Then Merete Suntook looked up, puzzled. "If that plumber left at ten-thirty, then who was that I saw?"

"Indeed. Who might it be?" Felipe smiled. "It won't take long until we suss him out." He pointed at that glued-up letter. "Now, back to your blackmailer. How do you usually communicate?"

"Usually they called."

"They never used to mail before?"

"No," Merete sighed. "I don't even know how they know this address."

"Are they based Down Under?"

"The numbers they use are Australian numbers."

"Let's have a closer look then." Felipe took up the page and chewed over it. "In this note, they are asking for one thousand pounds in cash, British sterling, to be precise. And you mentioned that previously you gave them a cheque, in AUD, I presume?"

"That's right."

"So why this sudden change in currency?"

"I don't know."

Patsy said worriedly, "I don't see where you are trying to get."

"I am very sensitive to pecuniary prospects." He turned to her. "In case you are unaware, Patsy, your GBP is depreciating quite sharply against the Australian dollar. One pound is only half of its value now compared to October the year before. Another consequence of steamrolling Brexit, without a shadow of a doubt."

"You're not here to lecture us on macroeconomics."

"Of course not. I want to know why these blackmailers are asking for pounds knowing they would lose out, not to mention the costs associated with currency exchange. A thousand quid is a small amount compared with their previous *modus operandi*." Felipe considered with a cunning smile. "Now, on to the second part."

"'Leave town asap'," Patsy read the line.

"Quite common to say in a blackmail note, don't you think?" he asked the two.

"I've already booked my ticket to go back tomorrow afternoon," Merete said. "That's why I wanted to make things up with you, Trish."

Felipe said with cavalier disregard, "My keen shopping eye tells me that the letters 'a' and 'S' were taken from a Sainsbury's circular and that the letter 'P' was from a Pizza Hut ad."

"Even I could see that, Sherlock Holmes," Patsy retorted. "But what can they tell us about Merete's blackmailers?"

"Plenty. And I have reason to think we are dealing with a copycat." He walked around and whispered to Merete.

"Is that wise?" she said.

"Señora Suntook, let me recount to you one of the most unfortunate incidents that happened to one of my friends. Once, he received a note demanding that he leave town, but he didn't budge. The next day, he got home and found that his clean bot had smeared his dog's poo all around the house. And while he was cleaning up this shitshow, he very *luckily* found a time bomb under his bed."

They cringed at this, and then Merete Suntook said, "Fine. I'll do it. I will leave as planned."

"Thank you. Our candid conversation led to a few questions I need to check very quickly. I know how to read the air and won't overstay my welcome."

"You were never welcomed," Patsy reminded him coldly.

Felipe showed himself out. "Patsy, enjoy your time shooting the breeze with your friend. Don't make a hash of it on my account, alright? Ciao~"

CHAPTER 8

Later.

Patsy enjoyed some time reminiscing with her long-lost friend before the latter left to attend a social call. Then she went to find Brendon at the Robinsons' flat.

When she found him, the boy was half crouched by an operating dishwasher.

"Aunt Pat," Brendon said excitedly, "I have learnt that if chewing gum sticks under your shoe, you can remove it easily with an ice cube. And I have been observing this dishwasher in motion, and I discovered that Sarnai might greatly benefit from an invention in the shape of a mantis to help her wipe the plates dry." He drew in the air and showed her. "Here we can have a thin frame, and the forelegs can help to grasp onto the plates to prevent them from falling. When not in use, it can also serve ornamental purposes."

Sarnai emerged. "It sounds very helpful, but I'm not sure if I want to have a giant insect working beside me. Some of my colleagues say that cleanliness is next to godliness, but I am not sure if I'm willing to go all that way to get my work done." She poured the boy some ice tea. "By the way, Brendon, do you want to hear a Mongolian story about a mysterious insect called 'Olgoi-khorkhoi' or, in English, the Mongolian Death Worm?"

"Deffo!"

"This is a story that my grandmother told me." She led him away and sent Patsy a small smile. "If you are looking for Mr Kazama, I saw him going back to his flat."

"I won't stay any longer," Patsy said irritably as she checked her wristwatch. As the two settled on the central carpet she added, "I still need to pick up Catherine's cat from her place."

"So eager to get back to your graceful Darcy? Patsy, you are more than welcome to explore my digs." Felipe appeared and leaned on the open door jamb. "You still haven't told me which charity you want me to donate to. How about the Fire Fighters Charity?"

"Uncle Feli, do you want to hear a Mongolian story about a mysterious insect called 'Ogee-Core-Quay'?"

Sarnai corrected him softly, "Olgoi-khorkhoi."

"No, Brendon, Uncle Feli will pass as your Aunt Pat and I have some other matters to discuss. Be sure to listen carefully so you can recount it to us later."

"Fine."

They entered the open-air atrium, and Patsy said quietly, "About that fire: I know now why you did it, but it still doesn't mean I approve of what you and I did."

"Patsy, there's no need to rake over the coals and turn your back on me. You mustn't feel so sentimental when chavs die young because of the fickle finger of fate and its itchy palm. Into each life some acid rain must fall, and some deadweight must lose*. Some people deserve

---

*   'Into each life some rain must fall, and some deadweight must lose.'
      Felipe adopts a quote from the poem 'Into Each Life Some Rain Must
      Fall' by Margaret Fishback.

dignity, some others only deserve dignity pants. One must like it or lump it, so just shed that millstone around your neck." He shrugged. "I wish I could tell you to forget it all, but I guess your conscience does not allow it. So, why don't you leave an anonymous supportive comment then?"

She heaved a weary sigh and sidestepped a bench. "If you are indeed an 'ethical blackmailer', as you called yourself, and not an unrepentant fly-by-night, I would appreciate it if you could stop drawing any fire-related references henceforth."

Just then, her stomach growled loudly. She had only had a chai latte since that morning.

"Come on in." Felipe led her to his flat and left the door open. "It is my belief that meaningful conversations should transpire on full stomachs."

She hesitated.

"Coming?" he asked nonchalantly. "Yes, no, maybe, never, always?"

Her conscience told her not to, but her inner self shushed that small voice.

"Come on," he gestured again. "Britain first."

She went in grudgingly. The first thing she noticed in the kitchen area was a well-worn butcher's block.

The room smelled of deliciously cooked rice.

Patsy watched as he unplugged a pressure cooker, took out a bone china bowl, filled it with hot, steaming sterile white rice, and added a generous ladle of simmered chicken fillets with eggs and chopped onion on top.

"Eat, please." He settled the bowl down and gestured for her to sit beside the countertop. "Unlike *some* cheapskates, I love to share my cooking with my friends." Felipe then brought her a spoon and a glass of mineral water.

She tried a spoonful. "Not so bad. What is it?"

"This is called *oyako-don* or the 'parent and child bowl', where you get to eat the mother and its kid in one go."

She rolled her eyes. "Mood killer."

"Oh, trust me, I can kill a lot more."

His callous comment left her apprehensive. Patsy finished her meal quietly. Afterwards, Felipe removed the empty dishware and asked, "So, what do you want? Coffee, tea, or me? How about some Kopi Luwak? I'm sure you don't want me to tell you what that is."

She sniped at him, "You are much more likeable when you are not talking."

"You don't half mean it."

He offered her a paper tissue as he brought her the coffee. Then Felipe said, "And now we can discuss business."

She looked at him. "Can't you just leave me out of this rum do?"

"Don't you want to do your old-time friend a favour? And don't you want to dive deep into others' innermost secrets? The cloak-and-dagger chambers of the heart that we are not allowed to mention, let alone visit?"

"No, never crossed my mind," she responded half-heartedly. "I'm an A&E nurse, not some private investigator."

"Ah, you mean you're not some down-and-out private investigator like Cormoran Strike, whose middle name is probably 'Pay Dirty Great'?"

She rolled her eyes profoundly. "I'm certain you didn't invite me here to discuss British crime fiction?"

"If I wanted that, I'd ring my friend Michael Dobbsy up."

"Now, who's the one who likes to play detective?"

"I'm no detective." He smiled. "I'm here to prevent something evil from happening. Detectives only solve a crime after it has happened. I'm prevenging. And this sort of stuff tends to be addictive."

She put down her cup. "Can't you discuss it with Chance? You two seemed to be more attuned to whatever it was that you were doing. Really, I wouldn't be surprised if you told me that you actually work in the protection rackets."

"Given my buddy is off to Somerset, I'd like to take counsel with you and count on your inwit."

"Fine." She had another sip. "But I thought you had your suspicion pinned on Liam Killngback already?"

"We have a funny feeling about his little habit. Anyone who has seen enough of Liam's videos would know that hand-wiping oddity of his," Felipe said. "While you renewed your companionship with Merete Suntook, I asked Sarnai some questions and got on the horn to make a few calls, so I'm beginning to see things more clearly."

"Really? Things like what?" she asked.

Felipe counted, "First, regarding the dog barks that she heard. It turned out that sometime during the summer, Sarnai discovered that Hannah's cleaning bot had various soundtracks mimicking cats, dogs, and Victorian servants. She knew that Hannah wanted a dog, but the apartments were pet-free, so she turned on the dog sounds, hoping it might lighten Hannah's mood. Yet, on September 19th, the clean bot was on the blink, and Sarnai couldn't get it up and running. In the end, she had to reset it."

"What are you suggesting?"

"Ikenua Joseph said he heard the dog barks that morning, but they halted all of a sudden. We can surmise that someone with very evil intentions entered Hannah's flat but somehow had to disable the mod con. Or he might have wanted to install some malicious add-ons," Felipe said. "Some researchers demonstrated that it is possible to spy on private conversations with a common hoover and its built-in light detection sensor."

"Okay." She winced at the allusion to espionage conducts. "What else have you found out?"

"Regarding your friend's account of some photographer flashing his camera at her on the rooftop across," Felipe said. "You know that a few of these flats are owned by a Saudi businessman, right? One of the tycoon's wives has eloped with one of his drivers, and he is after them both. So, it's possible that some stalkerazzo was tasked to see if the poor couple is hiding in the flats here."

Patsy sifted through the possibilities. "If they are indeed after these two, then why did Hannah's clean bot get involved?"

"Maybe they got the wrong door." Felipe showed her a photo on his phone, of a pebble-shaped object with jiggered wires projecting out. "Yesterday, we gave this place a once-over and found this bug. If professionals were involved, they wouldn't make such a blunder."

She finished her coffee. "It still beggars my belief that in princely apartments like these, something horrible happens, and there's no way to figure out just how it happened…"

"That's why it takes unhinged minds like mine to put shit together and iron out the wrinkles." He prattled on, "And brilliant minds like yours. Patsy, you were, after all, not the stick-in-the-mud you present yourself to be. Why am I not surprised?"

"Cajolery cuts no ice with me."

"Perhaps. But you can catch more flies with honey than with vinegar. Blandishments did help me to get my feet into the Royal Circle."

"Stop pouring it on thick, and you are diverging." Patsy took her cup and swilled it out in the sink.

"Okay. Back to business," Felipe said without hesitation. "Aside from Liam Killingback and any possible sidekicks of that photographer, someone else has cropped up on my radar."

"Who?"

"Travisy Newman," he told her. "He made a Freudian slip when we first met."

Patsy tried to recall that night when Sophie held her soirée. "What did he say?"

"He said to Hannah, 'why have a dog when you already have a clean bot?'."

"Your inference does sound a bit half-baked and not so cogent." She reflected, "Perhaps he had visited her beforehand."

Felipe smiled. "Are you hinting that Travis is a gigolo?"

"Of course not! She could have told him how efficient or funny her clean bot is, and that's why he came to know that the thing could mimic dog barks."

"There is more than meets the eye about him." Felipe smiled again wickedly. "Another hinky business about Travis is that he might not be the humdinger he purports to be."

"What do you mean?"

"There's something about Travis that's JDLR. I have a friend that I met at Harvard. By then, she was doing her PhD at MIT and now heads a Unit at the Global Environment Faculty. I called her to dig dirt, and it turned out that no one called 'Travis Newman' ever worked at the GEF. And other people named 'Travis' have a completely different profile than our Travis."

"Well..." Patsy stopped and hesitated. "Maybe he has his reasons."

"So, you agree that what he is doing is not cricket? Or are you giving him the benefit of the doubt? Even if his LinkedIn is too gussy to be true, even for LinkedIn?"

"Look, I know someone who wanted a glitzy profile, so she got a novelty degree and said she was an advisor to the WHO when she only attended a few workshops there." Patsy considered, "But I do think discretion is a desideratum."

He mused, "It's time we get down to the ABCs. You heard what Brendon said: Travis had asked Hannah for money."

"He didn't ask for money. He *borrowed* some."

"Fine. If you insist on disabusing me: he borrowed money from her with or *without* intending to return it."

She smiled cattily. "Oh. I know what it is – you're fixing your sneaking suspicion on Travis because Brendon said he preferred him to you. Or else why are you trying so desperately to prove Travis is unworthy?"

"You are not taking this situation seriously."

Suddenly Patsy felt a tingly headache. "Let's not quibble."

"I rang up an admissions officer at Harvard to see if Travis had truly studied there." He showed her another item on his phone. "This is the only photo of him that I found on his social media that has any remote reference to Harvard."

Patsy leaned in to look closer: it was a group photo with a dozen whippersnappers masquerading for a comedy society known as the Harvard Hasty Pudding Club. She couldn't make out which of them was Travis.

"Besides, there is another matter that I want to ask you," Felipe added. "On that night when Sophie had her soirée, Travis mentioned something about the tragic case of some GP. What was the case about?"

"Oh." She considered. "In 2011, Hadiza Bawa-Garba was working as a paediatrician in a hospital in Leicester. One day, her ward admitted a child patient. Due to a series of problems, including IT system glitches, miscommunication, understaffing, and admin errors, the patient died, and she was convicted of manslaughter. The nurse on duty was also convicted, I think. I need to look it up in more detail."

"I see. Another fatality resulting from the NHS corporate anorexia."

She shot him a sharp look. "I'm leaving."

He calmed her, "We are not done yet. That night, after Travis brought up this tragic GP, he also mentioned something about another nurse related to an infant death in a hospital in Cheshire. Are you aware of such a case?"

Patsy recalled, "I'm not in any capacity to know all the medical misconduct cases that have happened around the country. Sometimes information is disclosed strictly to protect the identity of the people involved. But if Travis had spent time over there, he might have heard some rumours."

"Right."

"Are we done now?"

"The best way to solve this mess is through elimination," Felipe suggested mysteriously. "I have a well-devised plan pending your assistance."

"What?"

"Are you willing to lend a listening ear?"

He told her what he wanted her to do, and Patsy flared. "I *knew* it! I knew you had some barmy traps set to goad me!" She stood up, almost irrepressibly shaking. "It's *not* happening!"

Felipe took up his phone, unlocked it, and showed it to her. "I sound very needy, I know. But look at this sweet two-shot of Joseph and his son and tell them that you won't do it for their sake. You yourself should know there is nothing more cruel than to take a beloved one away."

"It's *not* happening and that's final! What you are doing is reprehensible moral abduction! God, how can you be so brazen as to railroad me into doing these mad things without scruples!"

"*Pardon* me for *living*, Patsy! If I may be less bold, why don't you stab me with a kitchen knife and see if I bleed? If you won't oblige, then I'll just so **brazenly** ask someone else," he said disgruntledly. "There's no need to be hotter than a two-dollar pistol."

Patsy sneered, "Cecil already knows what I did with his wallet, and you no longer have a hold over me."

She set to leave, and he told her without guile, "Go home now, before we tear up each other. Just don't forget those wheat-free baps."

She turned and spat, "I'll bake them because I *promised* Hannah and not because I comply with **whatever** you wish!"

He watched as she left in a bate and considered for a moment. Then he took up his phone and dialled a number.

The call connected, and he said, "Hello? Hello. Is this Gladys? Well, hello, Gladys. This is Felipe Kazama, yes, aka the 'Chicken Connoisseur'. Oh, I am well. Are you free tonight?"

***

Nighttime.

Sean Reeves had had a long day that day.

After work, he put all his trouble behind him and stepped into the local pub he frequented.

Someone bumped into him, nearly knocking him down.

"Disculpe! Terribly sorry!" the culprit apologised with a drunken grin, followed by a foul-smelling belch. He reached out his hand and patted Sean's shoulder sharply. "Lemme buy you a drink. Cerveza? Tequila?"

"There's no need." He brushed the man's hand away. "I'm fine–"

"Oh, come on!" the idiot waylaid him.

"Really, just leave me alone." Sean smoothed his nubuck jacket and settled on a seat by the counter.

"Fine. I will make myself disappear."

The drunkard left, and Sean sat there, enjoying the live football and the noisy yet comforting ambience. Soon someone caught his attention – a sad-looking buxom young woman across the counter. His lumber for the night.

He walked around. "Hi, are you by yourself?" Then he noticed the woman had a ring on her ring finger.

"Sorta."

"Don't see you around here often," he observed as he nurtured his bitter.

"No," she said. "I came on a whim."

"Well, we all need some time to ourselves now and then. I'm Sean, by the way."

"Melissa," she replied. "Are you a regular here?"

"I usually clock in after work. Well, Melissa, pleasure meeting you." He looked at her delicate hand holding her glass. "Forgive me for asking, Melissa, and you might find me quite forward, but might I hold your lovely hand for a moment?"

She seemed surprised and frightened. "No."

"This is what I do for a living." He took a card from the back pouch on his phone and gave it to her. "I run a hand modelling agency."

"Oh." The woman took his card and let down her guard. "For a moment, I thought…"

"I did say forgive me for being so forward." He inched closer and thought: *The old trick always worked.*

"So, are you trying to scout me?" Melissa regarded him with interest.

"You do have a lovely pair of hands."

"Perhaps," she admitted, "but they didn't stop my husband from cheating on me with a floozy."

"Oh, that's torn it. Really, there's no need to cry into your mocktail." He had snaked his arm around her curvaceous back by now. "Do you want another dram, dearie? My shout. Something stronger, maybe? Calvados or grappa? Or mother's ruin? My personal favourite is Whitley Neill."

"Tell me, is making money as a hand model easy?"

"It's fair whack given you don't need to take your kit off." He shrugged. "Though you need good references, and nice commercial opportunities are rare." He added earnestly, "I can see you have some potential. I have an eye for *true* beauty, you know."

"Tell me more about your work," she invited.

"Apart from my hand modelling agency, I also take on photo shoots for the great and the good." He sent her a lop-sided smile. "Important events, linchpins, and such. Oh, and HENRYs, of course."

This caught her interest. "What's that?"

His eyes crinkled. "You know, 'High Earners, Not Rich Yet' that sort of lot."

"Do you make a lot, then?"

"It's too cynical if we sort everything according to its monetary value. It's a diminishing act to limit ourselves."

"Perhaps you are right, Sean." She put her hand on top of his. "Forgive me for saying this, and you might find me quite forward, but how would you like a very bonny sum in exchange for something?"

This puzzled him. He withdrew his hand tentatively. "Like what?"

"I know who you are," Melissa said. "I live in the Kean Street Apartments, and I saw you on my balcony on the morning of September 19th. You flashed your camera quite *insistently* at me." She added, "If my husband sent you, then I'm willing to shell out double – no, triple in exchange for those photos."

"Look, Melissa..." Realisation dawned on him. "I'm not...I did not..." He collected himself. "You must be mistaken. I was there for a school event, not to snoop on you...or anyone else."

"Sean." She looked at him sternly. "Do us a favour and stop lying."

"I swear!" He looked around, making sure no one was eavesdropping. "Truth be told, I was there to snoop on someone, but not you. I don't remember seeing you at all."

"Who then?"

"I can't say!" he pleaded. "But this much I can say: I don't have anything your husband might hold against you."

"You better be telling the truth."

"I *am*! My plan came unglued, and I didn't get any valuable shots."

"If I find you lying bald-faced," Melissa said as she made sure no one overheard, "Sean, you have such a nice, sturdy pair of hands, and I'd hate to see any fingers missing from them."

Later.

She found the car park, spotted the familiar Aston Martin, and got in.

"That was brilliantly done," Felipe complimented her from the driver's seat. "Classic playacting! If I were a dog, I'd wag my tail non-stop for you!"

"Thanks. I didn't expect him to be such a pushover." She settled down and warmed her hands with the takeaway coffee cup he handed her. "I did wonder if I had appropriately gauged Melissa's sentiment. So, I tried adding some Uta Hagen elements in there," Gladys explained as she had a small sip of coffee. "Pity that he resisted showing me those photos. Do you think I should have layered up on my threatening?" Something sparked in her head. "I could have said, 'Sean, you have such a nice, sturdy pair of hands, and I'd hate to see any fingers missing from them. I do have a quite nicey-nicey stiletto collection' or do you think I should have said cigar cutters–"

Before the starlet worked herself into a lather, he chipped in, "Well, Gladys, you might be pleased to know that while you and our Peeping Tom Pepper chatted, I sneaked into his office–"

She almost choked. "You did *what*?"

"I found nothing helpful to our case, but we can safely conclude that Sean Reeves didn't have any sidekicks who might have broken into the apartments."

"At least my efforts weren't in vain," Gladys contemplated. "But how did you sneak into his office?"

"Don't tell me you have never been a distraction thief? I snatched his keys when bumping into him." Felipe clicked his tongue with reproof. "If my buddy were here, we'd resort to more snappy techniques, of course."

"And did you see the photos? Maybe Sean accidentally filmed the intruder?"

"Sadly, no." He explained, "I went through them, but the flat in question looks out to the London Eye and Southbank, whereas the Saudi's flat looks out to Covent Garden and the Royal Opera House."

"That's a shame, then."

***

Meanwhile.

"*A-choooo!*" Chance sneezed as he removed his jacket and unbuttoned his cardigan.

Catherine emerged from the washroom and said, "Chinese superstition has that whenever you sneeze, it means someone misses you, or you are a topic for discussion."

"Or that our room is too mitey." He observed the interior of their rented chalet for the night that was surrounded by uplighters.

"And a bit draughty." Catherine wrapped her arms around herself and teased him, "I happen to see a pile of red bricks in the courtyard, so perhaps we can become brickies for the night and make ourselves a warm, heatable brick bed?"

"Not if we want to have any decent shut-eye for tonight." He unpacked the duffel bag they'd packed and brought out a well-folded aluminium emergency blanket. "We can put this under us, and it'll keep us warm."

"I know a way to keep warm in bed."

He cocked an eye at her intently. "What might that be?"

"By enforcing a hard-and-fast 'No Talking and Only Singing Rule'," she twitted.

He laughed quietly. "Really, kitty cat, for sure you don't want us ousted from here so soon."

"Your singing is quite up to snuff. I'm sure the guests here would enjoy a moonlit serenade. Oh, I miss home and our cuddly Darcy already." She joined him on the bed. "Budge up, tiger."

The couple had had a busy day. In the morning, they took turns driving to Salisbury, where Catherine's friends Mick and Sam were participating in a local musical production. They enjoyed a hearty luncheon with bonhomie and had a city centre tour before going to Dyrham Park, where they indulged in a bit of film tourism under the hazy blue sky. Then they drove to Somerset for Yining's netball game.

Their friend's daughter hadn't changed much from the last meeting, except her hair had grown longer. They chatted briefly before the gamine girl was called away to prepare for her match.

Soon the game started, and they watched as Yining played Wing Defence. In the end, her team lost to another independent school.

After the game, they waited some time for Yining to get changed. Finally, Catherine decided to seek her out. She found the girl sobbing alone in a corner of the changing room.

"Oh, Yining, is everything all right?" she consoled the girl. "You did great, but the other team is quite strong."

"It's not about losing, really," Yining told her as she wiped her tears away with her bib. "It's about Sanniang the cat. My dad messaged me that they discovered she has a nasty skin ulcer on her face. And they are looking for a way to catch her so they can take her to a vet."

Catherine remembered the stray Dragon Li mother cat that she saw in China. "Skin ulcers can be treated easily with care, so don't worry too much."

Then the girl wailed, "It's not only about Sanniang, Aunt Catherine. Do you remember Lin Min Huan? He has the fried chicken shop by my mom's bakery that I once took you to. Recently, some terrible rumours have been going around back home that he *somehow* is responsible for those three *awful* deaths in that seaside ruin." The girl shed more tears. "And they say he escaped to Korea to avoid punishment." She added,

"They also say that he coerced some parents not to tell the truth because if they did, then they would be admitting that their son pulled pranks on him. Then the boy's school records would be blemished. I don't believe Mr Lin is capable of doing all **this**. There must be some terrible mistake!"

"Oh, Yining," Catherine commiserated with her as she reflected on her summer and those three awful deaths. "Let's hope that everything will turn out all right."

She consoled the girl for another moment, and they reconvened with Chance. Then they had dinner in a nearby Chinese restaurant and went for a knickerbocker glory at a café.

The girl was a lot more composed as they drove her back to her school, and they saw her back at her dormitory's gate. Chance handed her a packed bag of snacks that he had prepared, along with a few books Catherine had bought her. "Have a good night's sleep. Tomorrow morning, we are going to Highclere Castle."

"Hmm...would it be okay if we skip the castle?" the girl asked. "I am looking forward to meeting Mr Darcy and visiting Bayswater tomorrow."

"No biggie." Catherine recalled, "Some friends are organising a barbecue luncheon tomorrow, so let's go straight back to London then."

"Thank you. I will wait at my school's front gate in the morning."

They bade her goodbye and went to their booked accommodation – a quiet lodge on the outskirts of Somerset. Then Catherine told Chance what had transpired, and they caught up with what was happening in London with two cups of valerian root tea.

"Sam told me a sorry episode earlier today," Catherine said. "It happened during the summer when Mick and Sam were on tour in Newcastle, where a local band performed for their production. After the finale, one band member invited the cast to his house to celebrate. As people arrived, they asked the host for their Wi-Fi password. The host claimed it was a complex combination, so he offered to enter it on everyone's device. He then discovered that an actor's device was automatically connected to his network, and that's when he began to doubt. Eventually, he realised that his wife had been having an affair with this cast member for a while."

Catherine ended her account and added, "Might there be a slight possibility that whoever sneaked into the apartments didn't use a jammer because he wanted to disrupt the CCTV system, but simply because he knew that his device might be logged by the Wi-Fi of one of the tenants?"

"Turning a device off is often the simplest way."

"That's good to know, then." Catherine mused, "At least Liam was travelling in Japan last month, or it wouldn't feel right for us to bring Yining to the barbecue tomorrow."

"Mm..." He hesitated, "Felipe found out that Liam was sighted in Soho sometime in mid-September, so I did a bit of social media sleuthing. I didn't find much, but Liam showed up at the jazz bar on the night of the 15th and he had a chat with Roddy. Liam said he attended an audition for a cameo role that was unsuccessful and mentioned that he was stood up by a fan. On the night of the 17th, Liam showed up at the Spearmint Rhino in Tottenham Court Road."

Then Chance hesitated to tell her what Felipe had found out about Travis Newman, but he did.

Catherine considered. "Travis might be sponging on Hannah in other ways." She remembered that small vial of honey the gym instructor gave her and dug it out from her bag. "Now I suspect that it might be mad honey, harvested from rhododendron plants. It has hallucinogenic effects."

They fell silent for a while, then she said enquiringly, "Perhaps we should get to the root cause of the problem."

"The root cause?"

"Uh-huh. The categorical 'Five Whys' approach." She listed: "First question, why did Joseph attack Sarnai?"

"Because he thought she had played a role in his son's death."

"Why was his son dead?"

"Because he and his girlfriend were engaged in dangerous driving, and he didn't have his seatbelt on. More so because someone goaded him over a phone call?"

"Why did Joseph lose his phone?"

"He had another job to go to and was in a hurry to get to it?"

"Why was Hannah not in her flat that morning?"

"She went for a flotation tank session?"

Catherine had something canny in her eyes. "And why did she go for a flotation tank experience?"

"That I'm not sure. She wanted to?"

"Hannah told me yesterday," Catherine said. "Because Travis had booked her a slot and told her it was a highly sought-after experience."

Later.

They each took a moment to complete their toilet and laid out a bedspread and a plush blanket they had brought. Neither wanted to discuss the case for the night.

"Yining told me something very interesting today." Catherine zhooshed up the pillows. "She said that she considers Sanniang, that stray cat that we saw around her house, to be her grandmother's reincarnation." Catherine settled down. "Apparently, the cat appeared exactly forty-nine days after her grandmother passed away."

Catherine took up her phone, examined her wallpaper that featured a junior Mr Darcy, and turned it off. "Do you think there is a slight possibility that Mr Darcy is my father's reincarnation? My father loved *pasta fatta in casa* with orange-infused olive oil, and our H Darcy is also very attentive whenever he watches us making pasta."

"And he's very good at *fare la pasta*. I've heard the Italians use this phrase to describe kneading cats?"

"That's right." She recalled the moments when her furball kneaded like a pastaio. Then Catherine laughed at her jejune idea and shook her head. "Though my father won't flip the blooming fridge door open and closed in the middle of the night."

Her account amused him. "I wonder what was the most mischief Mr Darcy ever made?"

Catherine reminisced: "When he was a kitten, he took a keen interest in our waste basket in the study. Somehow, he got on top of my uncle's bureau, tipped over his ink bottle, and then Mr Darcy left his inky paws all over my uncle's favourite dinner jacket."

"I see why your uncle doesn't appreciate him very much now."

"There was another time when my uncle's pen caps disappeared mysteriously one by one, until we found them under a sofa cushion."

"I wonder if Mr Darcy still hides a treasure trove somewhere, for some of my stationery has disappeared quite strangely. By the way–" her partner settled beside her and remembered– "I got a message from Amani today. She invites you and our furball to participate in a Halloween costume competition for pets."

"Sounds super! Of course, we shall enter. Is Watson entering?"

"Yes, but Amani and the students are having different ideas on how to dress him up."

"A black cat is remarkably suitable to dress up like a mighty vampire," she mused. "We need to give some thought to our furball's costume."

"A lion, maybe?"

"Or Puss in Boots if we go down the badass cutie path." Catherine thought. "We can make a felt cavalier hat for him using his fallen fur."

Her husband smiled. "Our H Darcy is remarkably suitable to dress up like a cool swordsman."

She momentarily regarded him and reflected, "You are not a thug."

He seemed surprised. "I should hope not."

Then Catherine told him once she and Yining had climbed on top of a seaside lookout tower in China and how the girl told her a story of how a teacher from her school was beaten up by some thugs one night on the beach.

"I thought I did the right thing, but I couldn't help wondering how things might turn out differently."

Catherine rubbed his washboard abdomen tenderly and felt his corded muscle there. "Whatever he did, he shouldn't have punched you."

"There's still time to find him. And I reserve the right to punch him back."

"I hope so."

"What did you do to that child abuser?"

"I used a putter," he told her sternly. "He had multiple fractures in the end."

"I can't blame you. I would have done the same." Then she told him how, as Yining had recounted to her, when the news of the badly beaten-up foreigner broke out, the local streaker who haunted the area at night had also ceased operation. "I think it was a very good deterrence."

Then Catherine changed her topic. "Sophie said that she'd seen some positive change in me. And sometimes, I mull over that hummingbird hawk-moth An and I saw."

They cuddled together. "Things will change for the better," he said. "Let's sleep for now."

A few minutes later, Catherine stirred, sat up, and grabbed her phone. "Can you forward me that message on the Halloween costumes competition so I can send it to Mr Spencer?"

"Of course, but can't we wait until tomorrow morning?" He invited with his arms.

"Darling, I'm not phubbing. I just remembered there's something we can do *even* as civilians. We can do some cybersleuthing." She straightened her posture and scrutinised her phone screen. "Travis sent me a friend request on Facebook yesterday. Let's check his Facebook to see if we can find anything useful to tell his whereabouts on September 19th." Catherine scrolled down the constantly loading page. "Boy, does he like to share content from BuzzFeed."

He watched her intently. "Why do I feel that you are deriving some thrill from playing detective?"

"Maybe I do. But isn't it important to pursue some answers given how fragile life is?"

They watched her screen together as she navigated between the posts and links Travis shared and finally arrived at his timeline for that critical day. "Here," Catherine pointed out, "he went for a private lesson at a client's place at Elephant and Castle that morning."

Chance read the post: "Pumping up for our weekly 3hr session! Do you want to enjoy private meditation lessons at your home with a square deal? Sign up today for £50 per session, obo! Zone 1, 2, 3, 4,

5, 6, 7, 8, 9, and wherever a bike can take me to!" Accompanied was a photo of an elderly couple whose names were tagged.

They scrolled on and saw more clips where Travis featured his clients, sometimes meditating, other times doing strenuous exercises with the equipment at his gym.

Catherine put her phone down. "Well, at least we verified."

"Sleep for now?" Her husband lay down and offered his arms.

"Now we can get the sleep of the just." They cuddled up again and soon drifted off.

***

Midnight.

He got back to his room, drenched.

"Trav, bruh, you okay?" His housemate, the landlord's son, lolled on the sofa and asked.

"Still breathing. Never made my peace with the London washout."

"It's tipping down." Ken sent him a daft smile. "Have you got more of that honey?"

"Not presently. Even if I did, you have had several jags with it, and I'm worried about it affecting your health. I don't want you to get shaking and trembling." He removed his helmet and raincoat and hung them by the fireplace to dry.

"Bang goes my sweet dreams."

"I can make you some spirulina tea if you want?"

"Nah, thanks. None of that deprivation cuisine, please. Thought I'd go to Fabric or Scala later. Wanna join me?"

"Nope. I've had a long day. And early tomorrow morning, I need to attend this volunteer fun run with Save the Children."

"Night then."

The layabout took up his phone and continued playing *Candy Crush*.

Travis descended the stairs but came up quickly, "Say, Ken, has anyone been to my room?"

"Yay, the geyser's not working again, so Mum sent for a pipefitter to replace the broken ferrule." Ken grumbled, "Apparently, the last guy bodged. But really, what more can you expect from these Georgian gewgaws? He offered to check yours for free, so we let him in."

"Night then."

He plodded back to his room, got rid of his wet clothes, put his phone on charge, had a cup of soluble starch, took out a small box of discounted sushi from his bag and enjoyed it with soy sauce and artificial wasabi.

Afterwards, he cleaned up and flumped on to his creaking camp bed.

Everything is well, he thought. He had managed to repay Hannah and the confirmation he was awaiting should arrive any second now.

He would pass this trial, just like he had done many times before.

Everything is still well, and I am making the world better, one day at a time, he thought as he lost himself in slumber.

CHAPTER 9

Next morning.

Patsy arrived at Kean Street at a quarter to twelve with a dozen home-baked buns and a bag of party rings.

She dialled the intercom and went in, only to see Brendon and Sarnai exiting the lift.

"Hullo, Aunt Pat." Brendon waved at her. "We're off to buy some olive oil and HP sauce."

"Oh, you could have messaged me; I would have brought them," Patsy said.

"Mr Kazama says he needs them," Sarnai offered. "He is with Liam Killingback now, and I thought that maybe..." She continued in a small voice, "Mrs Robinson has been kind enough to invite my daughter here today, but I don't feel comfortable...you know...with him..." She trailed off.

The boy told her, "We're just going to the offie around the corner; we won't be long. When we return, I shall tell you the story of 'Olgoi-khorkhoi'."

Patsy saw the pair leaving and went up. As soon as she stepped out of the lift, she could hear a Spanish song blasting.

"Really, can't you turn it down a bit? It's acoustic pollution–" She pushed the wooden door that led to the open atrium forcefully and stopped abruptly as she saw a half-dressed Felipe standing in front of a smoking gas grill. A line of empty stainless steel buffet warmers stood beside the grill together with a Formica table on which were several cold food pans.

"Oh, Patsy, aren't you finding me in an *indisposed* state? I better put a top on before you claim my drop-dead-sex fine figure stings your eyes."

"And make sure you shush your unmusical piece!"

"He who pays the piper calls the banger~ And he who DJs is in the groove~" Having said this, Felipe disappeared into his flat.

Then Patsy heard someone greeting her from behind. "Hi, may I relieve you of your bag?"

She turned and found Liam Kilingback coming out of the Robinsons'. He had a lilting, magnetic voice and sported a simple vest under an apron and low-slung baggy jeans.

"Right, of course. You must be Eddy's brother."

He wiped his hands on his apron before receiving the zip bags that contained the buns. As she handed them to him, he said, "I thought the answer was quite obvious?"

"I mean, well," Patsy collected her thoughts, "my partner also works in the legal space, so I have met Eddy on a few occasions. You certainly share a resemblance."

"Someone told me that I'm *almost* a dead ringer of Eddy," Liam Killingback said as he stacked the zip bags on a nearby preparatory table. "My foster mom likes to bake as well. She would bake many burger buns in one go, and later, when they become very dry, she'd revive their texture with a panini press. Sometimes she also likes to procrastibake–"

"Be careful there," Patsy pointed out with asperity. "Let's not get the red zip bags mixed with the blue one. That's for Hannah's niece, who has a wheat allergy."

"Right." Liam carefully sorted the two piles.

Patsy sat on a nearby balsa-wood bench and chatted with him. "Did you grow up in the States then? I know someone adopted Eddy in New Hampshire."

"I lived with my foster parents in Bed-Stuy for a while before we moved to Amsterdam. That's where I lived up to eighteen. They never knew I had a twin brother, and they were as surprised as I was when Eddy first got in touch."

"We are sorry for your loss." Patsy explained, "Perhaps you don't know, but Sophie was also injured on the day of the Brussels Bombings."

"It was a terrible day." Liam chewed it over. "I only wish I could have known him better."

"Good men always die young," she offered softly.

The music halted and they fell silent for a moment, yet she could still hear the ringing earworm.

Then Patsy heard some finger whistling. Felipe called out from an opening over her head, "Patsy, does that mean you already consider Cecil to be 'old and dicky' then? Do you know in China, people say that the older the ginger, the spicier its aftertaste?"

"I find Cecil *quite* the silver fox."

"And are you a stone-cold fox in a fox trap who's starved for fun? Why don't you spare a moment and come up?"

She snarled, "I'm busy!"

The calling died down, and a moment later, a paper plane landed squarely on her bench, on it a large, emboldened '**WHY**?'.

Patsy sighed and unfolded the plane. Another line was written inside:

*Why are you banishing my lumps of delight? Heavens to Patsy, you don't look so **busy** to me!*

"Come on up, Patsy!" Felipe called out again. "You won't regret it!"

She found her way up the newels and saw the sunroom had many pressboard taborets that hosted peyotes and succulents of varying sizes. Felipe plumed himself before a pier glass, and he now wore a foppish bombazine calypso shirt.

A painting hung on the nearby wall; she recognised it as a duplicate of *The Dead Lovers*. Underneath the painting was something akin to a papier-mâché Godzilla.

An awful piece for inner decor, she thought.

"That's me after purgatory, basically," he gestured at the painting and said briskly. "Now, before you tell me to take a running jump, Patsy." His hands fidgeted with a small, japanned tin box. "I know your birthday is coming up, and I always make good on my promises. Since you didn't want a rabbit with cute and functional ears, I got you this."

She reached for the quaint box tentatively and opened it. In it was a boxwood carved *netsuke* swan.

She examined the small object, which was lighter than she had imagined.

"By the way, Patsy, do you know what a netsuke is for?"

She rolled her eyes. "For attaching medicine boxes and tobacco pouches onto the sash of one's kimono."

"Given that you are unlikely to own a kimono, why don't you put it on your dresser to remind Cecil that he is only an ugly toad with bandy legs lusting after a swan?"

"So," she stated, "are you finally admitting I have swan-like elegance?"

He shrugged. "More to remind you that you are only a stalwart, helpless creature who has wrapped yourself in the flag and are struggling in the iron grip of your Queen and her stultifying swan-uppers."

This provoked her ire. "Can't we have a proper conversation without you becoming a pontificating boor?"

He grinned at her. "Don't you know that the anagram of 'pitmaster' is 'trampiest'?" Felipe gestured her out. "Come on, let's go down and see those buns. Now is time to put my quality control hat on."

***

They went down and saw Liam with a cocktail shaker and various jiggers. "You guys fancy some homemade tipples?" He took up the shaker. "I have a friend who won this year's national cocktail contest in Belgium, and I got this dilly of a recipe from her. As we speak, she's competing in the World Cocktail Championship in Tokyo."

"I wouldn't mind one to ease the week's woes." Felipe checked the rotisserie's temperature. "But first, I'll have a skinful of rum. *A palo seco.*"

Liam poured him a snifter of the stiff drink. "There you go."

Patsy scolded him. "Felipe, I would advise against getting rat-arsed before lunch."

"I know what this is about, Patsy. You are enjoying your schadenfreude. Have I dragged you down to my level?" Felipe drank deep of his rum.

"Now, as cynical as you are, you might want to believe that there are people who are concerned for your health, financial health, and dipsomaniac tendencies."

"You should concern yourself about your onerous Stone. Is he in good nick and does he need a conservator? I am fain to sacrifice myself and take on this responsibility. Should I tell you the story of how I once drank Cecil under the table?" He took another swig. "My lust for life is ho-hum without sotting. I don't even have anyone to message when I see a cute cat meme and want to share it. Perhaps I shouldn't have put the kibosh on my budding relationship so early."

"As you brew, so shall you bake," she countered. "Maybe all you need to do is start to behave and stop being a looning cuss off the back of your previous poor performance."

"Sex without 's' only leaves us with 'ex'. Patsy, you are too stroppy to understand us millennials. Don't be a killjoy and don't tell me you have never walked on the wild side. I'll wager that the most adventurous thing your poor plod ever did was to wear brown shoes to the Magic Circle and dad-dancing to antwacky Buzzcocks. A barrister is dead inside by definition."

Liam watched their feud for a while and finally stepped in. "By the way, is Barrister Stone coming as well?"

"He is, later. He is, as we speak, at his cricket club to interview a new club candidate."

"Right, I never understood why there has to be so much poncy red tape even when people just want to enjoy a sport."

"We are a nice country with a different home-grown humour."

"I have heard that QCs are sworn in wearing wigs that date back half a century. Is that true?"

"Yes. Some of them are even more dated."

Felipe said, "The Brits are known for their inferiority complex, but they are arrogant and sensitive at the same time. Stats say that the average Brit says 'sorry' eight times a day. As a so-called 'Johnny Foreigner', I have a lot to chunter on the various occasions when I was lorded over."

Liam smiled slightly. "Anyway, I will make sure that we have enough saveloys. And Madeira wine for dessert, of course. I can make ice-cream floats for the children."

"You've reminded me," Felipe said as he examined the grill's internal temperature, "I once passed port in a renowned household anti-clockwise, and I was never invited to their place again. Perhaps they thought me to be gauche? To hell with the politesse! I'm cutting my wolf loose today!"

She cringed. "Honestly, you can just put anyone's back up."

"Now, isn't that a titillating image?" He waggled his glass at them. "I'm renaming my work-in-process to *Comet Wine, Women, and Song*! With much swashing and buckling and featuring a rags-to-riches, sagacious scalawag!"

"Anything for you, Nurse Bennett?"

She tamped down her urge to giggle. "Don't worry about me. I'll fix myself a snakebite."

Liam looked at her strangely and stated, "You think I'm filthy. You think what I do is filthy."

"Oh." Patsy realised. "Really, you mustn't feel that...I mean, I don't want you to feel that...I have nothing against you and your...profession as long as you work within legal confines. I don't want you to feel you must do all *this* bartending because you are a guest."

"You're also a guest, yet you still baked those buns."

"Sometimes we do potluck, so I felt I needed to contribute."

Liam nodded in understanding. "I feel the same. Let me be part of this Dutch treat. So, you'll let me fix that drink for you?"

"Gladly."

"Thank you." Liam took up a bottle of cider. "Let's see...where did I put that cap opener? No matter." He cracked it open with his belt buckle.

"Patsy, let's try not to bring your presenteeism here. We are here to have it large on this barn-burning autumn-spring day. Oh, and Liam, save those beer caps for me, will you? I'm gonna upcycle some wonderful toothpaste extruders with them. Hereby, I declare myself as the President of the Rum Drinkers Association in Lushington." As he breezed nearer her with a compostable plate, Felipe said, "Care to try some dainties before the feast starts? My buddy might be running late."

She glanced at the plate with two halves of roasted squab and some drizzling skewers. "Just to see if you have seasoned it enough." She took a bite of the squab. "Quite gamey."

"Glad to hear. Caught it on my balcony this morning—"

"Bleurgh!" She put the plate down in haste. "*Drat you!*"

"Just kidding." He laughed. "Really, shoot me if I'm lying. I had them delivered from the Fine Food Specialist store two fresh hours ago."

She announced with annoyance, "It is bad form to joke about things like that."

"But aren't you going to compliment my thrift, cheese-paring Patsy, for I have saved the giblets to make stock for our carvery?" Felipe gestured. "Now, some proper introductions. Liam, let me introduce you to Miss Patricia Bennett, the same Bennett as in 'Elizabeth Bennet', whose temper is also harder than treated ox hide."

She took up the challenge. "You are a bumptious, overweening Mr FixIt who thinks his bungled attempts at bon mots are funny when they are deadly dull, extremely long-winded, and outright offensive."

"Really? Is this your best attempt at sarky put-downs, Patsy?" Felipe joked again, "The burnt bird who rises from ashes is called phoenix, and the burnt bird who rises from chives is called *yakitori*. Now the skewer, please."

They complied unwillingly and refrained from commenting.

"I won't tell you such and such in case I ruin your voracious appetite again. A good nose-to-tail demon cook never reveals his secret." Felipe winked and offered the plate to Liam. "Care to try? It's called *shirako* in Japanese and supposed to be good for virility."

"Can I add some of this wasabi and soy sauce?" Liam pointed to the row of condiments on the side.

"Dive in."

"And what's this red sauce here?"

"Salbitxada, made from Catalan *calçots*. And the other is chimichurri sauce. As you can see, I am quite the saucebox." Felipe smirked as they ate. "I happen to know a simple remedy for lack of virility – all you need is a tiger and some water. And do you guys know that in Japan, to prevent deer from rambling onto the train tracks, people would spread lion faeces on the tracks as a deterrence–"

"Am I invited to this party?" They turned, and Merete Suntook approached.

"Huzzah, whoop, all are welcome! Roses, roses, float my boat, and push it out all the way!" Felipe introduced, "Lemme introduce. This is Liam Killingback, hailing from the land of the triple x. He's the long-lost twin brother of the late Mr Robinson."

She regarded him. "How are you?"

"Lovely to meet you." They shook hands.

"Did you know Eddy as well?" he asked as he handed Patsy her drink.

"Not really," Merete Suntook replied. "I spend most of my time with my family in Melbourne."

"I have a timeshare in Goolwa, and sometimes my team and I go there for a shoot."

"Like a photo shoot?"

"Erm... yes. I'm a–"

Felipe patted his shoulder. "Señora Suntook, perhaps you don't know, but Liam here is an acclaimed, louche adult action film phenom."

Liam smiled dryly. "Yes, I suppose you could say that."

"Adult action film...like Jackie Chan? I'm impressed."

Felipe laughed and took out his cigarette box. "Exactly like Jackie Chan: a hardman whose money is also hard-earned."

"Hold it, mister," Merete told him off. "This is a *non-smoking* residence."

"Fine, fine." He put the cigarillo back hastily into its case.

She then said, "Well, my boys love Jackie Chan. You must show us some of your moves one day."

"Umm..." Liam said, "my work has never been shown publicly. They are mostly small productions for home entertainment."

Felipe snickered, "And Liam is our cocktail master for the day."

"Finally, some good news! What do you recommend?"

"A Love Juice? Gimlet? Daiquiri? Appletini? Or the most fitting choice – Covent Garden? You name it, I have it."

"I think I will go with a good and old gin and tonic first."

"Right away, madam."

***

Patsy dragged her reconnected friend aside. "Merete, I must warn you about 'Paul Hogan' or whoever he may be. Whatever deal you struck with Felipe, you must be aware that the consequences may be...severe."

"Take it easy, gal," her friend said. "I haven't struck any 'deals' with that grape on the business. He thinks he's smartish and he's only a rat with a gold tooth. The temerity of him! I called my solicitor last night and we decided to go to the police. Perhaps I had it all wrong. Perhaps I should have consulted the police in the first place. How did I end up being so silly?"

"You said your blackmailers were holding something you said against your family?"

"Yes, something I regret having said. It wouldn't have mattered so much if a random nobody said it, but coming from my mouth, it would sway our share's market price."

"There's something that I must tell you. I want us to get above board again." Patsy confessed, "Felipe followed you the day before when you went to send the cash."

"Many thanks." Merete reached for the drink Liam handed to her. Her face remained impassive.

Patsy took a deep breath. "I was there at that Post Office counter as well. He said someone might be blackmailing you, and I wanted to know if that was indeed the case. Chance and I opened your envelope."

"God, Trish! Are you involved with some kind of scheme that I need to be aware of?"

"I'm sorry! I really am! But if there was a way to help you, I wanted to try it!" Patsy said. "And we did something that might help you trace and identify your blackmailers."

"What did you do?"

She murmured, "He sprayed your notes with an invisible dye, so it will taint the fingers of whoever touches them."

"Why, you clever clogs!" Merete praised, to Patsy's surprise.

"Anyhow. I wish we had met in better circumstances."

"Do you still like to take a dip in the Serpentine or in other lidos?" her friend asked.

"Well, now I usually swim at my hospital's facility."

"You should visit me on your next leave."

"Chance would be a fine thing."

"I'll make sure you get some proper spine-bash and recharge."

"I'll be counting on you then." She added, "I'm glad we made up."

"Me too."

They nurtured their drinks. After a moment, Merete said, "We have a stonking Olympic-size pool at home; you can take as many skinny dips as you want. My oldest is training to become a professional swimmer. I heard just now that you still like to bake?"

"Yes; mainly for fun."

"Ever thought about entering *The Great British Bake Off*? I watched an episode of Nadiya Hussain and I thought about you. Are you still a punter, by the way?"

"Horse betting from time to time."

"You always liked horse operas. We have a maiden that ran like a hairy goat. Maybe you can offer us some advice? Really, I never imagined that I would get involved with the sport of kings."

The blasting music was back on, and they could hear the other two talking intermittently.

Felipe joked, "If you are a human and someone tells you 'well done', you rock. If you are a steak and someone tells you 'well done', you are fucked up. Burn, *burn*, **burn**!"

Liam Kilingback offered a smarmy reply, and they heard Felipe saying, "Oh, that's why I'm such a fan of yours."

Merete sipped her gin and tonic and asked Patsy, "I must admit that I've never heard of him. Quite a dreamboat. Have you watched any of his films? Any titles to recommend?"

"Not really," Patsy replied, "with my work being quite busy." She added quickly, "And you know that I prefer to read."

"Quite so."

She couldn't bear to continue this façade of lies, so she edged closer and whispered in Merete's ear.

"He is a **WOT**?!"

She shushed her, "Keep it down, will you? It's only a kind white lie."

"You're telling me!" Merete threw her a sceptical look. "I bet you're having a laugh!"

She sighed as if asking, 'Which part of the euphemism did you fail to grasp?'

Then they heard the other two again. "I'm no slouch in the sports department, either," Felipe said. "I do believe that skills matter more than size. What's your favourite position?"

Another mumble.

Felipe maundered on, "That requires miles of stamina, and my back always hurts afterwards."

Patsy was fed up with their bawdy, near-the-knuckle conversation. "People, can't you cut it out?"

Felipe turned, a faint smile on his face. "Really, prudish Patsy, stop giving us a hard time. We are talking about soccer. By the way, did you know that in the Osaka street soccer scene, I'm known as 'Fermín F'?"

"I like soccer!" Brendon returned as he rolled a small pumpkin into the atrium, trying to catch it like a goalkeeper would his ball.

"A stall was selling these Halloween pumpkins, I thought maybe the children could make lanterns." Sarnai followed him with their purchase in hand.

"Who else is coming?" Merete asked.

"Mrs Robinson's sister and niece. She went to Heathrow Airport to pick them up," Sarnai explained, then Patsy added, "And also Chance, Catherine, and their friends' daughter."

"I see. Quite a cosy pack you have here."

Felipe clicked something on his phone. "Now it's time that we loop 'Let's Get Loud'." He sent a pointed look to Patsy. "Or should we loop 'La Tortura'?"

"Just keep it down!"

Sarnai went in and came out again as Brendon played around with the tiny pumpkins. She offered the pair a plate: "Do you want to try some quark that I brought?"

"Sure; it looks wonderful."

"It might not taste as nice as the ones I made back home," she said. "Back home in Mongolia, I can use fresh milk – still warm from the udder."

"Well, that does sound au naturel." Patsy took a piece with her right hand, remembering an etiquette book she had read once on taking food from a communal plate. *Always with your right hand...*

"Mongolia seems such a far, far-away place," Merete commented casually.

"I think it takes roughly the same time to travel from London to Ulaanbaatar as to Melbourne. If you fly directly, that is."

"Do you raise livestock back home?"

"Yes."

"I saw from documentaries that Mongolians are dab hands with horse keeping."

"They say horses outnumber people two to one in Mongolia. And we have even more sheep."

Merete became interested. "I was just telling Patricia we have a maiden horse that naps and jibs."

Sarnai offered earnestly, "With maiden horses, you can find them a husband, and after they give birth, you can make kumiss with their milk; very nutritious."

"Oh, she didn't mean–" Patsy tried to explain.

Felipe cut in, "Patsy, let's just fast forward to the part where you tell her off for telling you any more of her *abominable* dining habits."

She was genuinely annoyed. "You just can't keep your mouth shut for a second?"

"More quark, anyone?"

Merete moved her satin-gloved fingers but said, "I better not overeat."

"For you, Nurse Bennett?"

"Thank you, I'll have another chunk." She tasted the soft cheese and watched as Sarnai offered the plate to Brendon. Then she looked at her re-connected friend and stared at her cadaverous face, getting paler by the minute. "Merete, are you still..."

"If you are thinking what I'm thinking, yes. I still do it, but only when under pressure."

Patsy swallowed hard, "How bad is it? I want to see..."

Merete considered, "Let's get back inside."

***

Sarnai walked around and asked Felipe anxiously, "Mr Kazama, do you need my help with anything?"

"We're good; enjoy yourself, please. We don't want you to think that us men don't make good short-order cooks," he assured her, "just watch us rock and have fun."

"Ok. Then perhaps I'll get back inside to collect the tumble-dried clothes. I also need to put some towels in Mrs Robinson's sister's room."

On the side, Liam asked him in a low tone, "So, what is a *shirako*?"

"It's fish milt; rumour has it that it is good for virility." Felipe told him discreetly, "Sorry about earlier. Hannah had asked us not to disclose your profession to her sister, so it wouldn't do if Señora Suntook learnt what you do for a living."

"Well...it could be cringeworthy for some. And trust me, I've had a lot of trolling." His companion laughed. "When I was in Japan, I learnt a smattering of Japanese, and I was told to have plenty of *chouchin* with a similar claimed effect. Oh, boy, I miss their hot springs and shiatsu treatments already."

"My favourite Japanese food is bukkake soba, but sadly its name is soiled with certain industry practices. What brought you to Japan? By the way, I've followed you on OnlyFans, so I'm looking for your next big release."

Liam smiled shyly. "Thanks. I was there for a series of JOI videos–"

"Uncle Feli!" Brendon hopped around their preparatory table and looked at a set of ceramic knives. "Can I borrow one of your knives to start carving my Halloween lantern?" He showed him with his puppy eyes.

"Now, lad. We don't want any of your precious blood on the plush carpets here, so why don't we find another way? Go to my study, and you can find a box of markers in the top right drawer on my desk. You draw the pattern you want on the pumpkin first, and later, Uncle Feli can help you carve it out?"

"Fine..."

Liam poured the boy some pomegranate juice, and they watched him leave. Then Felipe continued, "I deal with JOI frequently in my work, but I suppose you didn't mean the 'Japan Institute for Overseas Investment'.

"Nope." Liam complained, "Boy, it is hot near the grill."

"Handy life hack," Felipe said, "a handful of starch around the chef's cheeks." He joked, "Gave them a nice massage and marinate, and you can cut them off and cook them the same way you make Rocky Mountain oysters. But don't worry, I've washed my hands."

"That's good to know."

Felipe then asked, "What do you want for your mini-burger? Beef or grilled chicken breast?"

"I'll go with beef and plenty of caramelised onions, please."

"I am a breast man myself," he said jokingly. "When I was doing my Master's in the US, the internet was so slow that it took on average three to five minutes to download a plain JPEG in my lab. So, the consequence was that I remained quite innocent of online erotica as there was no room for bad influence. But boy, Japan had fast internet!"

Liam smirked. "So, which video of mine do you like the most?"

"So many. 'Shut up and Shtup' and a short clip titled 'The Best Ways to Catch Unshirted Hell'."

"It's one of my favourites as well. A mixture of erotica and sexual tension."

They saw the boy returning with markers, and Felipe called out, "Brendon, do you mind passing Uncle Feli a marker so I can have Uncle BG's autograph on the back of my shirt?"

The boy threw him one, and Liam asked him questioningly, "Are you sure about this?"

"Yeap, put your John Hancock down there. Or you can write, 'From John Thomas with Love'."

He signed the back of his shirt.

Felipe carried on as he capped the marker, "Do you mind me asking you a question as a devoted fan?"

"Well, if it has to do with asking for any of my co-stars' numbers, then I'm afraid 'nothing doing' is the answer."

"Nothing like that," he said. "I have watched many of your videos, and I want to ask why you always wipe your left hand on your trousers?"

"Oh, that. Quite observant." Liam smiled. "My producers always chide me for that quirk." He explained, "It might appear on camera that I am wiping my hand, but in reality, I had an anti-static key chain in my pocket that I used before entering the rooms. I just hate static."

"I see."

"Static can also be a headache when filming. If you don't mind me asking, where are you originally from in Japan?"

"Well, my great-great-great-great-granddad went to Peru on the *Sakura Maru* to work as a farm help. He was from the Kinki region."

"That's around Osaka, right?"

"Uh-huh, whenever I tell people that I'm an avid Kinki man, they automatically think that I'm an 'avidly kinky man', so I just say I'm an avidly kinky man."

"Well, I wouldn't blame them for the blunder."

"How did you find Japan?"

"I really liked going to the *karaoke*. Everyone I've worked with is very professional. They certainly know what they are doing and the industry is developed." Liam added, "I've heard there are even vending machines in Japan that sell...hmm...worn underthings, unwashed."

"Besides your perception of Japan, there's something else I'm interested to know." Felipe inched closer and became serious. "How did you find Eddy?"

"Oh. The truth is, he found me out." Liam recalled, "Eddy said one of his clients had seen one of my videos and dropped a lot of innuendos in their meetings. When Eddy demanded to know what was going on, that was when he learnt of my existence."

"Sarnai told me that once she saw you going through the late Mr Robinson's things."

"I did, yes." Liam hurried, wiping his cocktail shaker. "I wanted to know what type of man Eddy was."

"You didn't learn enough about him when you met face to face?"

"People always present themselves in their projected images: to their family, to their friends, to their colleagues, to strangers." He sighed. "Eddy lamented how we were brought up differently."

"How so?"

"That I had both of my foster parents, and he only had a father. He'd ask me how it felt to have a caring mother around and how it felt to be pampered. He said he never had the opportunity to be a child."

"I've always wondered if Eddy was named after Eddie in the play *A View from the Bridge*, but Hannah told me he was named after a hydro-engineering term. Do you know about the play?"

"Can't say I do."

"It's about a man who has fallen in love with his wife's niece, and so tragedy ensues."

Liam spoke softly, "Although I might not have the noblest career, there are certain rules that I follow, and there are certain activities that I will never take part in."

"But the good news was that the niece in question was over the legal age, and nothing untoward had really happened."

"That's a relief to know."

Felipe asked, "Wanna lend me a hand with the seafood in the fridge?"

"Sure."

He led Liam into the vestibule of his flat and told him, "Let's talk turkey. I didn't ask you here because I needed your help but also because I don't want to wash Eddy's dirty linen in public."

"I don't understand."

"Are you investigating Eddy? Are you worried he wasn't the honest John he purported to be?" Felipe asked, then added boldly, "Are you worried that he was a nonce?"

Liam looked at him wide-eyed. "That's a very serious claim."

"But I think you are already inclined to draw your conclusions."

Liam Killingback leaned back against the patterned wood panel. "The day Eddy died, I was filming, and I told him to wait for me in that hostel lobby. The hostel keeper is a friend and he saw Eddy having a row with a woman who had a pram with her. She said she'd let everyone know what Eddy was, and then he had his stroke."

"Maybe he had an illegitimate child?"

"I wish it were as simple as that. We were in a hurry to get AED and call the ambulance and she just vanished out of sight." Liam took a deep breath. "Then I figured that if Eddy knew that woman, it was likely that she had met up with him at his posh hotel. So, I pulled some strings and poked around. People had heard infant cries and childish whimpering from his room."

They heard an exchange of pleasantries coming from the atrium, indicating that Hannah had returned from the airport with her sister and niece.

Felipe prompted, "Back in June, Hannah asked me about accessing a bank vault that Eddy had kept. She never told me what was in there. But judging by her subdued state over the summer, she might have some clues about what Eddy was."

"I can't just march out there and ask her!"

"Perhaps not; subtlety is what we need, and here's how we will approach it."

CHAPTER 10

A moment later.

When they emerged again, Brendon was nowhere to be seen, and they saw Travis squatting beside one of the terracotta pots in the corner, where the boy had buried his Twiggy.

"Do you know what's happened?" Travis asked as he cleared away a few rotten leaves that had fallen around the little wooden cross.

"Long story short," Felipe said, "the ghost insect is now a ghost."

Hannah had gone inside with her relatives to wash off their grime, and Liam and Sarnai helped them with their luggage.

"Hi, Liam. Nice meeting you. You almost scared the shit out of me. I mean, you and Eddy! And oh, you must be the janitor. My sister has told me *so* much about you and how you have helped her! Is there a hall tree somewhere inside? And where's the receptacle? I need to charge my phone."

"Let me, mam."

They watched them disappear. "Ah, but I have glad tidings to give the pescatarian!" Felipe announced as he lowered a Styrofoam box onto the preparatory table. "I've got you some freshly ground wasabi so we can enjoy authentic, sea-fresh sushi."

"That's great!" The young man was excited.

Felipe joked, "If there are men-eating fish, there should be fish-eating men."

"I'm not sure my vegan clients would agree with you."

"One man's meat is another man's poisson. I once had some piranhas with béchamel sauce. Didn't like them; too many bones."

"Really? I heard they contain high levels of mercury and other heavy metal elements because of river pollution." Travis reflected, "Sadly, the sushi fishes are becoming critically endangered. And there are rumours that the Japanese government is dumping the Fukushima nuclear wastewater into their sea."

"Let's pray they will remain in their right mind, which is challenging, given how little prudence they have exercised throughout the years." Felipe showcased the contents of the iced box to him. "A sushi master I met at Hawker House made everything and some more. Look at them makis! Do you know the traditional way to grind wasabi for sushi? People use sharkskin graters." He watched in his peripheral vision as Patsy and Merete Suntook came into the atrium, lost in their thoughts. "Wooh! Patsy, look at these squirting shells I got from Billingsgate!"

She pretended not to have heard him and picked up what Travis said instead. "By the way, is the double-parked Aston Martin downstairs yours? You just got a ticket, I'm afraid."

"How unfortunate; I guess those traffic cops won't listen that some dumbass had parked in *my* spot in the first place." Felipe laughed wickedly. "Maybe I should tow their car."

"Hold on a sec." Travis went inside and returned quickly. "I think they're gone. The slot is empty now."

Felipe took out his car key ring from his trouser pocket and swirled it casually on his finger. He waited until the youngster offered tentatively, "Hrm...do you want me to park it for you?"

"That'd be great. If you don't mind, of course."

"Not really; I mean, it's okay to be a valet once in a while in exchange for some soul-crashing sushi."

"While you are on it, kid, do you mind bringing me my lighter? It's a silver DuPont; I think it's inside the cup holder."

"Sure." Travis went down quickly.

Brendon exited his room a moment later, and his hair all slick and shiny. He neared the bench where Patsy and Merete Suntook sat. He approached the pair and asked gingerly, "Mrs Suntook, Mum and I have been searching for schools, and Aunt Pat said it is important to hear people's thoughts on their schools. Did you like your school?"

Her lips twitched, and she said, after taking a sharp breath: "I think a school is a very limiting place for some." She then said, "My mother was ill when I was a child, and my classmates would say, 'How could Merete laugh so loud when her mother is so ill?' or 'How could Merete eat so much when her mother is so ill?' or 'How could Merete look so chubby when her mother is so ill?'. To them, I was defined by my mother's illness and not who I was."

The boy slowly nodded. "I see. Thank you." He turned and observed, "Aunt Pat, are you alright? You look peaky."

"I'm fine." Patsy felt tears welling up in her eyes and choking her throat. "I just need the washroom." She took flight and sensed Merete following.

"Brendon Boy, here's another life hack for you," Felipe called out. "Always break up broccoli and cauliflowers with your hands rather than with knives, especially metal ones; they will make these vegetables taste bad. And did you know that if you add a few pieces of sliced raw ginger when frying fish, the skin won't break so easily? And here's a question to the entomologist-to-be: why is it better to eat well-cooked fish?"

"Because fishes can have parasites living in them?"

"That's right. When bears eat fish, they run a risk. Have you seen a bear infected by a long tapeworm? The worm grows inside the bear's belly and eventually drops out of its jacksie. Don't tell your Aunt Pat I said this."

"I won't. Uncle Feli, if you don't mind, I'd like to work more on my pumpkin now."

Travis returned a few minutes later and passed Felipe his car key and lighter. "All set, guv."

"Cheers." He pocketed the items. "Allow me to disappear for a few minutes to have a sneaky drag on my balcony. Watch the fish so it doesn't turn into charcoal, won't you?"

"I'll do my best."

Felipe returned a few minutes later and asked Travis, "How did you find her?"

"Oh, quite a nice car."

"As rakish as its owner and truly rambunctious when redlining. Huge bang for my buck." Felipe cooked as he chatted casually. "No offence, but you look like a Tesla owner to me."

"Oh, no. I never had a car, and I don't have much use for them. Public transport and biking often take me wherever I want to go."

"That's not a very murican attitude. What happened to the 'Nation on Wheels' and its citizens?"

"Well. There were spring breaks when I'd rent a car with friends to Pascagoula, but that was it. Also, given how ridesharing and pooling are becoming prevalent, there will likely be a time when private car ownership ceases to exist. If everyone uses Uber, there won't be so much transport-generated GHGs."

"Ah. An Uber fanfarer, then." Felipe sprinkled a pinch of salt and pepper onto the fish. "But haven't you heard that deadheading Uber riders emit much more GHGs than personal trips? Even compared with trip-chaining practices."

"That's something worth looking into then. The algorithms could reduce the chances of drivers not having passengers in their cars. And this may come as a surprise for many, but if they only eat food grown and produced in their local region, emissions would halve."

"So you are not only a Uber fanfarer but also a locavore!"

"Though I find it very difficult to practise buying locally in London, especially when a lot of foodstuffs here are imported. I already spend the thick end of my budget on everyday expenses and the things at Planet Organic are effing expensive–"

"I don't want to go downstairs; I'm **SLEEPY**!"

They heard Hannah's niece complaining through the open door.

***

"But honey, it's already a bright morning back home. Let's grab a bite, and you should meet Brendon. He's a very nice boy."

Bella came out grudgingly while Hannah Robinson held her hand. The girl looked no more than six or seven. She wore a pink chiffon dress and had a pink Minnie Mouse barrette in her hair.

"Ah. Brendon, come and meet Rosabella." She asked them, "What are you doing with your pumpkin?"

"I'm marking my patterns on them so Uncle Feli can carve them out for me later." The boy squatted down and explained, "This is a daddy longlegs, and this one is a monitor, and this long shape with lines branching out is my Twiggy, my pet ghost insect, and this super long one is a tapeworm. It's so long that it goes around."

"Yucky!" Bella exclaimed.

"Don't mind her," Hannah Robinson said. "Bella's always gets a bit upset when she doesn't sleep well." She rummaged in her jacket. "Here, a gluten-free candy corn for each of you."

Bella rubbed her eyes, still adjusting to the jet lag. She looked at Brendon as she unwrapped the candy. "What's a ghost insect? Like a bug that's dead?"

"It's a very thin and long insect that looks like a twig. It's also known as *Phobaeticus chani*. It's the world's longest insect. My grandpa got me it on my birthday." The boy scratched his nose. "Though I'd have preferred a hisser or a peach-throated monitor."

The girl murmured, "My granny gave me a gopher for my birthday. She's a city manager."

"My grandpa is a barrister, and he works in Pump Court."

"Oh." The girl made a double turn. "Does he have to pump his water then?"

"I'm sorry?"

"Your grandpa is a barista. Does he have to pump the water as well?"

"How dare you! My grandpa is a *barrister*, not a barista–"

"You goofball!"

Felipe intervened, "Come on, Brendon, where are your niceties? While we don't expect you to be on your best behaviour, we also don't want your peer from across the pond to think that the 'B' in 'Brendon' stands for brat, right?"

"Fine." The boy said firmly, "I'm sorry." He offered his candy to the girl.

Travis walked over and sat between them. "Brendon, why don't you tell our Rosabella here what a barrister does?"

The boy shrugged. "He goes to courts."

"So, is he a lawyer?" Bella asked.

"Not just any lawyer; he's a Queen's Counsel."

"Does he live in Buckingham Palace then?"

The boy gave a small laugh. "No. He doesn't want to, even if the Queen invites him."

She looked at him pop-eyed. "Auntie Hannah promised we would go to Buckingham Palace and Harry Potter World!"

"I've been there already, many times."

Travis asked, "What about *Harry Potter* do you like the most? I think the Invisibility Cloak is very cool."

"I like the magical creatures," Bella replied.

Brendon thought. "Uncle Feli doesn't believe in magic, and he says that Hogwarts isn't worth going to."

They heard Felipe's voice: "I only believe in one kind of magic: the one where you pull a rabbit out of a bag." He approached. "Children, you should write in with my inquiry. Question number one: what is it with British authors and their fixation on the 'darkness' in Peru? I suppose they'd find the 'brownness' in India or the 'yellowness' in Japan equally amusing? Question number two: Why is Voldemort dressing up like a Zen monk, consequently offending the other half of my parentage?"

Liam came down and joined them. "*Harry Potter* might be forever remembered as a box office blockbuster, yet not many people know that the actor who did stunts for Harry Potter was hurt in an on-set explosion and ended up paralysed."

Felipe concurred, "*Twilight* only tells the story of a stalker. *Harry Potter* is a big, fat hypocrisy on nepo babies, and *Peter Pan* features a serial kidnapper with mommy issues. Convince me otherwise."

***

A couple of seconds later, they heard Hannah and her sister. "I'm telling you, Wren, that the proper way of heating water here is to use a kettle and not a microwave."

"But it's quick and effortless. Besides, I don't want it too hot."

They came out, and Hannah's younger sister brought with her an aura of cachet. She swaddled herself in a fine woollen shawl fastened by a bow brooch.

"Mommy! I want to sleep!"

"Aren't you hungry, honey?"

"No, I only want to sleep!"

"Very well, have some water and go to bed then. I have unpacked, and you can find your toothbrush in the upstairs bathroom. Remember to brush your teeth, alright? If you feel peckish, just come down."

The girl scampered back to her bedroom. Soon, Brendon grew bored with his pumpkin. "Uncle Feli, can I play *Uncharted* on your PlayStation?"

"Of course. Use the controller with a black sticker; that one's fully charged." He directed his attention back to Hannah's sister. "Great to meet you. The name is Felipe Kazama. 'Kazama' is a Japanese word that means the time when wind passes, not passing wind."

A moment later, Patsy and Merete Suntook re-emerged. The latter had her luggage in tow. They could hear Felipe saying, "Diana was quite fond of Camilla, and yet–"

She flared up. "Really, of *all* the things to say, you find bloviating *cheap* gossip so interesting?!"

"Patsy, we are having a nice discussion on Roman mythology, and haven't you heard that gossip is only an inter-subjective presence among people?" He looked at her challengingly. "Unlike some who get a bang out of speech-policing, I can at least take some venial solace in food. As they say, food is the new three-letter, verboten word. Oh, I better use the lav before our feast starts. My philosophy is one meal in, one meal out. I'm crowning here."

Patsy pulled a face at him. "Get lost!"

"No love lost, just forgive me for trumping."

When Felipe returned, Wren told the group about one of her recent visits to Japan. She told him, "I've heard that *The Tale of Genji* was the world's first novel and was written by a woman."

"What is it about?" Patsy asked.

"Pretty much about a handsome young courtier shagging around," Felipe said. "Base instincts, Patsy."

Wren showed him a small charm on her phone: "I bought this *omamori* lucky charm at a famous Shinto shrine."

"Japanese culture has always been up for sale." He smiled. "Do you know that ninety-nine per cent of the lucky charms sold in Japan are made in China, so you are better off praying in Chinese temples."

"Donald Trump is warning us all not to flood our country with more 'Made in China' stuff."

Patsy brought up, "Donald Trump champions selfishness pathologically, yet he thinks he's the big enchilada."

"Well, we have a choice between a man who promises to help us and a woman who calls us 'deplorable'. I think the answer is obvious."

Patsy shrugged. "There is a fat chance of small, rotten apples."

Wren added, "Speaking of Chinese temples, my mother-in-law was in China a few years back on a junket visiting our sister city. She was at a temple, and her cross necklace just snapped in the middle. There was apparently some taboo about wearing crosses at a Buddhist temple. Some unseen forces at battle, that sort of thing."

"I remember an episode when I was working in China," Patsy said with mirth. "Rumour has it was a common practice for the large public hospitals, especially the military-affiliated ones, to send their surgeons to the US for a visiting fellowship before they were promoted. Naturally, this drew some opposition, but the ones responsible for the programme said that there was simply no way they could get that many patients with gunshot wounds in China to provide their doctors with more hands-on experience."

"It's so lovely of you to share your story with us, Global Britsy. Britain is truly global! What more to ask when the London Black Cabs and Thames Water are owned by the Chinese, the *Financial Times* is owned by the Japanese, British Airways is owned by the Spaniards, the Royal Family is funded by the Saudis, and the Premier League teams sponsored by Latino drug cartels? You should commend your Tories for buttering up your sunlit uplands twisting in the wind. And Patsy, Donald may have a bubbling mouth, but what's not been said matters the most. Suppose you have a choice between tea with Donald or with Prince Andrew, I would go for Donald all the time."

Wren stretched over dramatically and raised her fists high in the air. "Oh, my neck is killing me! Hannie, do you have any pain relief patches? Ten hours of flying economy is no joke. Next time I won't skimp on trans-Atlantic transport."

"I'll get you one right away."

Liam said, "I always book the exit row for more legroom. Gosh, I just remembered that I must fly back to Tokyo in under 72 hours."

Patsy thought of a way to put his nose out of joint. "Felipe, what happened to your free air miles? Surely you can do our friends a favour?"

He looked at her and smiled. "Brilliant, Patsy. Of course, where are my manners? Folks, I have accumulated quite a lot of air miles, so if anyone is interested in free first-class tickets, let me know right away!"

"That's so sweet," Wren said. "But ours is a roundtrip, and I don't want the second part to go to waste."

"Can you indulge me then?" Liam asked bashfully. "I haven't yet booked my ticket as I hoped to grab a cheap last-minute one."

"I'll be more than glad. Send me your full name, date of birth, and passport number, and I will sort it out for you."

"I can just send you a copy of my passport to your addy if that will make things easier." He swiped something on his phone.

"You do just that." Felipe confirmed, "Got it. I take it that I have permission to use your personal data? I remember Japan Airlines has an afternoon direct flight from Heathrow to Haneda, is that alright?"

"Course: JAL is great, and they have great service."

Felipe checked his phone and waved his hand. "Catherine and my buddy should be here soon, so let's get the chairs out."

They went in to help, with Travis and Liam taking the foldable dining table and the ladies responsible for the spindle-legged chairs and cutlery.

Soon, the buffet warmers and cold food pans were filled with pigs in a blanket decorated with Italian spices and mini burgers, cherry tomatoes of varying colours stuffed with mascarpone, braised burdock root salad, jamón slices wrapped around tender asparagus spears, rolls of sushi makis, and grilled fish fillets and Cancun-flavoured chicken breasts and thighs. There was also a three-stack seafood tower packed with mussels, oysters, half lobsters, and king prawns, garnished with lemon slices and lime wedges.

As they laid on a spread, Hannah's sister asked Travis, "So, was it your father or another family member?"

"I'm sorry?"

"The ring you are wearing. I can spot a West Point Class Ring when I see one. My husband graduated as a cadet and has one."

"Right." Travis touched his ring self-consciously. "My grandfather passed it to me. Both of my grandfathers were military men through and through. My other grandpa served on the USS Peterson in the mid-nineties and toured the Mediterranean Sea."

"Do you know that there is a scheme now where old graduates can donate their rings to have them melted down to make new ones for the graduating cadets?"

"Really? I must look into that."

They chatted as they helped Sarnai with a fine tablecloth and the cutlery. Finally, when everything was set, Sarnai told Hannah, "Mrs Robinson, everything is ready and prepared, so I don't think I should stay for lunch–"

"Oh, nonsense. I'm not your employer today. I'm your friend!"

"You are very kind, and I so wish to stay..." The cleaner buried her face in her hands as if in shame. "It's just...it's just that I can't *bear* to continue to keep a big secret from you!"

They were very surprised by this outburst, and Hannah put her arm around her friend. "What is the matter, Sarnai? Is anything wrong?"

"Something is very *wrong*!" She settled on a chair nearby and snivelled, "I can't keep it in me, no matter what Mr Kazama says!"

Felipe cleared his throat with a grunt as all eyes fixed on him. "Hnn... Sarnai, I thought we agreed–"

Hannah Robinson looked daggers at him. "I'd like an explanation, please."

Sarnai blew her nose with a paper napkin and said in broken sobs, "Mrs Robinson, I will tell you *everything*. Do you remember that last month, there was a morning that you went for a flotation tank session?"

"Yes." Hannah sat beside her; her haggard face clouded with concern.

"That morning, you told me to use your spare key and do my work. My daughter had a fever that morning, so instead of working here, I sent my friend instead."

"Oh, Sarnai, darling, this is no problem at all–"

"Let me finish. That morning, you also said that a plumber was coming to attend to something in the atrium, and it turned out that he left his phone here. My friend found it and returned it to the main reception, but earlier this month, the plumber found me and said that someone had tampered with his phone. Someone other than me, my friend, and not even Mrs Suntook, so...so..."

"Calm down, dear, here, have some water. You lost me there for a moment," Hannah said, casting a glance at Merete Suntook. "What does Mrs Suntook have to do with this big secret?"

"That plumber, that Joseph man he calls himself, says that his son called him that morning and that someone else had answered the call. It seemed that this someone had a row with his son, and his son ended up dying in a car crash. And he blamed me first, then Mrs Suntook, thinking we had played him false and answered his son's call, except it couldn't be us..." Sarnai wavered. "And so, Mr Kazama began to investigate, and he found out that a mysterious man had broken into the apartments on that day–"

"That is enough," Felipe stopped her coldly. "It's an incident that is still under investigation."

Hannah spun and looked around. "And none of you cared to let me know this? I'm being kept in the dark? What the actual fuck?! None of you thought maybe I had a right to know what was going on?" She spoke with a harsh fervour.

"My apologies," Felipe offered. "Truly. There's no need to get yourself into a paddy. We decided not to trouble you as you'll be moving out soon. And with the dragnet I've put up, I'm starting to grasp what happened that day. Some of the flats here are the property of a Saudi businessman, and one of his wives had eloped with one of his drivers, so he might have sent someone to check if the poor couple were hiding here. As for what happened with that plumber's phone, there is no telling if the John Doe in question was whacked out and possibly in drink; hence, we cannot buy everything he says. Maybe he wanted some quick money."

"What about the CCTV footage? I bet you could find something useful on there?" Hannah demanded.

"Well..." Felipe looked down. "The cameras were out of order for a short while on that morning."

Merete Suntook huffed and said querulously, "If only people had done their job properly, it wouldn't end up in such omnishambles. I have had enough of this place. Last year, it was a fire and a suicide, and now this debacle."

She left to catch her plane, and Patsy saw her to the lift.

"It's a tricky situation," she heard Felipe explaining. "It's been weeks since it happened. If it were only a few days, then I have a friend who works in forensics at Interpol, and he can reconstruct fingerprints from phone screens, even if the offender wore gloves, but now such a long time has passed, and hence the possibility is slim."

This piqued Travis' interest. "Surely, this technology only applies to smartphones and not dumbphones?"

"I really shouldn't be telling you this." Felipe looked around again. "Please don't bother yourselves making a meal out of this spot of bother. I'm sure truth will out very soon. New CCTV cameras have been installed and we have taken all precautions necessary to ensure no further breaches to security will happen again."

***

Sarnai's confession had cast a chill over the whole party. Thus, when Sophie and her father walked through the wooden door leading to the open-air atrium, they could not find a reason for the wretched mood suffusing the familiar atmosphere.

They shook hands with the relatively new faces, and Sophie said, "Hey, nice to meet you. I'm Sophie. I always like to ice-break with a game called 'Three Truths and One Lie'. Ready? Here it goes: which is accurate about me, and which is a lie? One – I once had dinner with Helen Sharman; Two – I was inspired to become a space engineer after watching *Deep Impact*; and Three – I was once accused of international business espionage."

Wren recounted the statements. "But there are only three of them. I thought there would be four?"

"Well, one of them is both true and false. I once had lunch with Helen Sharman, not dinner."

"Who's Helen Sharman, anyways?" Travis asked.

"She was the first Brit in space."

"She must be very brave then," Wren said. "As a kid, I watched the *Challenger* explode on live TV. It's forever my nightmare. So it's true that you've been accused of international business espionage?"

"That story is for another time, and I'm glad to tell you that all charges have been cleared."

"Thank goodness!"

"Regarding the *Challenger* explosion," Cecil chimed in, "do you know that the families didn't have a legal basis to sue because the participants had been properly informed of the risks involved and the possibilities of explosion?"

"Having a senior moment, are we, Cecil?" Felipe corrected him: "They died because of oxygen depletion, not so much because of the explosion. Though it doesn't matter too much, I suppose."

"Well, thanks for Space History 101," Travis said. "And perhaps I should get going."

"Not so quick, Mr Pescatarian," Felipe protested. "The feast hasn't started, and we haven't even rolled in the sushi."

"Can I have some to go then?" Travis seemed conflicted. "Is just that my gym manager wants me to–"

"You are taking a day off, aren't you? So, sod them all." Felipe joked, "Or are you secretly meeting some cool dolly bird from our meditation class?"

Travis blushed and smiled. "Yes, it's my day off, so perhaps I will stay a bit longer. And no, I keep a very professional line with my class participants," he said rather pointedly. "However, Felipe, I was under the impression that you are on *quite* friendly terms with Jennifer."

Hannah gasped. "Jennifer *Jennifer*? Your gym manager?"

"That's right."

"Tush! She's what, counting sixty the coming month?"

Felipe admitted, "Mommy issues, can't help it. Jennifer's got great pillars to the temple; don't you think?"

Hannah's lips twitched. "No comment there, mister."

"Judge me all you want, but I don't give a tinker's cuss."

Travis added, "He even brings her lunch with homemade tea-stained egg."

"Talking about lunch, maybe we can start?" Sophie suggested. "How long do you think Catherine and Chance will be?"

"Any minute."

Travis told Sophie about Brendon's reaction when Rosabella misunderstood 'barrister' and 'barista'. Sophie laughed and said, "There's some truth in there, I suppose. I received the best education, and I'm getting paid as much as a barista."

Chance, Catherine, and Yining joined them shortly after, and their luncheon started.

Liam tended them to their choice of drinks, and Felipe raised his glass. "A toast is in place, I believe." He cleared his throat again. "'To stay youthful and stay useful'. From John Keats. And to a life full of vim." He clinked his class with Hannah sitting on his right, Liam on his left, and then with Sarnai on the other side of their table. "*Cincin!*"

Catherine recalled some trivia from her Mandarin Beginner's Class materials. "The Italians adopted 'cincin' from Chinese, meaning 'please, please' or simply 'after you'."

"It sounds similar to a Japanese word I've heard, though its meaning might not be so...innocuous," Liam suggested.

Felipe barked a laugh. "I think I know exactly the word you're thinking."

"Sorry to keep you all waiting," Chance said as they dined. "We were shopping in Chinatown. If we'd known everyone was here already, we'd have come straight from Catherine's house."

"Oh, what did you buy?"

"Mostly snacks," Yining said. "There is a rather limited offering in my school's tuck shop."

"I thought you went to Highclere Castle, so that's why you're delayed?"

"No, we didn't," Catherine explained. "We came from Somerset early in the morning and spent some time with Mr Darcy."

Wren became interested. "Highclere Castle? Isn't that where they filmed *Downton Abbey*?"

"That's right."

"I'd love to see it. Hannah, let's add it to our itinerary." She asked, "Was *Downton Abbey* as big here as it was in the States?"

Patsy offered, "I suppose so; at least all my colleagues spoke of it highly."

Felipe commented, "I don't understand the fuzz for Downton Abbey is only a high old toxic workplace. And populist entertainment is like poorly made popsicles. It tastes nice when you first try it, but you will suffer from gippy tummy afterwards." He continued, "Except that only this time, it is Tutankhamun's Revenge. By the way, did you know that it was the Carnarvon family, owner of Highclere Castle, who funded the looting of the Tutankhamun Tomb?"

"I didn't know that," Yining murmured. "Now I'm really glad we didn't go."

"And we should be asking Lord Grantham and his valet John Bates if they didn't interrogate civilians, set up concentration camps, and burn crops to starve the locals during the Boer War. I suppose this was the British application of 'fighting fire with fire'?"

Patsy was annoyed. "Who are you to lambast and pick holes in British television? Surely you can't apply the same moral calibre we have today to life back a century ago?"

"So says the do-gooder," he said. "Patsy, imagine that you find a junior nurse in your ward gets raped, and by a patient, no less. You wouldn't do anything? Other than telling her to clean after herself?"

"Of course, I'd do something!"

"I'll drink to your probity." Felipe raised his glass again.

"I like Anna and Mr Bates very much, and I am sorry to see their hardships and struggles," Yining said. "Though sometimes I feel their storyline was a bit...arbitrary; they are suffering because the show producers wanted them to suffer. And the whole thing with the way Mrs Bates died was just drastic and not very convincing."

"I remember having a similar conversation with An," Patsy said. "Some of my colleagues have discussed this, and they think that the former Mrs Bates might have acted that way because she displayed symptoms of overt neurosyphilis. The worst include hallucinations and paranoia."

"But that's just perpetuating the same platitude," Wren reflected, "that the only way to account for Mrs Bates' behaviour is to belittle her further."

Yining nodded. "You are quite right. Anna and Mr Bates had their on-screen first kiss in the show's second season. In the original scripts, they had their first kiss in episode six in the first season, and this was a letdown for me – this is when Mr Bates hadn't separated from his former wife."

"One of my friends who works in the Met has an interesting theory regarding Mrs Bates' death," Felipe said, "that it was Mrs Bates senior who had poisoned her."

"Mrs Bates senior? But how? She had already died then."

"Who knows? Maybe she left a sullied bottle of wine languishing in their cellar? Stats have shown that women tend to use poison more often than men to kill themselves – or others." Felipe refilled his glass. "But you mustn't feel bad, Yining, for no one can get away with murder, and the execution of a murderer does not violate their right to life because they forfeited that right the moment they committed a murder."

Patsy glared at him. "Stop harassing us with your value system."

"Hardly *mine*, Patsy. John Locke said it: ask your steadfast Stone if you don't believe me. Cecil, someday I'd like your opinion on the Lockerbie Trial. Do you consider it a travesty of justice?" He then turned his attention to Travis. "Travis, you've been unusually quiet. Why are you withdrawn from our cosy chat?"

"Oh...huh..." Travis said nervously as he rotated his right shoulder. "I'm fine. I'm just enjoying my sushi. Truth be told, my frozen shoulder is giving me some trouble."

"I can think of another type of frozen shoulder that will leave you uncomfortable," Felipe said. "When you feel better later, can you entertain us by explaining how the tradition of naming the Harvard Houses after their presidents was discontinued?"

"I'm not sure that's proper table talk, Felipe. It's too coarse, even for you." Travis pulled a face at him.

"Fine. Then have plenty of everything of my moreish food, please! I wasn't a chef de partie for nothing. Here, have some of this freshly grated wasabi."

"Do you want a pain patch as well, Travis?" Hannah asked him as he added the wasabi into his sauce plate.

"Oh, no. I'm fine. I already took some painkillers and I feel like a million bucks."

"I wonder," Yining voiced on the side, "what it was like to study at Harvard?"

Travis mused, "Let's just say not everyone who got in deserved to be there."

"Getting an MBA from Harvard Business School was like the educational equivalent of *The Hunger Games* for me." Felipe reflected, "We hid books in the library so our classmates couldn't find them."

"I wish I could be seventeen again," Hannah said, "when all I thought about was flowers, hootenannies, trending romcoms, shimmying to Madonna, and my passing fancy for the boy next door, not mortgages, sleepless nights, and other complexities."

"If it is any solace," Cecil told her tenderly, "my life became all dull and dreary when my wife passed away, but I met someone who picked up the pieces and I found light and love again." He took up Patsy's hand. "It's never too late to enjoy beer and skittles."

CHAPTER 11

Soon, they were engaged in small talk with the persons sitting next to them.

Catherine looked around, and Liam was telling Felipe that he had learned that in Japan, people perceived the neck as the sexiest part of the human anatomy, while Patsy and Hannah discussed their favourite gunpowder green tea brands.

At one end of the table, Yining was teaching Brendon a form of martial arts that originated in Yantai City called mantis boxing. At the other end, Sophie and Sarnai compared the differences in their experiences between a ride on a parabolic flight simulator and a roller coaster, using a salt dispenser to illustrate.

Catherine then asked Wren, who sat on her left: "Hannah tells me that you are a writer?"

She dabbed her mouth with a napkin. "That's right. I'm here partly because I have a book coming out with Mills & Boon. I'm not sure if you've heard of it. It's a publishing house specialising in romance."

"How wonderful, and many congratulations! Of course, I know it. What's your book called? I'll be sure to grab a copy when it's out."

"You can already pre-order it." Wren clicked something on her phone and showed her the book title. She clicked once more and told her discreetly, "I also write hot, heavy, spicy, and steamy stuff under this alias. Just don't let my sister know; she disapproves."

"I see." Catherine glanced at Liam and was starting to find the situation funny, if not oddly coincidental.

Wren threw her a few questions about the new Duke of Westminster and allegedly Britain's newest billionaire-cum-media darling before turning her attention to Liam.

"So, Liam. Hannah tells me that you are an actor?"

"That's...right."

"What films have you been in?"

"Oh. I did a cameo for a hokey Dutch series you probably haven't heard of. And also, some body double work." He shifted uncomfortably, "Filming is very different from living the life. I recall that with some of the more intimate scenes I've made, many expected me to be a contortionist, but some of the demands are just so horrible, and if you did that in real life, you'd end up with a fractured bone."

"Reminds me of that shy pair of body doubles in *Love Actually*."

Catherine then saw Yining helping herself to more grilled chicken, and she said to the girl, "Yining, I'm sorry if the *Downton Abbey* scripts I sent you had caused you any...distress. No one is perfect in Downton Abbey, which makes them so human."

"Oh, no, don't get me wrong, Aunt Catherine," the girl replied. "I certainly enjoyed the scripts, and they helped me to refine my fanfic stories. It's just that I had always viewed the relationship between Anna and Mr Bates as platonic in the first season." She then said, "At least *Downton Abbey* was straightforward to follow. *Gosford Park* has so many actors and characters, I lost track of who was who."

Hannah asked across the table, "Do you find yourself experiencing any culture shock? I had loads when I first came to live in London."

"Oh, actually, I have," the girl said. "For one, I have never heard of a green tea called the 'gunpowder green'. And the fact that you need to pay for ketchup in McDonald's and KFC. Back home, they are free."

Then Yining remembered something else, "and that the police here can have tattoos." She went on, "The other day, I got lost in Sedgemoor, and one officer helped me to find my bearings. He had both arms full of tattoos, and for a moment, I didn't know if I could trust him. In China, the police can't have tattoos or piercings, and you'd never pass the preliminary physical examination if you had any."

"I guess that's just a minor degree of administrative freedom," Patsy said. "But then, a tattoo ban could make more sense so that no bad guys could infiltrate the forces."

"It's alarming how much confidence people place in uniforms," Felipe commented.

"Uncle Feli, I have figured out your chicken nuggets problem, and the answer is 43," Brendon announced proudly. "And I didn't Google it. I did the calculations on my own."

"What was the problem about?" Yining asked him.

He told her and explained the logic behind his reasoning. A moment later, Felipe was conversing in a low voice with Liam on what ancient words gave rise to the city name 'Manchester'. At the same time, Chance and Sophie were discussing their college days at Imperial and how Chance had a friend who founded a cereology society.

"What do people do in a cereology society?" Yining asked her. "Do they study cereals?"

"No," Catherine smiled. "They study crop circles. You know, the mysterious shapes and patterns left in wheat fields."

"Like by aliens?"

"Yep, you know those."

Brendon roared, "Uncle Feli, if you don't believe in magic, how come you believe in aliens?"

"Brendon Boy, I believe in scientific approaches toward studying unidentified anomalous phenomena. That does not mean I believe in the so-called 'magic' as manifested in *Harry Potter*. Similarly, I may well believe in the existence of ghouls, banshees, and squonks, but not the cultural appropriations in *Harry Potter*."

"Ha!" Patsy pointed out, "Felipe, have you not heard that extraterrestrial belief is an outlet for spiritual longing?"

He huffed in reply, "I can tell you this much, Patsy. When I pray to the Buddha, I tell him how many flies I've killed."

Liam asked on the other end, "Barrister Stone, would you like some soy sauce with your sushi?"

"Oh, no. I've been operating on a strict low-sodium diet for some time. Nurse's orders."

"Well... Could you pass me the soy sauce, then? It's just that I've heard that British etiquette demands one to phrase such a request in this particular way."

"Certainly." He passed it but nearly dropped it in the middle of the table.

"Getting butterfingered, are we, Cecil?" Felipe quickly caught the glass bottle. "Is the old noodle still working?"

Catherine looked around, and now Patsy was telling Hannah that, initially, Eli Lilly didn't know whether to market Prozac as a weight-loss medicine or as an anti-depressant.

"How are you finding your school, Yining?" Sophie asked the girl. "My son and I have been doing some school visits."

"I find it quite nice, though it is a bit small compared with my school in China," Yining reflected. "We also have some free time to do a personal project of our choice. One of my classmates is researching sea shanties in the nineteenth century. Another is exploring the possibility of mass-producing silk dental floss. Apparently, it is bio-degradable and eco-friendly, though he still needs to overcome the cost-effectiveness side of things."

"I see. What are you working on?"

"I haven't decided. I was planning to read more on household service in England in the early 1900s. But I don't think it will be meaningful except for my interest in *Downton Abbey*. I'm thinking of something relevant and related to the UK and China."

"Here's a thought," Patsy said. "If you are interested in history, you can look up the illegal deportation of Chinese sailors in Liverpool during the 1940s. These seamen had served in the British Navy during World War Two, and after the war ended, they settled in Liverpool. But sometime later, the Home Office deemed them to be 'unwelcome' and 'undesirable' and deported them, leaving many children fatherless. The government didn't even notify their families, so many of their wives believed their husbands had died at sea or ditched them."

"Oh, this is so sad; I certainly didn't know about this deportation."

"One of my neighbours' grandmother had married such a Chinese sailor, and she'd warned her children never to marry a Chinese person again for 'you'll never know when the government decides to take them away from you'."

"I will definitely look more into this," Yining said. "Many of my family were sailors and fishermen. Some of them had served in the Navy."

Catherine caught her husband's soft eyes across the table and felt loved and lost all at once.

***

A moment later, Sophie was conversing with Wren. "'Big Bang' is a term that gives people the wrong idea. Back then, the Universe was just an expanse of heat, not a big firecracker. So, the Big Bang Theory is fun but does not stand up to scrutiny."

"What is your view on Elon Musk's SpaceX? Will it allow us to travel in space soon? Even have space hotels?"

Sophie shrugged. "There are many challenges ahead, not to mention that the Starlink initiative has been slated by astronomers. Also, I'm not sure if you've ever heard about Kessler syndrome; it is when objects collide with each other in Low Earth orbit and thus further increase possibilities of collision. Debris objects can travel very fast and cause much damage – a one-centimetre-sized object travelling at ten kilometres per second can release the same amount of energy as a small sedan crashing at forty kilometres per hour."

Wren responded, "The metric system is so confusing."

Felipe said, "Perhaps let me use a more down-to-earth example, no pun intended. A typical five-storey building is about fifty to fifty-five feet tall. I have heard that for anyone to jump off this building onto gravel, the result is to feel your body puncturing like a pierced water mattress. To jump off a ten-storey building onto asphalt, you'll hear a pop."

Wren grimaced. "I suppose the pop is more...deadly."

Travis cut in disdainfully: "Felipe, I wish you would speak of such cases with more respect and discretion. I had a friend who threw herself off a building."

CHAPTER 11

"Oh, that's terrible to hear. Did she end up alright?"

He shook his head feebly. "No. They couldn't do anything; she was pronounced dead at the scene."

"It's just sad," Sophie reflected, "that one of the former tenants of my flat died in there at her own hands."

Sarnai paled and whined, "I never want to think back on that day again..." She shuddered.

"You know what we should do?" Wren proposed. "We could use a Ouija board, and who knows, we can communicate with Eddy and this girl." She asked Chance and Yining, "What are some of China's most famous ghost stories? I'm doing a paranormal round-robin for Halloween and am looking for exotic inspirations."

"Oh," Yining said, "there are many famous ones. But in terms of mythical romance, I think *The Legend of White Snake* is best-known."

"What is it about?"

"During the Song Dynasty, there was a white snake who took a human form, and she fell in love with a young scholar. The couple ran a pharmacy together, but a Buddhist monk in the city had learned about this snake's presence, so he sought a way to purge her because their union was forbidden. He told the scholar to bring some wine to his wife, and the scholar didn't know that the wine contained realgar, which can reveal snakes' forms. The scholar was terrified at seeing his wife becoming a snake, and he died at the scene. The snake was utterly devastated, and she risked stealing heavenly herbs to bring him back to life. Then the monk holds the scholar hostage at a temple, so the snake causes a flood, trying to destroy the temple. However, when she did this, the flooding also killed many civilians living in the city, and for this, she was caught and sealed under a pagoda by the West Lake in Hangzhou. She then gave birth to a boy and entrusted the baby to her husband. Many years later, when the boy grew up, he became another famed scholar, and he went back to the pagoda, offering himself in place of his mother so she no longer suffered. His piety moved the gods, and the pagoda crumpled, mirabile dictu, releasing the snake lady to reunite with her family."

"Wow," Wren said. "This is certainly a lot to take in." She typed some notes on her phone. Her manicured fingers made small scratching noises all along the smart screen. "So, when you say 'sealed under a pagoda', do you mean that they locked her in a basement?"

"It's like having the entire pagoda placed on your shoulder," Yining said. "There's another mythical legend that the Buddha sealed Monkey King under a mountain for five hundred years."

"Okey-dokey. Any more recommendations?" she asked Chance.

"There is one story I heard," he said. "But it's not a ghost story in the strictest sense and certainly not a romance."

"I'll be glad to hear it anyway."

"Fine." Chance sat up straight and recounted, "In China, we have different folklore and legends varying from region to region. In Northeast China, where my grandfather came from, people believe in the 'Four Great Spirits':

- Foxes as the Red Spirits.
- Yellow-bellied weasels as the Yellow Spirits.
- Hedgehogs as the White Spirits.
- Snakes as the Cyan Spirits.

Each of them brings their skills and knowledge to the effective functioning of nature. For instance, I have heard of hedgehogs transforming themselves into elderly ladies wearing white, and they would walk down a country path. When they meet anyone who is ill, they will offer them herbal remedies."

Wren typed more on her phone. "Carry on, please."

"People are generally very cautious in their encounters with these Spirits, for they don't want to offend them." Chance continued, "Some fifteen years ago, my aunt set up an apple juice factory and hired a helper. He was an army veteran who had encountered bears and wolves, but he forbade me and my sister to mention or speak ill of any of these Great Spirits. Once we asked him why, and he told us the following story:

"In the 1980s, when he was a young lad, there was a time when he worked as part of a forest patrol in Daxing'anling, an area of very dense forest in Northeast China. One day, their forestry services received a scientific expedition team from Shanghai, who were there to record the local fauna and flora for better conservation efforts. After a long day's trekking, they returned to their base and began cooking dinner. That was when he heard some researchers making fun of yellow-bellied weasels and taunting how 'stinky' they were. Naturally, my aunt's friend told them off for such caustic comments, but the team leader told him they didn't buy such superstitious nonsense in the big cities where they came from."

"Then what happened?" Catherine prompted him.

"That night, when they were sound asleep, they heard a shriek, then some screaming," Chance said. "Our young veteran woke up abruptly and saw a human on their ceiling."

"You mean on top of their roof?"

"No, a human was transfixed on their indoor ceiling as if his clothes were superglued to it. And so they hurried to get a ladder to release him. While they were at it, some asked the person how on earth he had ended up there, and he said that he had felt a 'great suction'. The ladder was brought in, but they could not remove the person from the ceiling, no matter how hard they tried. Soon, the poor fellow began to sing and laugh uncontrollably. It was evident that he was under some…influence. Then, our veteran friend remembered how yellow-bellied weasels came to possess people's souls and how to rectify the situation when it happens."

"What did he do?"

"Apparently, in moments like this, you need to apply acupuncture to the possessed person's armpits. So he found a sewing needle and did just that. Then the poor fellow shrieked again, saying, 'Don't hurt me, don't hurt me!' And the young veteran told him, 'We won't hurt you; please release your control over this lad's soul, and we will bring you something delicious as our token of gratitude.' Then the person said he was hiding in a haystack in a nearby barn and would only relent his control when they brought him the food. They went out to find the haystack exactly where it was described to be and found a weasel in it. By then, none of that scientific expedition team dared to go near it, so our young veteran took up this challenge and offered some chicken to this Great Spirit. By the time they returned, the poor fellow was lying on his bed, and he was in a trance for two days."

Chance finished his story and looked around at the attentive faces. "Out of all the supernatural stories I have heard, I found this to be the most interesting and disturbing, more so because it came from someone I trust deeply. I can't think of any more logical explanations besides it being a true supernatural occurrence."

"Uncle Yang, I know how to explain it perfectly!" Brendon was excited. "This person was *magicked*, and the weasel is a wizard and an animagus!"

He nodded. "I think it is safe to say that stranger things have happened before."

"That's a great story, thanks a lot!" Wren put away her phone and declared, "God, I'm stuffed to the gills! As they say, exciting literature after a meal is not the best digestive."

"I have some Gaviscon if you want it?" Hannah offered.

"Yeah." She reached out to take the tablets and chewed them carefully.

"I heard a story in Japan that will give you goosebumps," Liam said eagerly. "It was said that when the Japanese *yakuza* gangsters want to dispose of a body, they'd put it in an empty oil barrel, cast it full of cement, then throw the thing into the Tokyo Bay. But someone I met at a bar in Shinjuku told me that the real yakuza no longer does this because the pressure will crack open the cement when the body rots and bloats. So, what they do is that they work with asphalt manufacturers, and they throw the body into the oven like molten asphalt, so it evaporates."

They shuddered at the thought.

"Grandpa, won't you tell us a ghost story?" Brendon asked.

"Well..." Cecil thought. "Alright. When I devilled, that is, when I worked as a junior assistant for another barrister, I was once tasked to examine whether ghosts exist under English law. In 1868, Mrs Lyon, a widow, engaged the services of a psychic medium, a certain Mr Home, hoping to communicate with her late husband. Mr Home told her that her deceased husband had wanted her to gift a majority of his assets to Mr Home himself and so she did, but later she regretted her decision. This case was brought to court, and they ruled that Mrs Lyon acted out of undue influence and the notion of the ghost of Mr Lyon was considered as not legally significant."

"That's very interesting to hear," Wren said. "I once read about a case in the Swedish courts in the seventeenth century where a woman claimed that she encountered a fairy in some concupiscent dreams and for whom she bore seven children. The courts, I believe, acknowledged the existence of such fairies at that time and had offered their prayers for the lady."

"There is also a US case that touches upon the existence of a 'psychic vampire'," Cecil brought up. "Preternatural occurrences and vampires remain a trendy subject among students. I recall a course on vampire studies being taught at UCL."

Hannah reminisced, "Our parents had a few neighbours who would put coloured hex signs on their barns to keep evil spirits away."

"I can share a short thriller if you want to hear it?" Felipe said meaningfully.

"Right, let's hear it." Wren was eager to gather more notes for her writing.

"Sometimes you hear tales of corporate scandals and contract killings in my work. Once, a serial kidnapper who targeted young girls kidnapped a billionaire's only daughter, so he hired a team of mercs to track this killer down. These private investigators followed the leads and clues, and soon, they discovered that this kidnapper was a pervert out-and-out. He would pull off his victims' nails, grind them up and mix them with his protein shake. So, when the mercenaries got him, they made sure that he died a very eventful death." Felipe took a sip from his glass. "They fixed him to a chair with sturdy ropes and strong rivets. Then they brought a pack of hungry mice and shovelled these rodents one by one into the offender's mouth. When the rats reached his caecum, they had no way out, so they burrowed their way out of his belly button."

Wren swallowed nervously. "Honestly, I have heard of strange tales, but this one tops them all."

Brendon asked, "Why didn't the mice come out of his jacksie?"

"Who knows? Maybe the rats didn't like his gut flora?" Felipe laughed wickedly. "Wouldn't that be a way to get rat-arsed properly?"

Sarnai checked her watch and pushed her chair aside. "If it is okay, I think I have had enough of ghosts and mice for now, so I will start cleaning up."

"We are all in on this," Catherine offered as she collected the cutlery.

"Move your butts, people!" Felipe stretched. "Then dessert inside for those who behave."

Soon, people moved in and out of Hannah's kitchen, bringing discarded bones and used glasses. Amid this domestic turmoil, Rosabella came downstairs. "Mommy, I'm hungry!"

"Honey," her mother said, "why don't you go to Uncle Liam, and he can help you get some food?"

She went out, stood on her toes, and looked at the remaining food in the buffet warmers.

"What do you want, Bella? Some fish, or chicken, or mini-burger? This bun is wheat-free."

"Thank you, sir. I'd like that and some sushi and salad, please."

"Right away."

***

In the next second, chaos reared.

They heard a loud 'bang' and found the girl collapsing, her face purple and her breathing short and uneven. One of her hands grabbed onto her swollen throat as if choking, and the other flayed at her side and knocked down a row of condiment containers and liquor bottles.

"Bella, dear. What's wrong?" Catherine heard Liam asking agitatedly, and then Wren ran like a whipping top out of control. "Oh, *no*! Where's my fucking handbag?" She sprinted upstairs. "I need an Epipen!"

Patsy moved quickly; she kneeled and supported the girl as she fell and cushioned her arm against her back. There, she felt her radius giving away and heard the bone snap. "Bella, don't worry, you are having an anaphylactic shock. Everything will be alright. I'm a trained nurse."

Wren stormed downstairs. "Epipen, epipen, epipen," she chanted repeatedly as she administered the auto-injector. "God help her, God help her, God help her…"

"What did you give her?" Travis demanded.

"Nothing! I swear!" Liam explained quickly, beads of sweat forming on his forehead. "Just some chicken and a mini-burger, and I swear it was a wheat-free bun, and some sushi with soy sau–"

"YOU *LUMMOX*!" Travis raged. "Don't you know that people with a wheat allergy can't have normal soy sauce?"

"No…" Liam collapsed. "I didn't know…"

"An ambulance is on its way," Cecil announced, ending his call to the emergency service as Chance and Felipe moved the table and chairs around to make more room.

"I'll wait for the paramedics downstairs!" Hannah rushed towards the lift.

Sarnai and Catherine went in briskly and came out with a hand broom, a dustpan, and a large refuse sack to clean the spillages and broken bottles on the floor.

"Brendon, will you step aside? Be careful of the shards."

The boy moved over and slipped but landed on a nearby chair. The chair moved sharply, and its backrest knocked the smoking gas grill off, toppling on top of Rosabella and Patsy.

Travis leapt, caught the grill's still searing grate edge singlehandedly, and cursed, "Hell, that hurts!"

He let go of the grate out of reflex, and Felipe grabbed and steadied the stove from behind. The remaining heat was too much to bear, so he twisted, turned, and dropped it.

Just as they thought this chain of commotion had finally ended, the grill landed on the stone-tiled floor with a thud and set the pool of spilt liquor on fire.

"Oh, *bloody* Nora!" Patsy swore. "Do *something!*"

Yining picked up a wet rag and whipped it over the raging flames while Chance went in to retrieve a small fire extinguisher.

Soon, the fire was doused, and Hannah had used her intercom to tell them that the paramedics were arriving.

Bella seemed to be recovering from her shock, and Patsy monitored her breathing and heart rate vigilantly while Wren squatted next to them, holding her daughter's frail hand, and patting her hair.

Patsy told her, "You can go with the ambulance. I will follow up shortly." She casted a reassuring glance at her partner. "Cecil, dearest, are you alright? No palpitations? Can you drive? Or should we call a cab? My arm...I don't think it will do any good."

"You need not worry, strawberry. I can drive us there."

Catherine had finished picking up most of the glass shards when Sarnai offered to take over. She stood up and saw Travis nurturing his burnt hand in an ice bucket.

She said sympathetically, "Oh, it must have hurt."

Felipe groaned, "Mine hurts more, *more, **more**!*"

"You guys must go to the hospital as well!" Wren cried.

"I don't think the ambulance will fit all of us," Felipe lamented. "There's a walk-in clinic in Soho; I'll go there." He looked at Travis. "Wanna tag along?"

"I want to go with Nurse Bennett if that's okay," Travis said. "I want to make sure Bella is safe before anything else."

They separated, with Travis, Patsy, Cecil, and Hannah going to the hospital after the ambulance and Chance, Catherine, Yining, and Liam accompanying Felipe to the clinic. Sarnai, Sophie, and Brendon chose to stay behind.

Chance drove them to the clinic in his SUV, and they queued for a while and waited for Felipe to have his burn treated. Afterwards, he joked as he showed them both his swaddled hands. "Guess no more cooking for me in a while. At least two fingers are working so I can still light and hold a cigarette."

They walked out, and the sky had darkened to a depressive grey with a sprinkling drizzle.

"It's all my fault," Liam murmured.

"Don't worry too much, Big Gun." Felipe led them through the Soho snickets as he pocketed his medication. "I'm the one to blame for not having acquired wheat-and-gluten-free soy sauce." He clicked his tongue. "Would you mind getting my phone from my jacket pocket?"

Liam handed him the device, and Felipe announced, "Aha. TouchID, marvellous invention." He quickly checked and clicked something on his screen and said, "Great, Bella is out of danger, and Travis is getting his burnt hand treated. And more good news from Patsy: she's taking sickness leave." He put back his phone, took out a cigarette, and held it in his mouth. "We all had quite an unforgettable afternoon, and I don't want us to remember it as nasty as it went. I know a karaoke place around the corner. Shall we go?"

"Oh, surely you could use some rest now?"

"Nah, Cathy. I could use some distraction to dull the edges of my gyp and pain."

They looked at each other, and finally, Yining said, "I don't mind, but don't insist on our behalf."

"Come on then, honestly, I don't want to return to the apartments just now. And Liam, didn't you say you're the last word in karaoke? Let's hear it." Felipe convinced them in the end.

They found the venue without any hassle and were lucky enough to secure a box without booking. Before they went in, Catherine got a call from Sophie.

"Hey, girl. Everything's been cleaned up, and Brendon and I will stay at Father's house tonight. I have Yining's tote bag with me so you can pick it up there later."

"Alright," Catherine then asked, "Why this sudden change of plan?"

"For the record, I'm not fazed by things that go bump in the night," Sophie said. "I only want to send a signal to Patsy to show goodwill."

***

Chance and Catherine watched as Liam mimicked Nick Carter, and Felipe sang through a few melancholic Japanese *enka* tunes. Then as Chance went to spend a penny and Felipe and Liam went out to smoke, Yining played a song and just watched as the MV rolled.

"Mr Lin sometimes looped this song in his deli," she told Catherine with a weak smile.

Then their topic changed to Sanniang, the cat; it turned out that she didn't have a face ulcer but rather a sticky spot around her mouth. After a proper bath and a deworming, she was ready to return with Yining's parents and settle into their home. Then the girl told Catherine how once a passing Lin Min Huan had driven away a few stray dogs who had attacked the cat's kittens.

Later, they exited the karaoke, exhausted yet mentally freshened up, and had a quick early dinner at a nearby Chinese wok-fried noodles place.

Yining asked Catherine halfway through their meal, "Aunt Catherine, when Ms Sophie took my bag, did she take my travel adaptor and phone charger as well? I left them in Mr Kazama's place."

"Let me ask."

A few minutes later, she heard back from Sophie: the adaptor and phone cable had been left behind.

"Don't worry, you can use mine," Catherine said.

"My phone is an old iPhone." Yining showed Catherine her phone's charging port.

"I'll go and get it," Chance offered. "You two can stay warm and cosy here."

"Thanks, darling. Get the car, won't you?"

"No, traffic is tailing back around Seven Dials."

"It seems my buddy will walk me back home. What about you, Big Gun?" Felipe said.

"I'll take the Tube and get back to my hostel," Liam said. "Look, forget about that ticket; I'm perfectly capable of getting my own."

"No big deal. I will get it done for you," Felipe said. "Let's not make more trouble than it's worth. Whatever the others say, you never dissemble, and I appreciate that."

CHAPTER II

"Thanks. That's comforting to know."

Felipe looked at his seamed forehead and said, "By the way, Liam, have you ever heard of the 'racy lacy story'?"

"Not that I remember. What's it about?"

"Given we have tender ears here, let's get out."

They came out of the diner and found a quiet corner, and Felipe started, "Once, a friend of mine suspected his wife was having an affair, so he went home early. Unfortunately, the woman alerted her lover, so the man quickly escaped from the back door. But one thing put my friend at his advantage, for, amidst the chaos, the seducer had put on his wife's underwear. My friend soon caught up with the loser, and he grabbed the man he suspected on the road, urging him to remove his trousers to show him his underwear. And the man pleaded, "Please, you've got it wrong! I'm not the one! I'm not wearing anything lacy!" And my friend was furious, shouting, 'How do you know it's *lacy*?'"

He waited for Liam's reaction. A few seconds later, Liam asked, "That was it?"

"Uh-huh. That's the 'racy lacy story'."

"It's not what I was expecting."

"Anyway," Felipe checked the time, "the pain is returning, so I guess we should say goodbye. Thanks again for your autograph."

"No big deal."

They bade him goodbye and walked towards Kean Street. The chilly rain had intensified, and windswept fallen leaves swirled as they crossed Long Acre without saying much and soon arrived at Kean Street.

For an instant, Chance thought he was being followed, but he brushed aside his paranoia. Felipe took out his phone and checked. "I want to stay behind for a drag. Here's the key: why don't you go up first?" He leaned on his Aston Martin.

"But it's raining."

"So what? Can't one enjoy the rain once in a while?"

"If you say so."

Chance grabbed his key ring and key card and opened the double glass door. The entrance hall was eerily quiet, and he called down the lift without giving it too much thought.

He got upstairs and went into the atrium. All was fine except for a circle of charcoal-like stain on the stone floor.

He found his way into Felipe's room. Jayden Peng's flat was not unlike his sister's, with a panorama of Covent Garden and its nightly splendour. Chance quickly located Yining's phone cables and charger. He put them inside his coat's inner pocket and got out.

As he locked the door, he saw a line of small pumpkins sitting on the windowsill of Hannah's kitchen and a glinting dancing shape of light through the kitchen's window.

He walked across the atrium and found Hannah's door slightly ajar. Chance opened it wide. He went in and found Travis kneeling in Hannah's kitchen, holding his phone with its flashlight on, looking high and low for something.

Chance did not make his presence known. Instead, he crept behind Travis stealthily and followed him into Hannah's living room. The pier glass by the wall gave off an unsettling reflection.

"What are you doing, Travis?"

"God, you scared me!" The young man turned abruptly and, upon seeing him, relaxed by a degree. "Mrs Robinson and her sister are staying at the hospital, and I'm here to get some clothes for Bella. Bella's hairpin fell out when she had her allergic reaction, and Sarnai said she had gathered and put away everything inside the house. I couldn't find it in the kitchen, so maybe she dropped it somewhere."

He continued his search. "Bella insists on having it back tonight or she won't sleep. Have you seen it? It's pink with a decorative Minnie Mouse."

"I'll keep an eye out for it. Maybe it's outside somewhere."

"Thanks," Travis said as he searched. "Look, I'm sorry about what happened to Johnny."

Chance stopped and turned slowly. "Beg your pardon?"

"I'm sorry about what happened to Johnny," Travis repeated earnestly.

"How did you know about Johnny?"

"Felipe told us. I didn't know why he had to keep it a secret from Mrs Robinson, though."

"Allow me to ask you this then, Travis." Chance brought out his taser and hid it behind him as he inched closer. "How did you know the boy in question was called *Johnny*?"

Travis spun sharply and pounced at him. Chance could see a mixture of fear, hate, and murderous determination in his eyes. Travis punched him across his face and cackled, "The mirror gave you away, dude."

Chance let out a frustrated cry as he felt an acute jab of pain and then his taser was prised out from his fingers. A second later, Travis had manoeuvred him into a tight full nelson. He heard the familiar 'zap' and felt a strike of lightning in his bones, and then he was fading away...

***

Later.

When he regained consciousness, Chance was aching all over his body as if he had shouldered a pagoda for a hundred years.

He opened his eyes and saw only darkness. He tried to move his fingers only to find his hands tied securely behind his back. He felt around with his limited reach and felt he was trapped in a small space suffused with dampness and the smell of washing-up liquid. He moved his neck and bumped his head.

"Damn it!" he cursed under his breath. He realised he was in the closet below the sink. But whose flat was he in? How long had he been out? And where was Travis?

"Knock, knock." Chance felt relief washing over him as he heard Felipe's throaty voice.

"Oh, Felipe. It's you."

"Trick or Treat?"

"Sorry," Travis said with his young, foolish-sounding tone, "I'm not really in the mood."

"How's the hand? I see you have it strapped up."

"I'm fine. Had a painkiller. It won't kill me."

"Have you seen my buddy around?"

"Not since this afternoon. Your flat's light was off just now, so he may have already left."

"No worries then," Felipe laughed. "I know he might be *tied up* at the moment."

Chance heard footsteps going away, and he tried bumping his head around and scratching with his fingers to make any sound.

"What's that bumping noise? Did you hear that?" Felipe asked.

"Must be the dishwasher. Funny that the Brits always put their washing machines in the kitchen. Baked beans with smelly socks, eh?"

Once again, the steps were going away...

"Oh, is that my set of ceramic knives on the counter?"

"I guess so. Sarnai must have left them there."

"I better take these away; knives are dangerous household items." The footsteps were coming back. "How nice of her; she even cleaned them for me." Chance pictured Felipe taking one out from its sheath and examining the knife's blade. "I once tried to show off my knife skills in front of Gordon Ramsay."

"Did you?"

"Said I wasn't the sharpest knife in the drawer."

"I'm sorry to hear that. But given his temperament, you should take it as a compliment."

"I doubt that much is true." Chance sensed Felipe's voice was nearby. "Let's cut the crap and open our kimonos. Who are you?"

"Really, you are racking my brains here. I'm Travis. Did your meds get into your head or what?"

"Oh, I intend to rack a lot more." Felipe listed: "You are 'Timothy Farrimond', Princeton graduate researcher in Cape Town; 'Tyler Wright', Stanford dropout in Milan; and 'Travis Newman', Harvard wokester in London; who is the stonewalling fabulist standing before me?"

"Come on, you're slaying me here."

"Be careful what you wish for."

Chance heard a racket, then fisticuffs, and Travis squeaked in agony.

"Aye yai yai," Felipe said, "What did I say about showing off your knife skills in front of Gordon Ramsay? Let me take that taser. Good boy."

More cursing and clashing, and Chance heard their low arguments intermittently.

"Dripping poison into her memories, defiling her husband—"

There was a heavy punch, a muffled yell, and something dropped and clinked in the sink. Chance thought it sounded awfully like a knocked-out tooth.

"–pathetic crumb-bum who wore diapers and begged to be bottle-fed–"

Then came a loud, heavy landing and the sounds of glass shattering.

"–wrong house to trick–"

"–He told Johnny never to bother him again–"

The fights died down, and Chance heard Felipe panting, "–you wanna know what happened to my last personal trainer, Travis? I dripped Drano into his eyes and poured boiling oil down his butthole, and *boy*, it stank. Then I made sure what was left of him made a perfect bone me–"

Felipe grunted, and Chance heard a thud, then silence resumed.

Chance frantically tried to unbind himself but could only sit and listen for any signs of life. Some long seconds later, he heard a crawling noise as if a body were being dragged along the carpet.

The sounds drew closer, and Chance got ready to butt Travis in his face.

The closet door cracked open, and he saw Felipe, the gauze on his swaddled hands tainted black.

"Still breathing?" He cut him loose with a knife, and Chance said, "Took you long enough."

"I don't have my usual dexterity–"

Just then, they heard footsteps escaping away.

They chased after Travis and barely made it when the lift door closed.

"See you, fuckers." Travis laughed and dangled Felipe's car key in front of their eyes. Then he whisked out of their sight.

Chance bolted for the emergency stairs when Felipe stopped him. "Let him go."

"What'd you mean–"

Felipe took out his phone; its screen cracked. "Still works. Good." He made a call and said, "Get him."

Eight hours later.

Chance pulled over in front of Cecil's garage, got out of the SUV, and thought about those Chinese sailors who never saw their families again.

The rain had stopped, leaving a gibbous moon hanging low in the inky sky.

Chance looked up and saw Yining's worried face disappear by the bedroom window on the second floor. Then the front door was pushed wide open, and Catherine rushed down the stone steps. Her eyes were red, and her voice hoarse. "Are you alright?"

He nodded numbly. "Nothing that won't snap back."

Her fingers were splayed on his face then, checking, reassuring. Only when she found nothing more severe than a cracked lip and a friction burn, she whispered, "We heard that... Felipe..."

Patsy came out, her right arm in a sling. "Is it true?"

"Yes." He took a deep breath, "His car plunged under Waterloo Bridge."

"Oh."

"And the driver was announced dead at the scene."

Patsy stumbled and steadied herself with Catherine's offered hand.

Silent sobs reigned, but not for long. They heard a car door slam open and closed and Felipe's guttural voice called out, "Why, miss me already, patootie?" He neared them. "Or were you thinking about what to wear to my funeral and found out that you don't have a proper number?"

"Shut up." Patsy broke into a teary smile. "I'm not without a soft side."

"I heard that my favourite A&E nurse was on sick leave. No more roasted squabs for you, Patsy. Next time, you'll be eating crow."

Cecil, clad in a bathrobe, stood by the doorway, and called out, "Get inside and get warm."

They huddled closer and moved towards the door. "Come on inside, Patsy, let's shut all chaos out before we get *windsore*." Felipe mocked.

She followed them up and shut the door firmly, and the inclement rain soon began.

EPILOGUE

THE DIARY OF A YOUNG DETECTIVE

(continued)

October 19th, Wednesday. Broken clouds.

There is more info on the case of the IC1 male who stole a Peruvian city banker's sports convertible that veered off course on Waterloo Bridge four days ago.

I have jotted down details in my previous entries on this incident that caught all the headlines. Preliminary investigations provided some ground for suspicious circumstances. The deceased had two disarticulated fingers on his left hand. Blood analysis showed residual mescaline, a substance found in some cactuses.

A work ID was found, and the male was identified as a US gym instructor volunteering in a fitness facility in Covent Garden.

October 21st, Friday. Partly sunny.

The gym's management was baffled that their star volunteer of the month possessed a forged passport (apparently, they didn't bother going after his DBS). It seems that 'Travis Newman' had carefully woven a web of lies around himself.

The post-mortem mugshot we sent to our US counterparts helped to confirm his identity – a certain Mr T G from Centreville, Illinois, aged 28, who had a record of battery charges and grifting and had been on the lam for nearly three years.

Whoever Travis Newman was, he had successfully hoodwinked the persons closest to him, letting them believe he was a recent Harvard graduate looking for small jobs to support and fund his Master's studies in London.

Meanwhile, more information has surfaced regarding the night of his death. Only minutes before the Aston Martin plunged into the Thames, City Police had discovered a suspicious Ford Mondeo recklessly pursuing him in his vehicle.

October 23rd, Sunday. Foggy.

The pursuers were found and identified. Both had been recently released from custody and lived in Eastcheap. One claimed to have a relative who had a skirmish with the Peruvian banker over the summer. They admitted to tailing the vehicle, hoping to teach its owner a lesson, and fled when they saw it crashing.

We all thought this explanation to be a bit thick. Then, to make the situation even more bizarre, we believe they might have tampered with their electronic tags to roam however they wanted when they were placed under curfew. Responsible officers and relevant staff at the EMS have been notified.

October 24th, Monday. Sunny.

It's nice to feel sunlight warming your face and fingers in these chilly winds. I have been trying to contact that Peruvian banker to answer a few of my questions, but I am still waiting to hear back.

I visited the house in Russell Square where Travis Newman had stayed. He lived in a basement room that was provided to him for free (while he had been telling his gym colleagues that he was dossing at a shelter as a helper). The room had already been searched thoroughly, and the house owner's son told me his mother had always seen Travis as the 'son she could never have'. He also revealed that Travis had been supplying him with various tranks and even dubious honey that 'made you feel so good'.

In the afternoon, I went to a place on 75 Rossmore Road to meet with Miss Gladys Parker, who works as a part-time self-defence trainer. She seemed to be a key figure of contention in the dispute between that Peruvian banker and his pursuers. Gladys agreed to have a chat off the record.

"I think it was in early June. I wanted to move out of my parents' place and started looking at rentable flats. Someone contacted me with a very enticing offer, but when I pitched up at his doorstep, he had sex-for-rent in mind. Soon, I found myself locked in a bathroom, and he yelled out expletives. I called my mother for help, and sometime later, Felipe and his friend came to my aid. Of course, I could have escaped. I made a rope from the shower curtains but didn't want to leave like a burglar. Felipe gave that landlord a nasty beating, but who can blame him? I'd have done the same."

I clarified a few other questions before she left. Out of personal interest, I asked, "What exactly do you do as a part-time self-defence trainer?"

"The heavy lifting is taken account of, so all I do is to scare people off."

"Come again?"

"We have another trainer who covers all the theoretical stuff and practical moves. Then, we let our students walk past a district one by one and tell them that we have arranged for people to ambush them, leaving them all tense. Then it's my job to frighten them."

Before we parted, she asked me, "DC Deborah, do you feel safe in your work?"

"Well, I have my years of training and my co-workers to rely on."

She nodded, "It's just that... I find it very difficult to feel safe again, even among my fellow actors and actresses. And feeling safe is such a significant element of a successful performance on stage."

The pieces were slowly coming together, and her account pointed out another direction for me. If I couldn't get my questions through to Felipe Kazama, who always seemed to be in a meeting, I could contact his friend, Mr Changxi Yang, who co-owns and runs a jazz bar in Covent Garden. Mr Yang also gave a statement regarding Travis Newman. I contacted him, and he agreed to meet me at his venue early tomorrow for another off-the-record chat.

October 25th, Tuesday. Drizzle.

I got to the deserted bar, and Mr Yang was waiting.

"Thank you for agreeing to see me," I said as I furled my umbrella.

"Take a seat, please." He gestured at a stool.

"I have a few questions." I flipped through my notes. "You mentioned that Travis attacked you with a taser gun when you asked him about 'Johnny'. I'm not seeing the whole context here."

"One night, as my wife and I discussed, it struck me that only a few people were aware of the specifics of what happened when Ikenua Joseph forgot his phone. You see, my wife seemed to have automatically assumed that the phone in question was a smartphone when it was in fact a very old model of Nokia." He crossed his legs. "So, Felipe, Sarnai, and I had decided to keep certain key information on the down-low."

"Joseph's son's name and the make of the phone."

"Yes."

"Going back to that taser we found at the crash-and-fall scene. Mrs Robinson told us that her niece had not needed her hairpin that night. What do you think Travis was actually looking for in her flat?"

"I'm not sure, but I have a theory," he said. "Felipe and Sarnai decided to sweep the apartments for bugs and found one. I think they might have planted an idea for whoever was eavesdropping."

"What idea?"

"That Sarnai was worried about another break-in, so she stashed away some of Mrs Robinson's valuables in a few safe spots."

"They thought the person who planted the bug would buy that?"

He shrugged. "Were you able to find any cash where Travis was staying?"

"How do you mean?" I asked back, aware that he did not know we had found a cookie jar full of rolled-up notes in Travis' locker at another gym.

"It's just that I have another theory," Mr Yang said. "Maybe it's worth you checking if you can find any traces of invisible thief detection spray in the shape of a fishbone. I believe Mrs Suntook is willing to have a conversation with you. She is staying at the nearby Savoy."

"She didn't fly out?"

"No. Felipe suggested to her that she just pretend to do so."

I jotted this down.

"Anything else?" he asked, "If not, then I must head out to buy my wife a half-birthday gift."

"One last question. I'm trying to get in touch with Mr Kazama so he can clear some of our doubts. I don't suppose you can put a word in for us?"

"I'll try."

Then I met Sarnai Ganbold for tea at a nearby Pret. She told me a delicious recipe for making milk tea the Mongolian way.

With regards to the case, she said, "They already had their suspicions fixed on either Liam or Travis, so Mr Kazama gave me a task during that luncheon."

"What sort of task?"

"First, I had to watch their reactions whenever the word 'John' was mentioned. Then, I had to pretend that I could no longer keep the secret and felt I had to tell everyone about what happened on the 19th of last month."

"And did this work?"

"I think so. Travis said something about dumbphones."

"The aglet that you found, we were able to cross-reference it with the pair of running shoes belonging to Mr Nelson, and they matched."

"So, it is true that morning when Travis taught his private class, he made his clients fall asleep and left to sneak into the apartments?"

"There is evidence indicating that this might have happened."

I watched as she buried her face in her hands. "He never looked like someone who would do that..."

During lunch, I returned to the office and Jean from FALCON* was there with someone I did not know.

"We have been examining Travis' digital devices. It seems he was quite the digilante," Jean said. "Fortunately, you can't hide everything with TOR. Hurray to the age of data." She projected a few files. "Multiple Kiwi Farms accounts; fake Peppa Pig videos with disturbing content; and cyber catfishing."

"He was a time management guru."

"By the way, are you still benching that girl from TfL?"

"I barely have time to eat, pray, and sleep."

"Either you advance, or you retreat to the friend zone."

That someone said, "Honestly, I CBA going down these leads. It's like your cat having a giant hairball; just as you thought it was over, another bit of evil Travis pops out."

"Did he claim to be a member of the Kennedy family?"

I dug out my notes again. "Yes. Felipe Kazama had suspicions about Travis: he could find no evidence supporting Travis's claim that he went to Harvard, so he shared his concerns with his friend Patricia Bennett. She saw Felipe bossing Travis around during their luncheon and then she mentioned to him that Felipe was looking into his background. Travis tells her not to worry and that he was only using a false name as a safety measure and was actually a member of the renowned Kennedy family."

"If she bought that, I could pass for Prince Harry."

---

*   FALCON: Fraud and Linked Crime Online

"I believe she hesitated. But it was just then that she heard Mrs Robinson's sister and Travis talking about how their family members had attended West Point Military Academy."

"But didn't he nick the ring off someone else?"

Yusuf pointed out on the whiteboard. "The reason he fled the US three years ago was that he was wanted for gaslighting a girl who committed suicide. Her family had found snippets of chats between them where Travis encouraged her to jones on cocaine."

"He had told Mrs Robinson that he knew a senior at Harvard who recently completed her JD at Yale and was founding a startup on carbon credits trading. He said they could fund it together and that carbon certificates would be all that the Fortune 500 companies would care about in the next three to five years."

"By the way, I have a question," said Zainab, our newest member. "How did you crack his phone? I've heard that Apple does not cooperate with the authorities when it comes to cracking criminals' phones."

"We didn't necessarily 'crack' it," Jean answered. "We just watched through all the CCTV footage we got from the gym's locker room and found footage of Travis unlocking his phone with a passcode."

"I see."

"The simplest way always works." Yusuf added, "We also found that Mrs Robinson had been using a hacked lightning cable that allowed Travis to access her phone distantly."

"Speaking of chat histories, there is something we found." Jean grabbed some papers. "With some people Travis had contacted, he had been urging them to release their negative energy. For example, if you work at an off-licence and are unhappy, you can secretly crush crisps and cookies to vent."

"Ten quid that Travis couldn't pass the M'Naghten rule."

"And in one of his chats, he used code like 'bid' and 'tid'."

"Aren't they medical terms for medications and injections?"

"Yes, but we don't know what for."

"Strictly speaking, this is the third death that the Kean Street apartments have seen in the last two years."

"What were the others?"

"One was in April 2014, during the Holborn Fire. Our record shows Miss Yan Joyce Peng, a Chinese national aged 27, had overdosed and was found dead in her room. She was the half-sister of You Jayden Peng–"

"Aka the 'Fair Canary'?"

"That's him."

"What's that?"

"He runs the Nan Peng Group that owns half of the commercial real estate in Mayfair and half of Canary Wharf, hence the moniker."

"Who was the other deceased?"

"The other was the late Mr Robinson. He died in Brussels on the day of the Brussels Bombings."

"He was a victim of the terrorist attack?"

"No, he had a heart condition."

"Are you saying they are all connected?"

"Doesn't strike me to be the case."

Sunita said, "Regarding the CCTV footage we got from the flats, it's clear that Felipe Kazama made two calls as they saw Travis take the lift downstairs." She played a video. "Here, he made the first call and hissed something; then he hung up, and a minute later, he called 999."

"What's his explanation?"

"The first time he had dialled '110'. Apparently, in China and Japan, they use 110 to reach the police." Sunita sighed. "He gave me a lengthy overview of why that was the case."

"Why was it?"

"In the old days, where you had dial phones, you only needed to dial the first two numbers quickly if you were in a hurry to get to the police, and the last zero came in to give you some time to think over what you have to deliver succinctly."

"Handy knowledge for a pub quiz."

"He said when he realised his mistake, he shouted 'damn'. We ran this over with our lip readers; they are not a hundred per cent certain that it was a 'damn'. They said it could also be 'get 'im'."

"What did his friend Yang say about this?"

"That he was still recovering from his taser shock, and he failed to register."

"Are you suggesting that Felipe Kazama somehow colluded with his pursuers to get rid of Travis?"

"I bet you'll find this interesting. Yesterday, a huge amount of money was deposited in their accounts from an offshore bank account in the Cayman Islands."

"Sounds like a put-off job."

"Maybe they wanted to intimidate Travis, but it got out of hand? So they got some hush money."

"The car was in mint condition, and we didn't find any mechanical shortcomings. The TfL experts suggested that the car might have swerved on a patch of black ice."

"But I don't think getting out from a convertible would be that difficult."

"The forensics are investigating whether Travis lost consciousness before the car plunged. You know, scratch marks on the steering wheel and seatbelt, etc."

"Should we invite Felipe Kazama in for a cup of tea?"

"His solicitor made it very clear that his client won't have time to chat unless it is an interview under caution. Says that the banker's hourly rate is on a par with a sought-after Roger Dubuis."

"And he has been dodging our attempts to contact him directly."

My phone beeped and I said, "Not anymore. He's agreed to a chat off the record."

October 31st, Halloween. Cloudy.

My meeting with Felipe Kazama took place that night at a pub in Soho that he suggested. I entered The Coach & Horses and found him conversing with a pubgoer nearby.

"Chaos was the first being created in Greek mythology–"

"Excuse me." I cleared my throat softly and declared my presence.

"Ah. DS Deborah. How nice to see you." He turned, and I saw the dark contusion around his left eye was still healing.

"DC Deborah," I corrected him.

"Well. I'm sure your promotion awaits promptly." He offered me something taken from his waistcoat. "Candy?"

"No, thank you."

"Very alert; I like that. Got it on the street just now, and who knows if it isn't spiked. Never trust strangers. It could get you killed."

I gulped.

"And never wolf whistle until you are out of the woods." He then said, "Did you know that once Halloween in Chicago nearly got cancelled because of some cases related to Tylenol poisoning?"

"No, sir."

"Don't call me 'sir'. Felipe, please." He took a swig from his glass. "My buddy says you have some questions for me." He looked at me meaningfully. "I myself don't see where your doubts lie. The dead one did it, obviously. Anything to drink?"

"No, I mean, don't trouble yourself." I opened my notepad. "A couple of things to clear. It's still a mystery to me why your pursuers hadn't recognised you that night when you smoked by your car, and instead, they mistook the fleeing Travis for you."

"Oh, I was simply not my dashing self that night and I was not in my glad rags. And DC Deborah, there are countless times when people thought I was just a chauffeur." He chuckled. "Funny that I just remembered Travis saying that he found the Invisibility Cloak the most helpful item in *Harry Potter*. Sometimes, the most powerful invisibility cloak is a three-piece Savile Row suit. Other times, it is a uniform."

"But surely they would have recognised you." I explained the facts to him: "They had a very close look at you that day when you returned from Billingsgate – they even parked their car in your spot!"

"Did they? That's interesting. Guess they don't have good eyesight, then?"

I decided on another question, "Why did you and your friend go forward with Ikenua Joseph's idea without seeking help from the police?"

"Because he asked us a simple question – what crime can you subject the imposter to?" Felipe looked at me. "I hardly think confessions extracted under duress make sound evidence in court, and I am not very keen to allow recidivists at large. I don't believe in restorative justice. Do you?"

"Well...I think different types of criminals need different types of assistance, and socioeconomic factors such as their upbringing play a major part in how they perceive the world. Take Travis, his mother–"

Felipe stopped me with a raised hand. "I neither know nor care. There is a karmic retribution to how Travis died, don't you think?"

"I will refrain from commenting."

"But you are dead right in observing that criminals have different motives. I have read that one per cent of the general population are psychopaths, and around a quarter of them are currently or once incarcerated individuals. Psychopathy focuses on goals and behaviour not influenced by incarceration, quite patently."

I flipped a page. "When did you begin to suspect Travis?"

"Pretty much the first time we met. He mentioned that he did his AB in Government, and I know a faculty member quite well. So I asked Travis how Professor Rodriguez was, and he told me 'he' was well. The professor is actually a *profesora* on her maternity leave."

"I see."

"At first, I thought Travis was only a gold-digger. And money is like manure, DC Deborah; *all* maggots come from it – teachers, medics, Ladder Gang members, churchwardens, and even police officers."

I raised an eyebrow.

"The Law is not justice, and the police do not always uphold duty. Or why do you think the missing Christian Dior earrings belonging to Martine Vik Magnussen ended up at some nark's wedding?"

"That case happened eight years ago. Many reforms have found their way into the Forces today."

"Something recent then," he said. "Ever heard of the Primrose Hill Cat Killer?

I nodded.

Earlier this year, a springspotter was found dead in her home in Primrose Hill. She was stabbed to death by a former colleague of hers with whom she had a fallout at work. The investigation was straightforward enough until boxes of dead cats' bodies turned up in the victim's backyard. At the time, a canard ran rife that it was the victim's neighbour, an adopted girl who was once a Sudanese child soldier, who had slayed those cats, but the case closed nonetheless without further inquiries.

"Priorities matter when it comes to police procedures." I steered our conversation back to the topic. "You suspected Travis, yet you did nothing?"

"I suspected him, and I had no evidence. Evidence is anything that helps us to form a belief. Good evidence helps us to form a sound belief. So, my buddy went through thirty days and nights' worth of CCTV footage we got from a furniture store and finally found that one time in early September Travis had accompanied an intoxicated Mrs Robinson home. He left soon afterwards, but I think seeing where she lived gave him some ideas. Hence, we started with the ABCs."

"The ABCs?"

"You must be familiar with them. Who am I to show off analytical skills before Jane Tennison?"

"Never liked that show," I said. "But I know about the ABC principle: assume nothing, believe nothing, challenge and check everything."

"Liam said he was in Japan, and we found he wasn't always there. So, we dug some more. And my friend Patsy made a brilliant move. I'm sure she did it to spite me, though." Felipe laughed boisterously. "I got hold of Liam's passport number, and we checked when he flew out and ascertained that he was not in London on the 19th of September. Even the world's top magicians can't disappear from Tokyo one moment and turn up in Central London a few minutes later without any theatrical trick. However, moving from Covent

Garden to Elephant & Castle on a decent bike in less than half an hour is perfectly manageable."

"Interesting thought."

"Being devious is always a compliment in my line of work. When people throw lemons at me, I make *limonada* for them; and if people put a dead pigeon with broken wings on my windshield, then I make roasted pigeon. It's that simple. By the way, I have a friend who wants to become a hobby bobby; maybe you can dissuade her? And DC Deborah, I don't suppose you can tell me where I can donate to place a couple more sleeping policemen on the roads around Central London, can you? I hate to see good, decent Londoners plummeting into the Thames like blue-arsed flies."

I threw him another line: "We found some money made its way into your pursuers' bank accounts, so we have fair reason to believe that their silence is being *paid* for."

"You think I turned my haters to take out Travis for me?" He laughed. "That's an achievement theoretical at its best." Felipe then considered. "So, what if I gave them some money? I take at least half of the responsibility that their uncle could never get a stiffie again. Something's gotta give, right?"

"Erm..." I flipped my notes back and forth. "Let me see..."

"DC Deborah, why don't you ask me how I felt when I heard about Travis's death?"

"How did you feel?"

"Like caviar bursting on the tip of my tongue."

"That is a very...precise description."

"Ethics and social codes don't apply to me because I don't have to abide by them." Felipe gave a smile; he had a missing eye tooth. "Pity; Travis and I were only talking about going to sea and not returning deadhead. Do you think they can retrieve that ring? It'd make a good dental implant."

"I'm not sure that is possible. The ring has to go back to its original owner." I continued, "Are you aware of the fact that Travis may have gaslighted a girl back in the US so that she committed suicide?"

"He'd told us how a friend threw herself off a building." Felipe sighed. "Lies are always best told when intertwined with fragments of truth." He then smiled. "You know, I'm not entirely certain that Travis had tried to save my friend Patsy from the doom of a falling grill for altruistic purposes. I think he did it to render his fingerprints unavailable. Poor Travis, he didn't know I already got his marks from my lighter."

"One last question. More of a request, really."

"I'll indulge you. It's Halloween."

"Can I see your phone, please?"

"My phone?" He became interested.

"Your calling history, to be precise."

"Fine." He unlocked his phone and handed it to me.

I quickly browsed through his calling history and found the entry made to '110' on the night of October 15th and re-dialled it. It was a broken line.

"Thank you for your time, Mr Kazama." I organised my notes and heaved my shoulder bag back on. "We'll be in touch."

"The pleasure is all mine, DC Deborah," he said with a hint of a smirk. "I'm sure we won't be seeing each other so soon...if not ever again."

"What do you mean?"

"I believe your diligence will soon be required elsewhere to tackle even more hideous crime. Surely the people at the Electronic

Monitoring Service don't want a brewing scandal to escalate so soon – not before Christmas, anyway." He offered his hand. "Lovely chatting with you." Then he sent me a wink. "Gave me plenty inspo for a short Ortonesque whodunit."

I got out and found the chilling night air refreshing. A Halloween parade was moving through the crowds, and I overheard a couple arguing about someone running late again.

Then something struck me. When my sister was in sixth form, her boyfriend two-timed her with a simple trick – he created a new phone contact that he labelled 'Dad' while using his other girlfriend's number. He had used another contact labelled 'Daddy' for his real dad, so whenever he was with my sister, he'd get calls from his 'dad' that he had to answer. Ideas began to sprint in my head: What if Felipe had used a similar trick with '110'?

The only way to make sure was to access his calling history from his carrier service. I made a mental note of this as I got a call from Jean.

"Hey, I'll report back very soon."

"No hurry," she said. "A few heads up from our side. We found that Travis had also been using a hacked lightning cable and given that he was unlikely to steal his own data, we ran this through with the others. Ken, the son of the family where Travis stayed, said that they had hired a plumber sometime before Travis died to fix something in their house. But the funny thing is, we asked that company and none of their workers fit Ken's description of that plumber."

Cold sweat began forming at the base of my neck. "Did Travis have any Tylenol?"

"Sorry?"

"He was on painkillers, right? Were they Tylenol?"

"I need to check."

"While you're on it," my mind worked quickly, "the gym lockers were lock and key type, right?"

"Yes."

"And you've heard people saying that Felipe Kazama has been going after the manager there?"

"I did. Though I'm not seeing where you're going with this."

"Yusuf went through the CCTV footage at the gym to see Travis using his passcode on his phone. Perhaps Felipe only pretended to be interested in Jennifer because he wanted her master key to see what was inside Travis' locker–"

"I'll ask you to stop there, gal. This is too much to process, and... the case is closing."

"WHAT?"

"The EMS deemed their investigation needs to be...independent from ours and hence..."

I ended my call, feeling all was lost again.

And so, as I scribble this last line on the case, the official investigations may have closed, but I will find answers, and the truth will come out, no matter what.

The only thing I can ascertain is that things are *far* from **over**.

ENJOYED THIS STORY?

Thank you for reading *Ciao, Ciao, Chaos* - Mercenaries in Suits Book 4.

We'd love to hear about your reading experience. Could you take a minute to share your thoughts on *Goodreads*? Thank you!

ALSO BY SHAWE RUCKUS

Discover a world of lost dynasties and legendary creatures where an unlikely group of heroes must face their destinies to save humanity from the grip of history's greatest foes.

Start the *Princess Rouran Adventures* with Book 1, *Princess Rouran and the Dragon Chariot of 10,000 Sages*, and join Moli as she discovers her connection to an ancient khanate in this Amazon Best Seller.

When Moli's connection to the Rouran Dynasty is revealed, she unexpectedly opens the door to a realm of shamans, rituals, conqueror worms and dragon chariots, where all magic and danger are possible...

What readers say about Princess Rouran and
the Dragon Chariot of 10,000 Sages:

*"The mixture of time travel, mythology, SF tropes, and a spirited youngster
in the lead makes for a truly wild narrative."* – **Kirkus Reviews**

*"With a precocious young protagonist navigating immense, sophisticated
ideas and feelings, this is a thoughtful story about choosing empathy
and hope in a world of grief and intolerance, written with eloquent
language and Alice-in-Wonderland-like flair."* – **IndieReader**

*"If you love adventure stories featuring dragons, shamans,
talking cats, and other fantastical elements, this will
be just up your alley."* – **Readers' Favorite**

*"Deeply meaningful and with a blend of needed fantasy, the
story flows in a wonderful spectrum of events."* – **Amazon**

*"A captivating read that will keep you on the edge of
your seat from start to finish."* – **Amazon**

*"This is an intriguing and action-packed novel. I was entertained
as much as I was compelled to think about the faults, failures,
and triumphs of humanity."* – **OnlineBookClub**

In Book 2, *Princess Rouran and the Book of the Living*, third-year university student Edith Orozco is unexpectedly thrown into chaos as she boards her train home, but finds herself thrust into Ancient Egypt.

Edith, her niece Moli, and two strangers must rely on each other for survival as they encounter treacherous slave merchants, frightening prehistoric dinosaurs, and mischievous ancient gods.

When bravery is no longer a choice and with the clock ticking, can they save the world from moving one step closer to mayhem and destruction?

Join these heroes as they trailblaze through a suspense-filled 24-hour battle for survival.

What readers say about Princess Rouran
and the Book of the Living:

"Four young people face an uphill struggle in saving the world against the forces of evil in this whimsical fantasy. The dozen or so pages of notes and references testify to the density of the prose." – **Kirkus Reviews**

"A well-written and intriguing fantasy and a highly literate puzzle of a book that weaves the threads of ancient and modern history into a time-traveling tapestry of conspiracy theories and old-fashioned adventure." – **IndieReader**

"Shawe Ruckus has created a magnificent world full of otherworldly creatures and futuristic technology, resulting in a uniquely engaging setting where you are completely immersed." – **Readers' Favorite**

"An epic tale of adventure, magic, and danger. What truly sets this book apart is its strong and inspiring female protagonist." – **Amazon**

"Combines excellent elements of fantasy and sci-fi, brilliantly woven throughout the course of a fascinating story that will keep readers hooked until the end." – **Amazon**

"Definitely a must-read for fantasy and adventure lovers." – **Goodreads**

ABOUT THE AUTHOR

Shawe Ruckus is an author of urban mysteries and YA science fantasy, in which cold cases and legendary creatures take centre stage. She is a former student at the Worshipful Society of Apothecaries in London, where Agatha Christie learned how to poison.

Shawe is a globetrotter born in Inner Mongolia. Having woven a rich tapestry of experiences from her diverse residencies—including China, the UK, Austria, South Korea, Switzerland, and Japan—Shawe brings a unique medley of humour, bad humour, suspense, and slices of everyday life to her stories.

Having attended King's College London and the University of Cambridge, Shawe also took courses at the International Space University, where she acquired much useful technical knowledge for her writing.

Her first book in the *Mercenaries in Suits* series was shortlisted for the 2023 Readers' Favorite Book Award in the Urban Fiction category. Shawe was also recognized as 1 of 15 sci-fi writers shortlisted for the 8th Masters of the Future Award.

When not writing, Shawe Ruckus indulges in culinary adventures, offers mentorship sessions to inspiring entrepreneurs to 'hunt' their next unicorn, and persistently attempts to cultivate a green thumb.

JOIN THE AWE AND RUCKUS VIP BOOK CLUB

STORIES LIKE NONE BEFORE...

Join thousands of like-minded readers from 63 countries and regions to receive monthly issues of FREE, FUN, FABULOUS books by awesome indie writers around the world!

Sign up today for your spot at *www.aweandruckus.com*